MW00643635

Praise for LARA ADRIAN

"Adrian has a gift for drawing her readers deeper and deeper into the amazing world she creates."

—Fresh Fiction

"With an Adrian novel, readers are assured of plenty of dangerous thrills and passionate chills."

—RT Book Reviews

"Nothing beats good writing and that is what ultimately makes Lara Adrian stand out amongst her peers . . . Adrian doesn't hold back with the intensity or the passion."

—Under the Covers

"Adrian has a style of writing that creates these worlds that are so realistic and believable . . . the characters are so rich and layered . . . the love stories are captivating and often gut-wrenching . . . edge of your seat stuff!"

—Scandalicious Book Reviews

"Adrian compels readers to get hooked on her storylines."

—Romance Reviews Today

Praise for Lara Adrian's books

"Adrian's strikingly original Midnight Breed series delivers an abundance of nail-biting suspenseful chills, red-hot sexy thrills, an intricately built world, and realistically complicated and conflicted protagonists, whose happily-ever-after ending proves to be all the sweeter after what they endure to get there."

—Booklist (starred review)

"(The Midnight Breed is) a well-written, action-packed series that is just getting better with age."

—Fiction Vixen

"Chocked full of action, suspense and romance, Adrian's Midnight Breed series is a winner . . . patent edgy characters, action-packed storylines, and smoking hot romances."

—*Smexy Books*

"Fantastic! We recommend to anyone who loves action packed, intense reads with gripping characters and spectacular storylines woven into a phenomenally crafted world. If you haven't started the Midnight Breed series yet, we highly suggest that you bump it up to the top of your list. "

—*Literal Addiction*

"If you like romance combined with heart-stopping paranormal suspense, you're going to love (Edge of Dawn)."

—*Bookpage*

"The Midnight Breed series is one of the consistently best paranormal series out there.... Adrian writes compelling individual stories (with wonderful happily ever afters) within a larger story arc that is unfolding with a refreshing lack of predictability."

–*Romance Novel News*

"Crave the Night is stunning in its flawless execution. Lara Adrian has the rare ability to lure readers right into her books, taking them on a ride they will never forget."

—*Under the Covers*

"Adrian has set up a really interesting and exciting plot arc that will hold strong for many more books to come."

—*The Book Pushers*

"It's official. Lara Adrian is brilliant."

—*Yummy Men and Kickass Chicks*

Praise for
THE 100 SERIES

"I wish I could give this more than 5 stars! Lara Adrian not only dips her toe into this genre with flare, she will take it over . . . I have found my new addiction, this series."

—The Sub Club Books

"There are twists that I want to say that I expect from a Lara Adrian book, and I say that because with any Adrian book you read, you know there's going to be a complex storyline. Adrian simply does billionaires better."

—Under the Covers

"This book had me completely addicted from page one!! There were several twists and turns throughout this super steamy read and I was surprised by how much mystery/suspense was woven in. Loved that! If you're looking for the perfect summer read, look no further than this book!"

—Steph and Chris Book Blog

"A complete erotic thrill! Lara Adrian has seduced me with every turn of the page. Just brilliant!"

—Shayna Renee's Spicy Reads

"For 100 Days is a sexy, sizzling, emotion-filled delight. It completely blew me away!"

—J. Kenner, New York Times bestselling author

The 100 Series

For 100 Days
For 100 Nights
For 100 Reasons
For 100 Forevers *(forthcoming)*

Run to You
Play My Game

Other books by Lara Adrian

Midnight Breed series

A Touch of Midnight
Kiss of Midnight
Kiss of Crimson
Midnight Awakening
Midnight Rising
Veil of Midnight
Ashes of Midnight
Shades of Midnight
Taken by Midnight
Deeper Than Midnight
A Taste of Midnight
Darker After Midnight
The Midnight Breed Series Companion
Edge of Dawn
Marked by Midnight
Crave the Night
Tempted by Midnight
Bound to Darkness
Stroke of Midnight
Defy the Dawn
Midnight Untamed
Midnight Unbound
Claimed in Shadows
Midnight Unleashed
Break The Day
Fall of Night
King of Midnight

Midnight Breed Spinoff

Hunter Legacy Series
Born of Darkness
Hour of Darkness
Edge of Darkness
Guardian of Darkness

Historical Romances

Dragon Chalice Series
Heart of the Hunter
Heart of the Flame
Heart of the Dove

Warrior Trilogy
White Lion's Lady
Black Lion's Bride
Lady of Valor

Lord of Vengeance

FOR 100 NIGHTS

NIGHTS

A 100 Series Novel

NEW YORK TIMES BESTSELLING AUTHOR

LARA ADRIAN

ISBN: 978-1-939193-43-8

FOR 100 NIGHTS
© 2017 by Lara Adrian, LLC
ISE-2404

All rights reserved. No part of this work may be used or reproduced in any manner whatsoever without permission, except in the case of brief quotations embodied in critical articles and reviews.

This book is a work of fiction. Names, characters, places and incidents are either products of the author's imagination or used fictitiously. Any resemblance to actual events, locales, or persons, living or dead, is entirely coincidental. No part of this publication can be reproduced or transmitted in any form or by any means, electronic or mechanical, without permission in writing from the Author.

www.LaraAdrian.com

Available in ebook, trade paperback, and unabridged audiobook editions.

For 100
Nights

DEDICATION

For John:

My personal hero for the past thirty years. You've
slain all my monsters. You've picked me up and
carried me off to your castle. You've saved me.
I love you, forever.

1

Sunrise glistens on the meandering curves of the East River, the golden light of the August morning gilding the elegant hotels, mansions, and other prime real estate that surrounds verdant Central Park ninety-three stories below me.

Lifting my head from my pillow, I sweep my bed-tossed tangle of blond hair away from my eyes, awed and breathless as I watch daybreak gently play over the city from my privileged vantage point far above it all.

I've been waking up to this view—in this bed on top of the world—for the past two weeks, yet I swear each morning is more spectacular than the last.

So are the nights.

As tempting as it may be to slip out from the silky sheets and savor the splendor of New York City's waking skyline, my body is languid and flushed, my limbs too weak to move. All of my senses are still thrumming from an incredible predawn orgasm that's only beginning to ebb.

I sigh in pleasure, and the firm, muscled arm that's wrapped around me from behind flexes to pull me closer. Warm lips and a beard-roughened face nuzzles my nape with a kiss that sends wet heat licking through me, straight to my core.

The view from the penthouse of the tallest building in Manhattan is a jaw-dropper to be sure, but it's the man holding my naked body against his who never fails to leave me amazed and breathless.

Dominic Baine.

He's still inside me, his cock still erect even after the climax that had him shouting my name like a curse only moments ago. His hips move against my ass and I arch into his lazy thrust on a moan I don't even attempt to bite back.

"So greedy, Ms. Ross. Such a sweet, demanding pussy you have." He withdraws slowly as he speaks, each retreating inch a torment, a threat of loss that makes my walls clench around him in protest. I feel the vibration of his amused chuckle against my spine, his mouth teasing the sensitive skin behind my ear. "I've made you come twice since you woke up and you're ready for me to fuck you all over again."

Not a question. No pretense of propriety, despite the urbane polish of his deep voice or the fact that he's one of the most respected, successful—wealthiest—men in the country.

We're long past all of that now.

"Tell me, Avery," he demands quietly, yet firmly, against the shell of my ear.

"I want you to fuck me, Nick. Right now. Again. I

don't ever want you to stop fucking me."

"Good girl." He rewards me with a tweak of my nipple as he pushes inside me all the way to the hilt.

I suck in my breath at the enormity of him, of how primal our need for each other is. It's burned white-hot for nearly four months now, since the moment we first met—a chance encounter in this very building, then another, more provocative exchange at Dominion, the art gallery Nick owns on Fifth Avenue.

The same gallery where several of my paintings had hung unsold for more than a year before they were culled at Nick's direction to make way for more promising artists.

I hadn't realized Nick was Dominion's owner that first night I ended up in his bed. As angered as I'd been to learn who he was a few days later, it hadn't kept me from wanting him, or from falling headlong into the kind of carnal, consuming—infinitely intense—relationship I'd never had with any man before him.

Nothing had.

But then, to be fair, there were things Nick hadn't known about me either. I'd been playing what I thought was a harmless game—pretending I was someone I wasn't, letting him think I was someone better, someone without my ugly past and the onerous baggage that came with it.

I'd been acting like I belonged in Nick's world when in reality I was a failed artist and struggling bartender living a temporary fairy tale existence as a house-sitter in his building.

For the first hundred days we were together, I let Nick believe all of my lies.

Even the worst ones.

When everything finally crashed down around me, I thought for sure he would be gone. Instead, he came after me. He found me. He forgave me.

And then he named his price for letting me back in. One hundred nights.

For each day I deceived him, he demanded a night in return. He wanted all of me. In his bed. On his terms. At his total mercy.

I can't imagine a more exquisite punishment.

He drives into me again, another long, hard thrust that wrings a broken cry from my throat. My body is spent, my sex swollen and sore from the fury of Nick's passion last night and again this morning. But I crave this ache. I crave this man with a depth of need that probably should terrify me. Instead it only makes me hunger for more.

Half in pleasure, half in pain, I tilt my body to take all of him as his next thrust goes even deeper—to the razor's edge of what I think I can bear. I want everything he'll give me, the pleasure and the pain. The raw possession.

The complete dominance that demands nothing less than my full surrender.

He grinds out a tight curse and I groan when I feel him withdraw too far, too fast for my liking. He shifts behind me, the flat of his palm coming down on my ass in a sharp smack. "On your hands and knees, baby."

As I hurry to comply, I register that he's disposing of the spent condom from our last bout of the morning and rolling on a fresh one. He returns a moment later, the heat of his body radiating over my bare backside, which is on full display for him in the thin light of morning.

"God, you're beautiful," he murmurs, skimming his hands up the outsides of my parted thighs, then onto the rounded curve of my ass.

Facing the floor-to-ceiling window, I watch the faint ghosts of our reflection in the glass as he looms behind me naked on his knees, his strong hands roaming all over my body. I arch and shudder as his fingers leave no inch of me untouched. The warm coil of need that held me a moment ago now twists tighter, hotter, aching with anticipation of the pleasure still to come.

"All of this belongs to me," he says, while his fingers skate back down to splay atop my bare cheeks, then squeeze, opening me wider to him. Then he releases my ass only so he can slide one palm along the length of my bowed spine while the other one delves into the drenched and pulsing cleft of my sex. "All of you, Avery. Mine."

"Yes." The word rushes out of me, both an admission and a plea.

I am his, even if I'm not quite certain what his possession will mean for me in the end. Although I'm falling in love with him—and I've confessed as much to him—we've made no promises to each other beyond these hundred nights.

Right now, all I need is the next moment. I need to feel him inside me.

"Nick, please." My voice is little more than a whimper, my breath panting and shallow.

He leans over me, pushing my shoulders down onto the mattress so that my backside is angled high. Lust floods me, animalistic and urgent. He is naturally dominant, and, in spite of my history, nothing turns me on faster or harder than submitting to Nick's carnal control.

He reaches down to caress my face with the back of his hand—the one that's riddled with angry scars, horrific wounds he's dismissed as the result of a foolish brawl when he was eighteen. They are the only flaws on his otherwise perfect body.

At times in these past few months we've been together, I've wondered if there are other scars he doesn't allow me to see. I know there must be, because the broken parts of me recognize the fractures in him, even if he hasn't permitted me close enough to touch them yet.

When his thumb brushes my lips, I stroke my tongue against it, then draw him into my mouth the way I want to—need to—draw him into my body.

His groan sounds ragged as I suck him deep. His pelvis bucks against my ass, his erection wedged between the slickness of my cleft.

"Ah, fuck," he snarls, rubbing the pad of his thumb against the cushion of my tongue as he guides his cock to my entrance. "Hang on, baby."

The low command is a warning. I feel his ferocity building even before he pushes inside me on a sharp roar. There is no gentleness in him as he pulls his hand away from my mouth and gathers my loose hair in his grasp. He winds the blond tresses tautly around his fist, until I feel the sting all over my scalp.

I am instantly lost to the violence of his passion—and my own.

He powers into me like a tempest, furious and unrelenting. His words rasp low and dark above me, praise and profanity, my name uttered like a prayer as he takes me over body, heart and soul.

Braced on my hands, with my head pulled back and my shoulders pinned to the mattress, I stare through pleasured tears at the carnality of our lovemaking reflected with fading clarity in the window glass and the warming colors of the summer morning now bursting to life on the other side.

My chest aches with emotion as my orgasm swiftly builds. This is when I feel most alive—held fast against this man, naked and surrendered to him completely. Feeling the full measure of his power and fury, yet knowing there is nowhere safer that I can be.

The sensations overwhelm me. The beauty and the pain and the pleasure.

I want to hold all of it close. I want to memorize every moment.

I want to paint everything I'm feeling, even though it's been weeks since I've worked on anything new.

"Oh, God . . . Nick." My grasp on lucid thought slips away as my climax chases up on me. Eyes closed, I bite down on my lip as Nick's merciless tempo pushes me right over the edge. The scream that rips from my throat is jagged, uncontrolled.

Nick's guttural shout a moment later is no less primal. With the fingers of one hand digging into my hip, the other still wound tightly in my hair, he rams deep, a hard shudder raking him as he comes.

Although I'm spent and trembling from my release, he continues to rock inside me, losing little of his hardness, despite the ferocity of his own orgasm. He moves slowly, patiently, gentling me now. Tender kisses light on my shoulder, then along my spine. He lets go of my hair, carefully unwinding it, then combing his fingers through the loosened strands.

As turbulent as our sex often is, his aftercare is impossibly sweet.

Gathering me to him, he takes us both down onto our sides on the mattress. His arms encircle me, strong and warm, a shelter I'd like to remain in all day if I could. Forever, if I'm being honest.

It takes some time before we're both breathing normally again and relaxed. Nick reaches up to stroke the side of my sweat-sheened face. When he speaks, his deep voice is thick like velvet, a caress I feel as palpably as his touch. "Better now?"

"Perfect."

It's not a word I'm accustomed to using, especially when it comes to my life. But these past few months—the two weeks I've been living with Nick in particular—have come pretty damn close. I never thought it could be like this with someone. I never imagined that I would ever feel this connected to anyone, this whole.

I've never felt this terrified either.

Because as deeply as I've fallen, I know that the bottom could drop out of this bliss at any moment.

It nearly did two weeks ago.

Nick and I came through some of my worst secrets together, but there is more he doesn't know. Things I don't dare tell him. A truth I intend to take to my grave.

He kisses my nape, drawing me out of the past that continues to haunt me.

"Now that I've satisfied one of your appetites, how about breakfast?"

My mouth waters at the thought. "Mm, sounds great." As gifted as he is in bed and at business, Nick's culinary talents are nothing short of spectacular.

Giving my shoulder a light nip, he carefully

withdraws from my sex. "Join me in the shower. I'll get the water started."

I moan as he rolls away from me, leaving cool air where his delicious heat had been. Pivoting around, I watch him move to the edge of the bed and dispose of the condom. The sight of his muscled back and broad shoulders makes my mouth water too.

How did I end up with this amazing man? It's a question I've asked myself numerous times since fate put me in his orbit.

Dominic Baine, a man who can have anything—and anyone—he desires, yet the only person he seems to want is me.

When he glances back to look at me, I am struck now, as always, by how handsome he is. An arresting mix of sharp angles and hard lines, his face is softened only by the lush line of his mouth. A mouth that knows every inch of my body and how to pleasure it. Under the ebony slashes of his brows and bed-tousled crown of dark hair, Nick's cerulean gaze makes my pulse kick with banked, but still smoldering, arousal.

One of those inky brows arches wryly. "If I didn't have a meeting I can't miss this morning, that look might get you fucked again right now, Ms. Ross. Whether you're ready or not."

I laugh, but my core throbs, knowing he means it.

He stands up, facing me with a hard-on I can't help but admire. "Shower and breakfast," he growls. "If I don't decide to skip the cooking and spread you out on the table before I leave."

"Promises, promises," I tease, sliding to the edge of the bed where he waits. Taking his cock in my hands, I flick my tongue against the tip. Before he can grab hold of me, I hop to my feet and dance out of his reach. "Shower and breakfast, Mr. Baine. I'll put the coffee on and join you."

His acknowledgment is little more than a snarl. "Make it quick."

I pad out of the spacious bedroom naked, feeling at home in the immense, luxurious penthouse that overlooks all of Manhattan from various angles. Passing the windows in the living room, which frame the iconic skyline of the city and the view I glimpsed the night Nick first kissed me here, I head for the kitchen with a smile lingering on my lips.

As I go to the coffee maker, I notice my cell phone peeking out of my small evening bag on the black granite counter where I left both last night after Nick and I returned from dinner and a play.

The text message light is blinking.

"Shit." I had silenced the phone in the theater and forgot to turn it back on.

I swipe the lock screen and tap the message icon. All the blood drains from my face when I see the phone number on the unread text. I've seen this Pennsylvania number before. It's been seared into my mind from the last time I saw it appear on my phone.

My finger trembles as I open the message and absorb the fresh threat I've just received.

U avoiding me?

Told u 2 wks ago we need 2 talk.

Im not going away Avery. Not this time.

Be in touch. Thats a promise.

My breath is racing, my heart banging so hard it might burst out of my chest.

I can't delete the text fast enough, but even when it's

gone, the terror of what it means presses down on me like a vise.

No matter how far I've run, no matter how much I want to believe I might deserve some shred of happiness in my future, my past is never going to let me go.

2

After Nick leaves for work, I realize I'm going to lose my mind if I stay in the penthouse alone with little to do. My nerves are too on edge. My panic after seeing that awful text message has put a knot in my stomach that's only tightened in the time since he's been gone.

Despite the fact that I was clean and semidressed for breakfast, I strip out of my short silk kimono and take another shower—this one scalding. Beneath the punishing spray of water I try to compartmentalize the hideous past that still clings to me and the fragile, hopeful present I've only begun to know.

To think I had almost convinced myself that the ugliness I left behind in Pennsylvania would never find me all these years later.

Until two weeks ago, I thought I was safe. I thought that part of my life—and the secrets I ran away from—

could never hurt me again.

How wrong I'd been.

There's only one person who can understand what I'm feeling right now, but I refuse to burden my mother with this new problem of mine. God knows she's already sacrificed more than enough where I'm concerned.

For my own sake, I need to immerse myself in the here and now, not withdraw into the fear and shame that's clawing at me in the wake of that text. I need the cacophony of the city around me. I need some semblance of the familiar in order to find my grounding again.

When I walk up an hour later to the locked glass entrance of Vendange, the restaurant where I worked as a bartender until three and a half months ago, my friend, Tasha Lopez, hurries toward the double doors to meet me. Her loose brown spiral curls frame her soft features and long-lashed brown eyes as she tilts her head to study me for a moment through the glass.

Using one of the manager's keys that hang from the neon green plastic coil around her wrist, Tasha opens the locks and lets me inside. Vendange doesn't open until lunch, but half a dozen servers are already at work prepping for business. Like Tasha, the waitstaff are all wearing fitted black button-down shirts with black tuxedo vests and black slacks, a polished, understated look that perfectly complements the trendy, upscale bar and restaurant.

Before she and I have a chance to greet each other, one of the employees calls out to her from the restaurant storage room.

"Hey, Tasha? Looks like we're down to the last three take-out boxes."

"Check out back. I placed an order for another case earlier this week. I think I saw it when I closed up last night." Without missing a beat, she turns to me and gives me a big hug. "You look gorgeous as usual."

Her gaze skims my loose white silk tank, slim-fitting tan pencil skirt, and flat, saddle-brown designer sandals—just part of the generous wardrobe Nick has gifted me with since we've been together. I opted to wear my blonde hair unbound, a habit I've begun since hooking up with him. He never allows it to stay tamed for long, anyway. Today it floats around my face and shoulders in a mass of air-dried, beachy waves instead of the orderly, blown-out ponytail that was my regular style when I worked at the restaurant.

Tasha seems to approve of my new look too. She fists her hands on her hips and grins at me. "Penthouse life definitely agrees with you—even if it means I haven't seen you in more than a week."

It's a none-too-subtle chide, but she's right. I have been spending a lot of time alone with Nick, especially since I moved into his place. Tasha has her family and a large social circle of her own, but she always makes me feel special and a part of her life.

After having worked together at Vendange five or more nights a week on average for the past year, she's not only my best friend but the closest thing to family I've had since I moved to this city.

"Speaking of gorgeous," she says, "where's your smokin' hot sex-god boyfriend today?"

"Meetings all day at his office." A couple of weeks ago, I recall scoffing at the idea that Nick and I were a couple in the boyfriend-girlfriend sense of the word. Even though I'm not entirely sure what to call us now, it's Tasha's wry smile that tugs my own mouth into a smirk. "As for the smoking hot sex-god part—accurate though it may be—is that really any way to talk about your new boss?"

"Good point." She purses her lips, looking far from contrite. "It's totally inappropriate for me to objectify Vendange's new owner like that. From now on, I'll refer to him as *mister* smokin' hot sex-god."

Her laugh is big and warm, one of the most comforting sounds I know. Hooking her arm through mine, she leads me farther into the restaurant. Male and female waitstaff buzz around us setting the tables, polishing fixtures, and wiping down surfaces. I gesture to the classic uniforms on the servers and bartenders.

"I like the new dress code, by the way. No more cleavage-baring shirts with black skinny jeans and heels for the women?"

Tasha rolls her eyes. "That was the first thing I changed after I took over as manager. I also added three new servers and trained two of them myself as bartending backup. I don't want anyone working mandatory doubles the way Joel made us do, especially those of us with kids at home. To make sure everyone gets the shifts they want, I reshuffled the schedule a bit and made a rotating call list of waitstaff who are looking for extra hours. So far, it's working out great."

"I can see that."

I can't help but be impressed. I remember how frenetic and stressful Vendange was before, when I worked here with Tasha under the previous manager's watch. Now the pace is efficient instead of hectic. The faces of the employees are focused, yet relaxed, not anxious that they'll earn the wrath of an overbearing jerk of a boss. Tasha appears infinitely happier, too, which makes me even more grateful for Nick's unexpected generosity where she's concerned.

There is a part of me that will always consider him my hero for the way he stepped in to protect my friend from Joel's unwanted advances. In true Dominic Baine fashion, he managed to purchase the restaurant out from under Joel and have the bastard tossed out on his ass—all in the space of a few hours.

Nick claimed it was all in the interest of a good business investment, but I know he also did it to help Tasha. He did it for me, even though we'd been in the middle of a big argument and on the verge of breaking up when Tasha arrived at Nick's building in tears after walking off the job following Joel's harassment of her.

She folds her arms and exhales a slow sigh. "I still can't believe I'm managing one of the most popular restaurants in the city."

"Why can't you believe it? You're good at this. You deserve this."

"Thanks." Her gaze lights on me with tender gratitude. But there is a question in her eyes too. "What about you, Ave?"

"What about me?"

She hesitates for a moment, studying me as we stand near the long bar where she and I so often worked together. "Everything okay with you?"

"Yeah. Everything's great."

My reply is automatic, honed by years of practice in pretending I'm fine despite the turmoil inside me. Maybe Tasha has experience doing the same, because she tilts her head, her eyes searching mine. It's all I can do to resist the urge to shutter myself from her scrutiny.

Not that it would work with her anyway. In the relatively short time we've been friends, she always seems to see right through me.

"How's your mom doing?"

Even though I confided in Tasha a couple of weeks ago, after Nick and I came back from the prison in Pennsylvania, it still jars me to hear someone ask about my mother. Her incarceration for murdering her abusive husband had been a secret I'd kept for a decade—one of many I wanted to leave behind me when I moved to New York. I'm certain I'd still be keeping her a secret, but then she took a bad fall and I had no choice but to rush to the prison to be with her.

Nick followed me there, even though it was the last place I wanted him to be. I didn't want anyone to see that part of my life, least of all him. But he stayed with me for as long as I needed. And then, when I was ready, he brought me back home.

"She's okay, all things considered," I tell Tasha. "Her broken ribs and pierced lung are on the mend, but her leg is healing slower than they hoped. They tell me she'll be in the infirmary for a while yet, possibly a month."

Tasha nods. "She's lucky. A fall down a flight of stairs like that could be deadly at her age."

"I know." And even as I say it, my thoughts turn to the threatening text I received this morning. The man who sent it had also called me soon after my mother's accident.

At the time I hadn't questioned how he knew about her fall so quickly. I was too shaken by the sound of his voice—and by the fact that he had found me—after so many years. Now, I have to wonder if he'd had something to do with harming my mom.

Could her fall have been something other than accidental? The very possibility makes the chill in my blood turn even colder.

I can't suppress my shudder, and I only hope Tasha doesn't spot my discomfort before one of the new bar staff comes over to speak with her. As they go over the day's specials on a tablet, I breathe a sigh of relief for the moment's distraction. I need it, if only to get a grip on my suddenly racing heartbeat and the clamminess that's gathering at the back of my neck.

"On second thought, I'd prefer a less obvious wine pairing with the roasted duck," Tasha says. "The Chardonnay is good, but can we try something more interesting?"

"We could do a red," the other woman suggests. "Cabernet or Pinot noir would both work equally well."

Tasha shakes her head. "Again, too expected."

"What about a Carménère?" When both women look at me, I shrug. "We tasted a nice Chilean one last spring, if I recall. Do we still stock it?"

"We do," Tasha says, a grin spreading over her face. "And you're right. It's perfect. Go with that one," she instructs the other employee before sending her off to change the menu. "God, I miss working with you, Avery. You ever want to come back, just say the word."

I slant her a look. "And work at the restaurant my boyfriend now owns? I don't think so. But I do need to find work soon. I'm going to go crazy if I don't have something productive to do during the day when Nick is working. Besides, I can't stand the idea of depending on him for room and board while I'm not contributing anything."

Tasha smirks. "I doubt he'd say you're not earning

your keep. Besides, what about your art? Haven't you been painting?"

"Not for a while."

"How long?"

"I don't know. A couple of weeks, maybe."

I try to sound nonchalant, but she catches on. "You mean, not since you moved in with him."

"Yeah. I guess so." At her contemplative, vaguely disapproving look, I rush to explain. "When Nick and I are together, there's no time for anything else. In case you haven't gathered, the man is . . . intense."

"I've gathered," she says, a droll look in her eyes. "What about when you two aren't tearing each other's clothes off? You said yourself you need something to do while he's busy being king of the corporate world."

"I want to paint," I admit. "But I can't exactly set up in the penthouse and do it."

"Why the hell not? Did Nick say you couldn't?"

"No, of course not. But there's no space—"

Her brows rise. "Don't tell me you can't find one little corner for yourself in an apartment that spans two floors and more than eight-thousand square feet."

"No, that's not the problem either. It's Nick. Really, the problem is me." I blow out a sigh. "I'm not ready for him to see my new work. I want it to be good first."

"Because he told you that it wasn't."

"He was right," I admit, surprised at how the sting of Nick's critique of my art has lessened over time. "He said I was holding back and that it showed on my canvas. He says he believes I have talent, that I have it inside me to be great."

He said a lot more than that, truths I'm only beginning to understand since we've been together. Nick said my art was self-conscious, afraid . . . like me.

But that doesn't mean I'm ready to let him in.

I can't. Not all the way.

Not when there are things I can't allow him to see.

Tasha puts her hand on my wrist, her eyes soft with sympathy, as if I've just spoken all of my fears aloud. "You *need* to paint, Avery. I've seen how much it means to you. It's part of you."

"I know." I nod, grateful for her understanding. "I'll find a way."

"What about renting a little studio somewhere?"

"I don't have the money for that."

"You made five grand from house-sitting for Claire Prentice four months ago."

"Yes, and after paying back rent on my old apartment in Brooklyn, then renting a car to go see my mom two weeks ago, plus dozens of other little expenses, I've got less than half of it left."

"Maybe I can help." Before I can ask what she means, she pulls her cell phone out of her back pocket and calls her husband, Antonio. "Hey, babe. Does Aunt Rosa have any friends who might have a small, unfurnished space to rent here in the city? I'm talking dirt cheap, but not dangerous cheap." She pauses and rolls her eyes. "Yeah, because we don't already have a perfectly good bedroom for that. I'm talking about a place for Avery to use as a studio for a while."

"What?" I shake my head in protest, but there's no stopping her.

"Okay, great. No, just have her call Avery if she finds something. I'll text you her number in a minute. Yep, love you, too, babe."

"Tasha—"

"Don't even start," she says, already slipping her phone back into her pocket. "You've done so much for me, this is the least I can do for you." As she speaks, someone calls out from the back office, alerting her to a delivery that needs a signature. "Listen, I gotta go take care of a few more things before we open."

"All right," I relent, as she pulls me into a brief hug.

"Come back and see me later this week, if you can manage to drag yourself away from your other favorite creative pursuit," she says with a wink. "We can chat about him over a glass of Carménère."

3

The warm summer weather is so nice when I leave Vendange, I decide to walk instead of hailing a taxi or riding the subway back to the Upper East Side. Hundreds of other people apparently have the same idea. Rather than fall in line with the corporate types and other Manhattanites who rush past me on Madison Avenue, I take my time, strolling along the broad sidewalk with the crowds of meandering tourists and window shoppers.

Up and down this bustling stretch of asphalt, concrete, and towering steel, exclusive boutiques stand side-by-side with national brands of all kinds, as well as upscale designer stores, and financial institutions. I'm not in the market for anything specific, but as I approach a luxe lingerie shop, I can't help myself from pausing at the brass-framed windows to admire all of the lacy, satiny things secreted inside.

It isn't hard to imagine how hot Nick's gaze would smolder if he saw me in one of those sexy undergarments . . . or how quickly his strong hands would work to peel it off me in his need to get inside me.

My nipples tighten at the thought. A flush of heat races through me, warmth I feel most intensely between my bare thighs, which now tremble a bit beneath my light linen skirt.

Curiosity, and the desire to drive Nick even a fraction as crazy as he makes me, finally gets the better of me. With a smile curving my lips, I open the glass doors and step inside.

Soft classical music and delicate perfume drift on the comfortably cool air of the boutique. I nod in greeting to one of the half-dozen elegantly outfitted saleswomen who are all busy with other customers. Glad for the privacy to browse on my own, I head toward the section in the back of the shop where the prettiest items are on display in mirrored glass alcoves and stacked glass drawers.

I'm immediately drawn to one of the bra and panty sets I saw in the window. Both comprised of delicate champagne lace and see-through mesh, each piece is embroidered with burgundy satin roses and dainty ribbon trim. The effect is sweetly innocent, yet decadently sexy.

"Lovely, isn't it?"

I turn to find one of the sales attendants approaching. The pretty black woman who smiled at me when I came in. She walks toward me with the fluid grace of a runway model, her stylish, slender figure, high cheekbones, and arresting light green eyes completing the effect.

I nod as she comes to stand beside me at the display. "It's perfect."

"Would you like to try them on? I'm Evelyn. I'll be happy to help you find your sizes and show you to a fitting room."

"Okay, thanks."

I tell her what I wear, then, after retrieving my sizes from within a pair of locked drawers, she brings me into a serene private dressing area that's practically the size of my old studio apartment in Brooklyn.

Evelyn carefully places the bra and panties on a glass vanity table. Next to it is a taupe velvet upholstered bench seat sitting atop a soft rug woven in a feminine pattern of soothing neutrals. Large mirrors and soft, boudoir lighting ensure every angle is presented in the most complimentary fashion.

"Make yourself comfortable," Evelyn says.

I sit down on the cushioned bench and skate my fingers over the barely-there translucent lace cups of the bra, shivering at the thought of Nick doing the same while I'm wearing it. He'll love this, I'm sure. And I'm excited at the idea of watching him unwrap me later tonight and discovering my surprise.

Excited, that is, until I see the price.

Nearly a thousand dollars for the two pieces.

If Evelyn catches my disappointed look, her expression never falters. "You have excellent taste. This set is part of our signature collection. It's a classic that will look beautiful on you for years to come."

When I only nod in response, she smiles kindly and gestures toward the front of the boutique. "If you don't feel this one suits you, we have something similar in our everyday collection that you might like too. Just let me know if you'd like to take a look."

"Thank you." At that same moment, my phone chimes with an incoming call. Nick's ringtone. I reach into my purse to retrieve it. "Sorry."

"Take your time," Evelyn says. She gestures to a brass hand bell sitting on the vanity. "If you need anything, just ring for me."

She walks away, closing the dressing room door behind her as I swipe the screen on my phone and answer Nick's call. "Hi."

"I've been thinking about you all morning."

Just the sound of his deep, raspy voice makes my pulse kick into a faster tempo. I glance at the decadent lacy underthings in front of me and smile wistfully. "I'm thinking about you too."

He makes a low, approving noise in the back of his throat. "Tell me more. Are you touching yourself while you're thinking of me?"

I laugh softly, a flush warming my cheeks. "Not at the moment. I don't think it would be appropriate."

"You know how I feel about being appropriate," he murmurs, and I can picture the wry twist of his mouth as he speaks. "Where are you?"

"On my way back from Vendange. I popped in on Tasha for a little while."

"I hear music in the background."

"I'm in a boutique on Madison."

"Which one?"

"L'opale."

"Nice," he says after a brief pause. "Find anything you like?"

I try to ignore the fact that he seems so readily familiar with the store. I know he's had a sex life before me, but the idea of him buying any of these things for another woman puts a pang of jealousy in my breast.

"Avery?"

"Hm?"

"You said you're shopping for lingerie and thinking of me. Christ, I'm already hard just picturing that." His voice lowers to that silken tone that always leaves me weak in the knees. "Indulge me before I have to head into another damn meeting. What sexy little things are you looking at? Better yet, try something on for me and let me see you in it. We can switch to video chat and see where things go."

Now the heat that had flushed my face travels down my neck and straight to my core. "I can't do that," I whisper, squirming a bit on the velvet bench seat. "Someone might see."

"The dressing rooms are completely private," he says with more certainty than I care to acknowledge. "Get into one, Avery."

"I already am."

"Then we're halfway there." He chuckles, but there's more heat than humor in his voice. "Are you already undressed too?"

"No. I brought in a bra and panties to try on, but I've changed my mind about them. I was going to put them back before you called."

"Why?"

I shrug, and even though he can't see me, he seems to home in on my discomfiture.

"Put them on for me. I'll call you back on video in two minutes."

He ends the call on that demand, and I exhale a sigh as I glance at the beautiful lingerie I have no business pretending I can afford. But I know Nick was serious that he expects me to show him what I selected, and there is a part of me that's hungry for his reaction. Hungry to see his desire for me, especially when he's busy with work, yet making time to play naughty games with me.

Stepping out of my sandals, I take off my silk tank top and linen skirt, then slip out of my pastel peach department store bra. The first wisp of expensive champagne lace and burgundy satin against my bare breasts feels like a caress. I fasten the front closure and adjust the delicate ribbon straps, then scoop my breasts so they're sitting high and plump in the pretty balconette cups.

Because I won't be buying the lingerie, I leave the three-hundred-dollar panties on the vanity table and walk over to the mirrors to see how I look before Nick calls. I thought my lace-edged peach thong had been cute enough when I left the penthouse, but seeing it next to the stunning bra makes it look as mundane as a pair of cotton briefs. On a frustrated huff, I reach down to take it off, just as my phone chimes with Nick's incoming call.

As promised, he's calling from a video app. His handsome face fills the screen, making my breath catch even though I've had the privilege of seeing those dark-lashed cerulean eyes and brutally sensual features practically every day and night for the past four months.

"That wasn't two minutes."

He smirks. "I didn't have the patience to wait that long."

He's not at his desk, but seated on the pale gray leather sofa in the conversation area of his large office.

Behind him, a broad wall of gleaming silver granite soars easily fifteen feet from the floor to the ceiling. The wall serves as a backdrop for a single work of art—a Jackson Pollock original painted in black enamel. The tangle of chaotic lines and bold splashes are a stark contrast to the steady, in-control titan of business seated in front of the masterwork.

Settled back against the clean lines of the sofa, Nick grips his phone in one hand as he loosens his tie with the other. His mouth quirks at one corner as he holds my gaze from inside his corporate headquarters across town. "Let me see you, baby."

I slowly extend my arm, giving him a view of the gorgeous bra. His low exhalation and thickly uttered curse tells me he approves.

"More," he commands over the lowered volume of the speaker. "Let me see all of you."

"I'm not wearing the panties."

"Show me."

I shake my head. "I'd have to try them on over my own underwear unless I intend to buy them."

Nick doesn't seem to care about my explanation. His eyes are blazing hot on me. He leans forward as if he wants to crawl through the phone. "Let me see your pussy, baby."

Pressing my lips together, I angle the camera so he can see all of me.

"Holy fuck." There is a fevered edge to his voice, a raw current of need that ignites the same in me. "You're so damn beautiful. You get me hot just thinking about you. I'm hard as fucking steel over here."

My body responds to his carnal praise as if he's here in the room with me, looking at me . . . caressing me.

Wanting me.

"Touch yourself. I want to see you stroke that pretty little clit."

"Nick," I whisper, worried that we'll get interrupted, yet astonished that it doesn't stop me from obeying him.

With my free hand, I slide my fingers down over the trimmed patch of curls between my legs, then into the wet cleft of my body. I'm drenched already, my sex aching for him. I can't hold back my moan.

His breath leaves him on a deep groan. "Jesus Christ, what you do to me."

I angle the phone so I can see him too. His jaw is clenched, his brows lowered over the intensity of his stare. I see him shift on the sofa, the camera's focus jostling with his movements. I hear the soft metallic jangle of his belt buckle, followed by the quiet rasp of the zipper on his suit pants.

The thought of him taking his cock in hand while I stroke myself several blocks away is almost too much to take. I want him so badly, I can hardly stand it. I bite down on my bottom lip to keep the cry from spilling off my tongue.

Nick hisses a sharp curse. "Fuck this. I've got a better idea."

"What?" My voice is thick, my blood roaring in my ears as I draw my fingers away from my throbbing flesh.

"I'm going to send Patrick to pick you up. I want you in my office. Right now."

"But your meeting—"

"Can wait," he says. "I, however, cannot. Look for the car in ten minutes. Bring the bra and panties with you."

I shake my head, embarrassed by the reminder that

I'm out of my league in this shop and with this man. "Nick, I can't afford them. They cost almost a thousand dollars."

"Have the store put them on my account."

His account? Disappointment does battle with my embarrassment, and I'm not sure which one bothers me more. "You have an account at L'opale?"

He arches a dark brow. "I have accounts at many nice places around the city."

"I'll bet you do." I'm sulking a little at that admission, but it's hard to be totally irritated with him when he's looking at me like I'm the only woman he's ever wanted this badly. The power of that heated, sensual smile is enough to melt everything except my desire for him.

"Ask for Evelyn, she's the manager. She'll take care of everything for you."

My lips flatten in reaction to that telling statement. "How many other women have you outfitted with expensive lingerie?"

"Do you really want to know?" His eyes hold mine unflinchingly.

I remain mute, because, damn him, I don't want to know the answer to that question. Not that it would change my mind, anyway. I trace my finger over one of the embroidered silk burgundy roses on the bra, taking far too much satisfaction in the way his hot gaze follows my every movement. "You're sure you have the time for this? For me?"

The look he gives me is so possessive, it obliterates all doubt.

"Ten minutes. In my office. And Avery, I intend to show you just how sure I am."

4

Nick's driver drops me off in front of the dark glass tower on West 57th Street that houses Baine International. Holding the door open for me as I climb out, he offers me a pleasant nod once I alight to the curb.

"Thank you, Patrick."

"My pleasure, as always, Ms. Ross."

I enter the lobby of the multi-use building—one of several Manhattan properties Nick owns—wishing I'd had the foresight to bring a larger handbag when I left the apartment this morning. My tiny cross-body is useless when it comes to concealing my boutique purchases, so I have no choice but to carry the pearl-white shopping bag from L'opale into the building with me, its logo emblazoned in gold foil on both sides for everyone to see.

As I walk to the security desk in the lobby, I wave to

the guard on duty. It's the same man who was posted here last week when Nick brought me to his office after-hours to pick up some last-minute paperwork he needed to sign.

Late-twenties, his hazel eyes sharp and serious beneath a crown of brown hair cut just a shade longer than military high-and-tight, there's no mistaking the muscular Baine International security guard for anything other than a recent veteran.

"Hello, Gabe."

"Morning, Ms. Ross." As I approach to sign in, he stands up and gestures me on to the elevators. "No need to register. Mr. Baine called down a few minutes ago to say he was expecting you."

"Oh. Okay, thanks."

I have to admit, it feels good to sail through the Baine International lobby as if I'm not just another random visitor to the building or guest of the very eligible bachelor who commands half the city from his office on the top floor. Of course, I don't imagine many of Nick's visitors come to see him at work carrying a bag of expensive lingerie in their hand.

At least, they damn sure better not.

Since I have no choice but to own the situation, I ride the elevator to the thirty-fourth floor with the ribbon handles of the shopping bag held casually in my grasp. Lily Fontana, Nick's personal assistant, is just finishing a phone call as I emerge from the lift. We've never been introduced, but I know of her through Nick, and, by accident once, I saw her pretty, heart-shaped face and long ebony hair in a photo on his phone's contact directory.

She catches my gaze and continues talking to the

person on the other end of the line. Her voice is professional, but cool, in contrast with the pleasant smile she gives me as I walk farther into the private reception area.

"Unfortunately, as I informed your press secretary earlier this week, Senator McCormack, Mr. Baine's calendar is quite full. He's asked me to convey his regrets that he will be unable to attend. Of course. Yes, I'll be sure to let Mr. Baine know."

Lily politely ends the call and turns the full impact of her dazzling smile on me.

"You must be Avery," she says, coming around her desk to offer me her hand in greeting.

I take it, surprised by her directness and the firmness of her grip for such a petite woman. Diminutive in size only, Nick's longtime assistant is clearly a force to be reckoned with—which makes sense. I know from experience that shrinking violets would not last long in Dominic Baine's world.

"Nice to meet you, Lily."

"Nice to meet you too. Nick should be out shortly," she tells me. "He's finishing up in the conference room down the hall. He said he'd like you to wait for him in his office."

"Okay."

"Been out doing a little shopping?" She glances at the bag in my hand as she leads me toward Nick's corner office at the end of the corridor. "I adore L'opale. But then, what woman wouldn't, right?"

I nod noncommittally, and, before I can reply, I hear Nick's voice coming from somewhere ahead of us. He steps out of a meeting room accompanied by three other men in suits and a middle-aged woman dressed in a blue nun's habit and white long-sleeved blouse. I recognize one of the men as Andrew Beckham, Nick's lawyer. The handsome black attorney helped orchestrate the purchase of Vendange. The other men are unfamiliar to me, but the way they defer to Nick leaves no question as to who's in charge.

They all look our way, and I'm not sure what makes my face turn redder with self-consciousness—Nick's smoldering glance, or the sister's curious stare from behind her round, wire-rimmed glasses.

Shit. Of all the damn luck.

Why couldn't I be strolling in with a bag of library books or baked goods in my hand? Or clothes to donate for the needy?

Lily keeps walking, and I have no choice but to follow.

Smiling and murmuring a polite, "Pardon us, please," she leads me past the group while I do my best to pretend I'm not heading into Nick's office with the full intent to sin as soon as I can get my hands on him.

His deep voice does little to help my focus. "Again, Sister Margaret, Commissioner Rhodes, gentlemen—I do apologize for cutting today's meeting short. Something urgent arose a few minutes ago and I must take care of it personally."

I barely stifle the grin that tugs at my lips over his very deliberate choice of words. Although I don't dare look behind me, I'm certain I feel the heat of Nick's gaze on my ass as I walk with Lily the rest of the way down the corridor.

She lets me into the expansive office and indicates the seating area in front of the Pollock painting. "Can I get you anything to drink while you wait, Avery?"

I return her smile and shake my head. "No, thank you."

Giving me a slight nod of acknowledgment, she leaves the room, closing the door quietly behind her. The far wall of Nick's office is one immense window affording the kind of spectacular views I've come to expect of the places he spends any significant amounts of time. Yet as large and impressive as the space is, it's almost clinical in its lack of personal effects or expressions of individual style.

When he brought me here briefly a few nights ago, I hadn't really paused to absorb the details. Or, rather, their lack. Now, I notice little else.

There are no photographs or trinkets on his desk. No mementoes or *objets d'art* on any of the consoles or cabinets. Except for the multimillion-dollar canvas that consumes nearly all of one wall in the room, there is nothing that provides so much as a glimpse into Dominic Xavier Baine the international business magnate—or the man.

And while his office is comfortably appointed and impeccably situated in one of the finest areas of the city, I feel an unshakable sense of sadness as I stand in the middle of so much emptiness. I feel alone and lost. Solitary.

Imprisoned, despite the openness of the city all around me.

Does he feel it too?

Will he ever allow me close enough to him to find out?

This isn't the first time I've wondered about his seemingly impenetrable remoteness and isolation. Not the first time I've questioned if allowing myself to fall for a man with the kind of demons and dark secrets I suspect Nick is harboring can be anything but foolish—even dangerous—when I have so many of my own.

If my heart would have it any other way, I'd have never let Nick in.

If I were smart, I'd still try to find the strength to walk away—now, before my past catches up with me. Before it has the chance to hurt Nick the way it's hurt everyone else I've loved.

If I didn't think he would come after me again, maybe I would go.

But there's an even more cowardly part of me that's terrified he won't.

Not if he knew the truth.

I've set my bag and purse down on the sofa to drift in front of the massive windows when I hear the door snick open behind me a few moments later. Every nerve ending in my body responds as if trained to know Nick's presence. I hold still, my breath caught in my lungs, waiting for the moment I feel him come close.

His arms wrap around me from behind. I sink into his embrace, my demons chased back into the shadows now that he's here. I exhale on a deep, tremulous sigh I feel I've been holding since I stepped out of the dressing room at L'opale.

His warmth and strength engulf me, comforting me as much as he arouses me. The rigid pressure of his growing erection resting snugly against my ass sends fire licking through my veins.

God, how I want him.

The need he stirred in me over the phone roars back tenfold now that I'm standing in his arms.

He nestles his face into the crook of my neck and

nips my tender flesh. "Do you have any idea how awkward it is sitting across from a nun when you've got a rampant hard-on hidden under the table?"

I laugh as I pivot in his loose grasp to face him. "You're the one who started it, insisting on a private peep show in your office."

"I trust Evelyn handled everything for you like I said she would?"

"Yes, Evelyn was great. She was very nice, extremely discreet. She hardly blinked when I told her you instructed her to put my things on your personal account."

"I'm glad to hear it." He grins, loosening his pewter-colored tie. "It's always good to have firsthand reports from satisfied customers."

I gape at him. "Are you saying you *own* L'opale?"

"Technically, I own the building. Beck owns the store." Beck, as in Andrew Beckham, Nick's attorney. "He bought the boutique for his sister to manage a few years ago, after Evelyn went through a rough patch in her personal life and needed to start over."

I close my eyes as understanding sinks in. Now that he's made the connection for me, I realize the strikingly similar features that Beck and his sister share, from their tall, lean bodies and dramatic facial structures, to their creamy brown skin tones and stunning, light-colored eyes.

And while I'm still not ready to ask if I'm the first woman he's purchased thousand-dollar lingerie for on his account at the boutique, the fact that he owns the building and his friend and colleague is the proprietor helps me to at least rationalize some of his apparent familiarity with the shop.

"So, you're telling me that Baine International invests in everything from five-star hotels and commercial properties around the world, to retail space for women's unmentionables?"

"Among other things." Nick's mouth quirks. "I have varied and eclectic interests."

I practically snort. "Not the first two words that pop into my mind."

He laughs, drawing my hand into his and guiding it down to his very impressive erection. "I don't suppose I need to elaborate on the words that are popping into my mind right now. Or less conveniently, during my meeting with the good sister."

I cup my hand around the bulge in his charcoal gray suit pants. "Serves you right, making me walk in here carrying lingerie in my hand, especially when you apparently knew damn well who was here."

He smirks, thoroughly unrepentant. "Could've been worse. There's an interesting sex shop in the Village I'd like you to see."

"I suppose you have an account there too?" I raise my brows. "More than an account?"

He holds my gaze without answering, and my imagination whirls with curiosity about this man and all the pieces of him that he has yet to reveal to me. What kinds of erotic things would he want to show me?

What kinds of carnal, rawly sexual things would he demand of me?

Memories of our time together on his sailboat in Miami several weeks ago now replay vividly in my mind. Memories of surrendering to him completely, my hands bound tight, my body belonging wholly to him.

My sex throbs at the recollection . . . at the possibility

of knowing that kind of dark pleasure with him again.

Trust me, he'd demanded.

And I had, even though it terrified me.

Even though trust is the one thing I've never been able to give a man.

In these past several months, I've given Nick more of me than I have anyone else in my entire twenty-five years. That should terrify me too. It does, but with him even fear has its own kind of allure.

With him, I'm dancing right up next to the flames of everything I'm afraid of and I'm learning that I can actually enjoy the burn.

With him, I'm learning that I crave it.

Nick's gaze is far too knowing as he slides his palm around to the back of my neck, his fingers strong and firm against my nape, yet infinitely tender. He makes a low noise in the back of his throat, then presses a light kiss to my brow. "We'll save that conversation for another time. Come."

He takes my hand and leads me back to the leather sofa, pausing to reach for a slim silver remote that closes the dark wood louvers on all of the room's corridor-facing glass. That same remote apparently locks the door, too, the faint metallic whisper sealing us inside.

"Won't your employees wonder what we're doing in here?"

"No. And if they do, none of them will dare let on one way or the other." He slants me a serious look. "I demand trust from the people around me as much as I demand excellent performance. I pay well for both."

I feel a cold pang as I glance over at the bag of ridiculously expensive lingerie, which is not the only extravagant gift I've received from him. Nick has spoiled me with fine things these past few months. Incredible dinners at the city's best restaurants. Romantic getaways. A long rope of exquisite pearls that must have easily cost him tens of thousands of dollars.

"Is that how you feel about the women you date too?"

He frowns. "That I expect trust and performance? Or that I'm willing to buy it?"

I shake my head, wishing I hadn't spoken my thoughts out loud. "I don't know. Both."

A certain hardness moves over his expression. "What are you really asking, Avery?"

Too late to pull the words back, I hold his searching gaze. "Is that how you feel about me?"

Instead of answering, he cups my face in his hands and pulls me into a slow, bone-melting kiss. When our lips finally part, he doesn't release me. His brows furrowed, he exhales a quiet curse and lowers his forehead to rest against mine. "*That* is how I feel about you. Never doubt that. Never doubt what we have together."

I manage a nod, but that doesn't seem good enough for him. Lifting my chin on the edge of his scarred hand, he searches my gaze. "Tell me you won't doubt what we have together."

"I won't," I promise, unsure why it means so much to him to hear it when he's never promised me more than a moment. His eyes vow more than that, however. Right from the start, those fathomless blue eyes have promised me everything I dare to grasp. I need only to reach for it. "I won't doubt you, Nick."

His thumb traces the line of my lower lip. "Good girl."

I meet his touch with the tip of my tongue. "I thought I was coming here to be a bad girl," I say, hoping to steer us back to the playfulness I saw in him before I let my insecurities dampen the mood. "I'm surprised Sister Margaret's habit didn't catch on fire from all of the dirty things I was thinking as I passed you in the hallway."

His voice drops to a thick rumble. "Is that right?"

I nod. "I have to admit, seeing you with a nun was . . . unexpected."

"Really, why?" He sits on the sofa, but doesn't coax me down with him. There's a teasing glimmer in his eyes that I can't resist. "Because I'm the devil incarnate?"

I give him an arch look, all too aware that my stance in front of him has now perfectly positioned my sex level with his face. "If you mean in bed, the answer is definitely yes."

He grunts, running his hands up my bare legs and under my linen skirt. "Some would argue in business too."

"I don't know, Sister Margaret seems to like you well enough. She seemed downright charmed, if you ask me." I suck in a gasp as his touch skims my inner thighs. "How often do you meet with her?"

"Only when we're talking about plans for the children's rec center I want to build."

I freeze in his arms. "That's the meeting you cancelled?"

Nick confided in me not long after we met that he's been trying to get permits and construction approvals for a recreation center for impoverished inner city kids. It's a pet project that obviously means a great deal to him, yet here he is, blowing off a meeting about it to mess around with me.

I seize his wandering hands from beneath my skirt and hold them still. "Why didn't you tell me that's what you were doing today? Jesus, Nick. I don't want to interrupt your work on that project." As important as the rec center construction is to him, it is me who's become his singular focus at this moment. I can't deny the thrill it gives me, even though I'll probably go to hell for tempting him away from doing good, charitable work with Sister Margaret. "You should have told me. I never would've agreed to come here like this if I'd known."

"What makes you think I would've let you refuse?" Wry words, but the dark glimmer in his deep blue eyes is intense with meaning. "Need I remind you of our agreement, Ms. Ross? You know the terms."

As if to emphasize his point, he brings his hands out from under mine to resume their upward slide under my skirt. His fingers move onto the curve of my ass and contract, kneading the bare mounds of my flesh. The thin fabric of my thong wedges into the crevice between my cheeks, making me hyperaware of every flex of his fingers, every caress that brings his touch achingly closer to my core.

"Anywhere I want, anything I ask of you," he murmurs, repeating the promise I gave him in that rain-soaked parking lot the day he came looking for me. "No boundaries. No barriers between what I desire and what you're willing to surrender to me."

I nod and release a shaky sigh, torn between wanting him to soothe the wet, throbbing ache of my sex, yet savoring the anticipation of the pleasure I know he will give me. I can't look away from his face. The combination of his low voice and sensual touch rivets me. That's all it takes for him to make the rest of the world fall away for me.

The fact that he can look at me and make me believe that somehow I do the same for him is the most powerful aphrodisiac I'll ever know.

His eyes rivet on mine, holding my gaze so possessively, I can hardly breathe. All I can think about is the need for him to touch me, to kiss me . . . to make me come the way I nearly did back at the L'opale dressing room.

But he isn't ready to give me that relief just yet. I see the truth of that in his ruthless gaze.

His hands slowly drift away from me. Yanking his tie loose, he tosses it carelessly aside, then unfastens the top two buttons on his shirt. He leans back now, draping his arms along the back of the sofa, his thighs spread. His knees cage me on both sides where I stand in front of him. With his cock straining in the confines of his pressed trousers, he looks at me with a profane mixture of hot lust and cool, aggravating control.

"Undress for me, Avery."

I shoot a sidelong glance at the door and the shuttered windows, the only things concealing us from an entire floor full of people. Muffled voices carry indistinctly from the corridor outside. At almost noon, the office is buzzing with activity and conversation.

"Don't think about them," he instructs me firmly. "There is no one else right now. Only us. And I want you naked."

There is no leniency in his command, only certitude that I will obey. Because he knows I will. Not because it's part of our agreement, but because I want desperately to please him.

Despite my fear of discovery—despite my awareness of all the reasons I shouldn't find a man's complete domination of me as seductive as I do with Nick—I nod my head in acquiescence and begin to do what he demands.

I remove my sandals, then slowly peel off my white silk tank and let it flutter to the cocktail table behind me. My breasts feel heavy, too constricted within the lacy cups of my bra. My nipples have been hard as pebbles ever since Nick entered the room with me.

Now I feel them pucker even more under the hungered blaze of his eyes as I reach around to unzip my skirt. The linen slides down my bare legs, pooling at my ankles. I step out of it, a move that brings me one pace closer to the edge of the sofa and Nick's erotic, negligent sprawl.

I shiver, not from any chill, but from the pure animal heat that pours off him as I stand before him. I can see what it's costing him not to reach for me, to deny himself the urge to snatch me up right now and throw me down beneath him. His hands are splayed on his spread thighs, his strong fingers curling into the muscle of his legs so intensely his knuckles are bone white.

"The rest, Avery." His voice is raw, coarse with desire.

With one arm laid across my breasts, I reach back with my other hand to unfasten the clasp on my bra. It springs loose, held in place only for a moment before I let it fall away. Nick's breath leaks out of him on a low curse.

That curse becomes a groan a moment later, as I slip my fingers into the front of my thong and slide it off my hips.

"Jesus Christ, baby. How many times have I seen you take off your clothes, and yet I'm never prepared for just how fucking beautiful you are."

He reaches for me at last, harshly dragging me toward him as he moves to the edge of the leather cushion. His hands grasp my wrists and push my arms behind me, leaving my body wide open to him. Then he is off the sofa and down on the floor on his knees, his mouth closing over my sex. Sensation rushes up on me in wave after wave as his tongue spears into the folds of my cleft, wet and hot and hungered.

My head drops back, a jagged mewl of pleasure tearing from my throat.

Nick shows me no mercy.

Thank God.

My body has been on the verge of exploding for what feels like hours, and now that Nick's mouth is on me, I know I won't last long. He kisses and licks and suckles me, his wicked tongue moving from the tight knot of my clit to the drenched seam of my body.

When his grasp on my hands goes lax, I know better than to risk moving them. I know his cues well enough by now. He has no rope to bind me, but he wants my surrender just the same. My reward is the deepening power of his lips and tongue on my quivering flesh, while his hands now roam freely over my body.

"Nick," I gasp brokenly. "Oh, fuck . . . I'm so close. I'm going to come."

He moans against my pussy, his tongue pushing inside now, adding fuel to the fire of my building release. I clutch my hands together behind my back, my legs starting to tremble violently under the sensual assault of his mouth. He pulls my clit between his lips, sucking the bundle of nerves so intensely I see stars behind my closed eyelids.

When his finger enters me and drives deep, my orgasm erupts. It takes me over the edge, splintering my senses. I cry out with the force of it, not caring if every person on the floor can hear me. This is what he does to me. Makes me shameless. Makes me bold.

With him, I've become someone I would never have recognized just four short months ago.

His name boils past my lips as hard tremors rock me. My legs feel boneless, my body wrung out and quaking under the relentless pleasure of his wicked mouth and skillful hands.

His gaze catches mine, his blue eyes stormy, as dark and wild as a tempest. The sight of him licking me so carnally while he watches my face twist in uncontrolled passion is nearly enough to make me come all over again.

I reach for his shoulders to steady myself, but in the next moment he's shifting between my parted legs, giving me one final, dizzying lash of his tongue before he moves back onto the edge of the sofa cushion.

His mouth is wet with my juices, those full, sensual lips held in a way that tells me he's just as fevered as I am. More, because while my climax is still echoing through me, his own is banked and burning. Waiting to be set loose.

On a wordless growl, he tugs me down to meet his kiss. His mouth ravishes mine. There's no gentleness in it. No gentleness in his hard grasp on my arms as he urges me to my knees before him now, his meaning unmistakable.

I fumble with the buckle on his smooth leather belt. I expect the metal to be cool, but it's heated from the inferno of his body. As I unfasten it and slide his zipper down, Nick's tongue thrusts deep into my mouth, sweet and musky, the taste of me still lingering there.

My fingers work quickly to free him, spurred by the awareness of his need and my own ravenous hunger to have him in my mouth. Thick and hot and heavy, he fills my greedy hands. I break away from our kiss on a moan, starving to feast my eyes on him.

His big cock thrusts out of his open trousers, jutting high against his abdomen. My core clenches at the sight. My mouth waters shamelessly. I lick my lips, then lower my head to take the broad crown into my mouth.

Usually, I like to tease him a little at first, but I have no patience for that now. Neither one of us does. I take all of him in a long, slow slide, not stopping until he hits the back of my throat.

"Ah, Christ." Nick's words are strangled, uttered through clenched teeth.

When I draw up to his tip, his pelvis bucks reflexively, a shudder racking him. His hands roam over the back of my head, tangling in my hair, his fingers flexing and contracting with every inch of him I devour as I go even deeper with him this time.

"Baby," he groans. "Yeah . . . take all of it. God, that's so fucking good."

I hum in response to his praise, bobbing my head faster, harder, taking him as deep into my throat as I can bear. I've never cared much for sucking a man off, and considering my history, that's probably little wonder. But I can't get enough of Nick. I can't get enough of his pleasure, or knowing that I have the power to deliver it.

His growl tells me he's close. Slick, salty liquid beads against my tongue as I reach the tip of him once more.

He thrusts into my mouth, hissing a curse as I tighten my lips around him and lower my head down to his groin.

"Avery . . ."

I don't let up for a moment. I'm obsessed with the need to make him come. Caressing his balls with one hand, I wrap the other around the hard stalk of his shaft, pumping him firmly while I lick and suck and worship every delicious inch of him.

His breath races out of his lungs, heavy pants that sharpen as I continue to work him. "Ah, fuck, baby. Your mouth is amazing."

His hands hold my head in place, his arms trembling with the force of his need. As I slide my mouth up to the crown of his cock again, his hips jerk, then begin to piston hard and fast and tight. A low roar builds inside him as he fucks my mouth.

When he shouts my name again, it's raw, jagged. And then the first hot burst of his semen erupts on my tongue. It jets against the back of my throat, thick and scalding, almost more than I can handle. I swallow and he fills my mouth again and again, his hips still bucking in a wild rhythm, his hands still fisted in my hair.

We're both panting, both spent and languid, when the last of his aftershocks have faded. Sagged against the leather cushion at his back, he pulls me up beside him. Tenderly, he cups my face in his hands and draws me close for an unrushed kiss. My lips are swollen, pulsing from the fevered intensity of our passion and the force of his climax.

Nick's tongue sweeps over mine in slow, gentling strokes. For long moments, we simply kiss and caress and hold each other. When he releases me, I nestle naked against his side, my legs drawn up onto the sofa.

I tip my head up and meet his hooded gaze. "So much for the private lingerie show you wanted."

He grunts, a smile tugging at the corner of his sinful mouth. "What are you talking about? I thought this was only the pre-show."

I laugh, my fingers toying idly in his mussed dark hair. His crisp white shirt is wrinkled and askew, his bespoke suit pants undone and bunched around his hips. "You look awfully sexy like this Mr. Baine, all spent and disheveled."

One black brow wings up in dark amusement. "Who says I'm spent?"

He leans toward me and cups my breast, flicking his thumb over the nipple and making a low sound of approval when the bud tightens in response to even that brief touch. Raising my chin on the tips of his fingers, he brushes his mouth over mine in a tender kiss that leaves me sighing for more. When he draws away from me a moment later, I can't curb my frown.

"Evidently I'm not the only one who's not spent just yet." He tweaks my nipple, then takes my hand and draws me up off the sofa. "Come with me."

"Where to?"

"To freshen up," he says. "Then I'm going to take you out for lunch. Eventually."

5

Nearly two hours later, Nick and I are seated at a cozy corner table, enjoying a late lunch in one of the finest restaurants in the Upper East Side. Even at the midafternoon hour, the dining room is packed. Because I've worked in the business for some time, I'm well aware that the wait for a reservation in any of the star chef's handful of locations around the city can be days or even a week or more in advance.

Yet Nick and I sailed right in moments after we arrived. And although the maitre d' was infinitely discreet as he led us away from the crowd of people waiting at the front of the house for their reservations, I don't doubt for a second that a table "just happens to be available" whenever Dominic Baine steps through the door.

I pick at my delicious meal of grilled sea bass, trying not to stare when I spy more than a few celebrities seated among the tables and banquettes occupied by assorted suits, titans of business and media, and ladies who lunch. For all my effort, I notice I'm not the only one trying not to gape. Nick and I have not gone unnoticed either, and the surreptitious glances from several directions across the room make me fidget a bit on the plush velvet chair beneath me.

My self-consciousness isn't helped any by the fact that beneath my blousy white silk tank, I'm wearing the new bra Nick bought for me. At his insistence, after we made love in the shower in his office's private bathroom, I gave him the lingerie show I promised.

I hadn't intended to wear the sexy underthings to lunch, but once he saw them on me, he refused to let me take them off. Now, I can't help feeling conspicuous for the way the tiny burgundy roses ghost beneath my top. To my mortification, I can also see my nipples, which are barely covered by the shallow balconette cups.

When I glance at Nick, he's staring at me as he brings his glass of Lagavulin twelve-year to his lips. "Stop worrying about what anyone thinks of you, Avery."

"That's easy for you to say," I tell him, my voice as quiet as his—not that anyone can hear us above the hubbub of lively conversation filling the dining room. "I guess I was picturing sandwiches at a tavern or deli somewhere, not . . . this."

He studies me over the rim of the wide-bowled glass of amber liquid. "You don't feel comfortable here?"

I scoff softly. "Not really, no." My gaze drops, unable to look at him as I whisper my chagrin. "If you knew we were coming here, why did you make me dress like this?"

"Because it pleases me." He sets his drink down

soundlessly on the cloth-covered table and reaches for my restless hand. His palm settles over my fingers, warm and firm. "Because I want every man in this place to look at you with the same lust that I feel for you. I want you to understand the kind of power you have."

"Power?" My head comes up in confusion.

I try to pull my hand away from him, but he holds me in place. Oddly, his touch grounds me, centers me, even while I feel panic and outrage building in my chest.

Nick knows my history. I've confided in him about my stepfather's repeated abuse, about my rape the night my mother killed the son of a bitch. The very last thing I want is to draw the attention of men I don't know.

Or that of people who might look at me in this rarefied place and see that I don't belong here. That I'm not like them.

That I'm less than them.

That I'm damaged . . . dirty.

"Nick, don't—"

"No hiding, Avery. Not with me, remember?" His gaze is intense in the muted light of the restaurant. His grasp on me doesn't lessen, but his strength is coaxing, not coercive. "You promised to trust me." He strokes the top of my hand, slow brushes of his thumb over my skin. "You agreed that for these hundred nights, you are mine. Whatever I ask, whatever pleases me. Not merely because I demand it of you, but because you trust me enough to let me lead you into places you've never gone."

I swallow, darting a glance anxiously around us. We're beginning to draw attention from the tables nearest to ours. I feel heat flood my cheeks.

Yet as self-conscious as I am, my panic is receding. I

feel the coldness of it melting away as Nick holds my hand, caressing my skin while his smoldering, yet coolly in-control gaze draws me in until he is all I see . . . all I feel. All I know.

"Do you trust me, Avery?"

"Yes." The word rushes over my tongue without hesitation. "Yes, Nick. I trust you."

His lips curve almost imperceptibly, satisfaction gleaming in his eyes. "You see? Power."

Gently pulling my hand to his mouth, he kisses the tips of my fingers, then releases me. Casually, he picks up his silverware and slices off a piece of his grilled lamb chop. "How's the sea bass, Ms. Ross?"

I stare at him, astonished that he can go from full-throttle intensity to relaxed nonchalance in the blink of an eye. His abrupt change tells me our conversation is over. He's made his point and I have to admit I do feel a certain defiance as I straighten my spine and take a sip of my Sauvignon blanc. I'm still not totally comfortable with the furtive glances—and, now, the flurry of whispers—circulating the room, but I am comfortable with Nick.

And, yes, I trust him.

"The sea bass is amazing, Mr. Baine."

"Good," he says, his tone heavy with sexual heat. "I promise I will never steer you wrong."

The look he gives me is pure sin. I squirm on my chair, eager with the anticipation of finding out just how far he intends to take that vow.

We fall into a comfortable silence, both of us enjoying our food and drinks. I hadn't realized how absolutely starved I was, but then again, Nick and I definitely know how to work up an appetite. I'm so engrossed in the joy of my five-star meal, I hardly register the muffled chime of my phone's ringtone.

"Sorry." Appalled to be that rude diner whose call disrupts the entire room, I hurry to reach into my purse and silence the damn thing. Nick watches me as I glance at the display, then send Tasha's aunt to voice mail.

"Nothing you need to handle?"

I shake my head. "I'll check my messages later."

"Because if it has something to do with your mother—"

"No," I reply quickly. "No, it's nothing like that. Just something Tasha and I talked about today."

He grunts, taking a sip of his whisky. "I've been thinking about her lately. Your mother, that is."

"You have?" I'm fiercely protective of my mom. Nick's tone is nothing if not concerned, but God help me, as hard as I try to sound merely curious, there is a tightness in my voice that I can only pray he won't detect. "What about her?"

He sets his glass down, pensively rubbing his thumb along the rim. "I know people, Avery. Lawyers who might be able to help. Between Beck and I, we know dozens of the top attorneys in the country—including criminal defense lawyers. We know some judges too."

I don't say anything for a moment, uncertain what he might be suggesting and reluctant to guess. "She's got a lawyer, Nick."

He scoffs. "A public defender, who from what I've gathered from you would hardly be fit to represent the local dogcatcher." As sharp as his opinion of Walter Stadler is, Nick's careful to keep his voice quiet enough for my ears only. "I think I might be able to help. I want to help, Avery. We can get your mother a new team of lawyers right away. From there, we can work on getting her a new trial—with the kind of representation she deserved in the first place."

I listen, stunned. Moved.

Terrified.

There's so much he doesn't understand. So much he doesn't know—can't know.

"Nick, the trial was hell on her. And now she's in the infirmary with no idea how long she might be recovering. I don't think she'll agree to any of this—"

"Then you'll have to convince her." He reaches out for my hand again. "Let me do this for her. For you."

"Nick, I just . . ." I shake my head lamely as his gaze bores into me. Nick is a man used to making the whole world bend to his wishes. I've seen him in action, so I know he's fully capable of moving mountains if that's what it takes to get what he wants.

This is different. I can hardly breathe as I look at his handsome face, so full of earnest conviction. So full of determination to fix something that cannot be fixed—not the way he thinks.

I'm touched that he wants to try, that he genuinely cares about my mother's situation, and, by extension, that he cares for me.

But there are a hundred reasons why I cannot allow him to get involved. They all jam up in my throat, along with the fear I have that one day, I won't be able to keep them inside anymore.

"Nick." I swallow, my mouth gone suddenly dry. My hand is still captured in his grasp, my gaze caught just as surely by the unwavering intensity of his unblinking eyes. "I don't . . . I don't know what to say—"

"Hello, Dominic."

The cultured female voice catches both of us unaware.

I feel the small jolt of Nick's pulse where his hand covers mine, but it's there and gone in an instant. Without removing his touch from me, his face remains impassive, impossible to read. But the toneless sound of his voice tells me just how displeased he is by the interruption.

"Kathryn."

My heart lurches in my breast. I know this woman's name. Granted, her name is essentially all I know about her. Nick has refused to discuss her with me, other than to admit that they had been intimate at one time, years ago, when he first came to New York.

He said she was only in his life for a short while, and although I try to reassure myself with that knowledge now, it's obvious from the change in his demeanor that this woman still has some power over him.

It's startling to realize it.

In the months I've been with him, I've known no one else who's been able to rattle Dominic Baine's flawless control.

She's come in with two other women, all of them dressed in classic New York black and dripping with elegant jewelry. She waves her companions ahead as she pauses at our table and gives Nick an uncertain smile. "You look well, Dominic."

He grunts. "You look tired, Kathryn."

He's rude, but he's right, I notice. There is a vaguely haggard quality to her refined, beautiful face. She is tall and lean, almost waiflike, with a thick mane of stylish gray waves that gleam like quicksilver in the flattering light of the restaurant. The lack of lines in her porcelain skin suggests an abundance of vanity and the means with which to indulge it, but no surgeon can remove the hauntedness that lives in her dark eyes.

She glances at me briefly, and I feel an inexplicable stab of sympathy for her. Nick is reputed to be merciless when it comes to his former lovers, a fact that isn't totally lost on me as I sit awkwardly in front of him while he freezes her out with his silence.

Kathryn affords me a pleasant, if uncertain, smile before returning her attention to Nick. He lifts his glass to his lips and drains the rest of the whisky as if she's already moved on from our table.

"Jared mentioned he saw you a few weeks ago at the mayor's party. It would've been nice if you'd come over to say hello."

I tense at the mention of Jared Rush. I met the charming, good-looking artist around the same time I met Nick. The two men are friends, which I find interesting considering Jared intimated he had something more than a strictly platonic relationship with Kathryn.

Jared also allowed that there was a time when Kathryn was practically family to Nick. Whatever he meant by that, I don't know, because Nick refused to elaborate.

Kathryn lifts her chin, still regal even under Nick's withering animosity. "I've heard about the rec center plans. It's a good thing you're doing. For the kids, and for you."

He glances up at her now, almost in afterthought. His eyes are steely. Cold with something I want to say is disregard, but it's not. Its edge is too sharp to be apathy.

Nick is seething.

"Is there something you want, Kathryn?"

His animosity toward this woman is obvious, if only to me. I'm not ashamed to admit that I've spent these past months studying him with almost worshipful interest. I know him. I like to think I know him better than most anyone else. But now that I'm feeling the glacial force of his reaction to Kathryn, I have my doubts.

"I only wanted to tell you that if you need my help at any point. If you need my backing—"

"I don't."

The clipped reply silences her. For a long moment, she just stands there, although I hesitate to call her defeated.

"All right, Dominic. I understand." She reaches up to smooth a nonexistent flaw in her perfectly coiffed hair. Light, mottled spots speckle the back of her slender, bejeweled hand, another small betrayal of her age. "Pardon me for interrupting your lunch."

She glances at me, and I wonder if there is anything she would say to me if Nick weren't sitting here, vibrating with leashed rage. Would she warn me away from him the way Margot, my friend who works at Nick's gallery, had?

Or would Kathryn take greater pleasure in watching me crash and burn once Nick tires of me the way he apparently had with her?

I don't realize I'm holding my breath until it rushes out of me in the wake of her departure. She glides fluidly away to join her chattering companions, while a pall settles over the corner I share with Nick.

"I'm sorry about that." He releases my hand, his own retreating smoothly, even casually, back to his side of the table. I feel the absence like a gust of cold air has just swept through the room. In fact, it has.

The chill that exists between Nick and Kathryn has now expanded to engulf me too.

We finish our meal in an awful, uncomfortable silence. As soon as the waiter appears to remove our plates, Nick requests the check.

I'm desperate for him to talk to me, to explain what just happened and why this woman still seems to have such a disturbingly strong hold on his emotions.

It's all I can do to keep my questions to myself as we get up from the table and head out to meet Nick's limo at the curb.

Patrick is waiting at the back passenger door for us as we step toward him, Nick's palm settled at the small of my spine. I'm relieved by the contact, and by the small kiss he places on my cheek as the driver opens the door for us.

I climb in first, waiting for Nick to slide in behind me.

Instead he pauses outside the car.

"Patrick, please take Avery back to Park Place. I've got a few things to finish up at the office. I'll catch a cab from here."

"What?" I peer out at him, confused. I don't doubt he's got plenty of work waiting for him at his office, but I know damn well that this is a brush off. An evasion. He doesn't want to deal the questions he must know I'll have, so he's shutting me out as surely as he did Kathryn. "Nick—"

"Patrick will make sure you get home safely. I'll see you later tonight."

He doesn't give me a chance to argue or respond.

Closing the door, he nods to his driver, then steps away to hail a taxi while the limo eases into traffic and speeds me off without him.

6

The doorman at the Park Place building meets me at the limo with his usual cheerfulness as Patrick drives under the glass-roofed porte cochère. Thick and barrel-chested, he's dressed in a dark suit with twin ribands of silver piping at the wrists, despite the August heat. "Good afternoon, Ms. Ross."

"Hello, Manny."

The big, middle-aged man with the quick smile and warm hazel eyes has been nothing but kind to me from the first night I showed up here. I'd come with Tasha in tow, the two of us eager to check out the apartment I'd been hired to housesit for another of the building's residents, Claire Prentice, an actress I'd met while working at Vendange.

That was also the same night I first laid eyes on Nick, after nearly crashing right into him in the elevator. Four and a half months ago seems like yesterday sometimes.

It seems like forever too.

He's become a part of my life, and there are days when I can't imagine what it would be like without him. When Nick looks at me sometimes, I want to think he feels the same inexorable connection to me. I *believe* he does.

Yet after today—after his almost visceral reaction to a woman from his past, followed by his abrupt dismissal of me—I wonder if I know anything about him at all. I wonder if he'll ever truly allow me in.

"Do you have any other packages with you today, Ms. Ross—er, Avery?"

I'm amused to note Manny's switch to less formality with me—something I insisted on soon after I moved in to the building. In spite of the confusion and anger I'm still carrying from lunch, it's not difficult to manage a smile for the one man who's always got a twinkling grin or a kind word for me.

"Just this one bag," I tell him as I step out of the limo. "I've got it, thanks."

Since I'm wearing my day's purchases, the L'opale bag I stowed in the vehicle over lunch contains the underthings I had on when I left the apartment this morning.

All of Nick's talk about wanting me to feel powerful and confident feels like a joke as Manny opens the door for me and I make my way through the lobby of the soaring tower high-rise that's just one more of Baine International's extensive holdings.

I feel like a joke.

How long before Nick tires of me and I find myself in Kathryn's place?

Am I going to be standing in front of him one day,

desperate to reach him but receiving only impenetrable, scathing contempt in return? Am I already heading toward that eventuality?

One hundred nights.

That's the only thing he's promised me.

Should I really be surprised if that's all I have in the end?

That thought haunts me as I push the elevator button and wait for the car to descend. While I stand there, I realize I haven't checked my voicemail since Tasha's aunt called. I pull my phone from my purse and play back the waiting message.

She's made some calls about cheap art studio space, but nothing's turned up. The only possibility she's found is a shared sublet situation in a developing section of East Harlem.

"There's a good chance I can call in a favor and get you an appointment to see it today, but I need to hear from you as soon as possible. Please let me know if you're interested."

Shit.

Her message was time-stamped almost two hours ago.

Stepping aside as the elevator arrives and a small group of people exit, I hit the callback and hope I'm not too late.

"Mrs. Vargas," I say when she picks up on the second ring. "Hi, this is Avery, Tasha's friend. I'm so sorry I missed your call earlier. Will it still be possible to see that sublet you found?"

She tells me the address and asks if I can meet her there in half an hour. Considering it's a fifteen minute subway ride to the East Harlem neighborhood, that means I have about ten minutes to change clothes and get to the station.

"The space is small and nothing fancy, dear. But from what I understand, you're mainly interested in price and a decent location, and this checks off both those boxes."

The idea of having space of my own in which to paint again invigorates me so much, I wouldn't care if the sublet is a rat-infested closet. I need to paint simply for my own sanity, but I can't deny that I'm still hopeful of one day seeing my art for sale in a gallery again. I'm practically vibrating with excitement as I step into the vacant elevator and push the button for the penthouse.

"It sounds great, Mrs. Vargas."

As eager as I am to look at the space, I'm also relieved to have something productive to do, rather than sit around licking my wounds and waiting for Nick to return.

Tasha was right when she said my art is a part of me. It's a part I've been neglecting for too long. If I learned anything today, it's that I can't afford to lose myself because I'm tangled up in someone else. Not even if that someone is Dominic Baine.

Hell, especially him.

"Thank you again, Mrs. Vargas. I'll see you in thirty minutes."

~ ~ ~

As it turns out, the sublet isn't rat-infested. It is, however, only slightly bigger than a closet. It's also a co-op studio being utilized by two other artists—a painter and a mixed-media sculptor. Only one of them, the sculptor, is there when we arrive at the one-room studio above a shoe repair shop on Lexington Avenue. She's a curvy girl with a beautiful face and a choppy pixie haircut dyed in the dark rainbow colors of an oil slick. Countless tattoos and piercings decorate her pale ivory skin.

"I'm Lita Frasier," she says, giving me a perfunctory handshake as Mrs. Vargas and I step inside the tight, cluttered space.

"Avery Ross. Thanks for letting me come by and take a look."

She shrugs and walks away from us, drifting over to mute the music that's blaring from a decrepit, paint-speckled boom box on the other side of the room. The CD playing is Mozart, which is a surprise, but something tells me Lita enjoys catching people off guard.

Two easels, one empty, the other with a half-completed painting on it, are set up on one side of the room. Most of the other side is overtaken by a collection of what I'm tempted to call junk. Plastic milk crates overflow with metal objects of all shapes and sizes, random chunks of wood, pieces of broken glass, bins of twisted wire, and assorted other materials.

On the long worktable sits an abstract sculpture made from many of those items. Its form is both disturbing for its many jagged edges and sharp protrusions, yet sublimely elegant in the way all of its pieces somehow combine to create a thing of beauty.

"I try to keep everything pretty chill around here," Lita informs me, catching me looking at her work. "This is my studio, but I lease out space on a short-term basis to other artists to help cover my rent, which is ridiculous, even for this section of town. Normally I only let people I know do this, but since my mom and Rosa are friends,

I told her I'm willing to make an exception with you. I guess."

I glance at Mrs. Vargas in question. "When you said you were calling in a favor to get me an appointment today—"

She lifts her shoulder. "My niece adores you and she said you needed help finding someplace to work. That's what favors are for."

"I charge two-eighty a month cash, plus a month's deposit for a copy of my key," Lita says. "If that sounds good, we'll settle things up, then you can come in whenever you want, set up your shit, and work here as often as you like."

It does sound good. It sounds pretty great to me.

"I'll take it."

I can't tell if the quirk of her pierced eyebrow means she's happy or disappointed. I hand over most of the cash I tucked into my cross-body bag before I left the penthouse, and she hands me a tarnished key for the door.

As I slip it into my pocket and Mrs. Vargas steps away to respond to an incoming text, Lita points a tattooed finger under my face, then delivers some terse instructions for how she expects me to conduct myself when I'm using her studio.

"No squatting in here. No screwing in here either. And absolutely no fucking stealing. Clear?"

I nod. "Yeah, of course. Has that been a problem for you before?"

She narrows her eyes at me, and I clear my throat before she decides to change her mind about this whole thing.

"Right. You don't have to worry about any of that

with me. I promise."

Without responding, she pulls her phone out of the back pocket of her shredded black jeans and starts tapping the screen. "Cell?"

As I rattle off my phone number, her colorful head tilts up at me.

"Pennsylvania area code? I grew up in Philly."

"Ah." I force a smile at the mention of my home state. "Small world."

For what isn't the first time, I wish I'd have had the forethought to get a New York number as soon as I moved here. I wanted to make it easy on my mom, so I kept the old number she knew by heart. The one I also registered with the prison on the day she was processed and locked away.

"Okay, all set." Lita gives me a faint nod, then taps something on her phone. Mine immediately buzzes with an incoming text. "That's the code for the building access. Half the time, my asshole neighbors leave it open, but just in case you ever come here and it's locked, punch 9-3-2-7 to get in."

"All right. Thanks."

Mrs. Vargas and I head out a few minutes later, pausing to say our goodbyes down at the street.

"Can I give you a ride somewhere, Avery? I've got a client meeting across town in a few minutes, but I'll be happy to drop you at the subway station."

I glance up at the clear afternoon sky and shake my head. "No, thanks. It's right up the street and it's such a nice day, I prefer to walk. Besides, it'll give me a chance to see what's around."

After she waves and heads off for the parking garage a couple of blocks away, I set out on a leisurely stroll for the subway station. This Spanish Harlem neighborhood seems a world away from the upscale blocks of the Upper East Side, but the change of scenery is refreshing. These sidewalks are lined with modest mom-and-pop retail shops and local eateries that tempt with everything from tacos to teriyaki.

Up ahead on the next block, a small grocery with fresh fruit and produce on display outside catches my eye. I walk that way, and pause under the red awnings to peruse the containers of ripe strawberries and aromatic oranges. It all looks so good, I can't resist picking up a few things to take home with me.

I'm not in the store more than ten minutes when my phone rings. Juggling my hand basket of groceries in one arm, I glance down at the display. Private number. I rarely ever answer them. Everything in me urges me to ignore this one too.

But it could be Lita. It could be someone from the prison infirmary calling about my mom. It could be anyone. Yet down to my marrow, I know it isn't just anyone, even as I swipe the lock screen and bring the phone to my ear.

"Hello?"

For a long moment he doesn't say anything. In the silence, I feel a spark of hope that maybe my paranoia is just that. The feeling doesn't last.

"Hello, Avery." My breath seizes in my lungs as the voice I dread—the one person I fear more than any other in my life right now—releases a thin chuckle. "Long time, no hear."

I glance nervously around the store, feeling cold panic begin to bubble up inside me. "Stop calling me, you hear me? Stop texting me." My voice is tight, clipped. I pray he'll take it as fury and not the terror I taste on my tongue as I hiss into the receiver. "I don't have anything to say to you."

"Ohh, now, see? That's where you're wrong. You and me, we got plenty to talk about." I hear him take a drag off a cigarette, then exhale slowly. "We can start by talkin' about August twenty-first."

A clamminess settles at my nape. Nine years ago on that date, my mother shot and killed her husband, Martin Coyle. He's the reason she's been living at Muncy State Prison all this time. *I* am the reason too. Because if my stepfather hadn't been abusing me—if he hadn't finally succeeded in doing more than that on August twenty-first—my mother wouldn't be serving a life sentence for murder.

My temples start to pound. I'm breathing hard and fast, but I can't seem to get air. The small store feels suddenly too hot, too crowded with other people.

"You still there, Avery?" He sounds amused. "Maybe you'd rather talk about your mom. Sounds like that fall really took a toll."

At his emotionless tone, a chill sweeps over me. The suspicion that's been eating at me regarding her accident at the prison two weeks ago now floods into my veins like ice water. "Did you have something to do with that?"

"Me?" He chuckles as if I just told a joke. "Now, what on earth would make you say something hurtful like that, Avery? I'm concerned about her, is all."

"Leave her alone." I lower my voice, trying not to be overheard inside the busy little market. "I want you to leave us both alone, damn you. Haven't we all suffered enough?"

"Not even close, baby girl."

The endearment grates over my senses even more than his threatening response, as I'm sure he intends. Bile surges up the back of my throat in reflex of hearing it again after so many years. "Stay away from my mother. Stay away from both of us, or I'm calling the police."

"We both know you won't. And we both know why."

I ignore this last threat. Not because it's untrue, but because of the sheer terror it ignites in me to hear him say those words. I need to protect my mom. I need to protect myself, and this new life I'm trying to create out of the ashes of my horrid past.

"I'm done with this conversation," I snap at him. "I don't know what you think you have to gain by harassing me or my mother, but you're mistaken."

"Yeah? I'm sure that rich prick you're fucking might have something more to say about that."

I scoff, appalled. "This is about money?"

"This is about debts, baby girl."

A violent shudder racks me. Instead of his voice, in my head now I hear another one crooning the nauseating endearment. A voice so similar to my current harasser, because it belonged to his father, Martin Coyle.

My temples start to pound. "Don't call me that. Don't ever fucking call me that, or I'll—"

"Or you'll what, Avery? Shoot me?"

If I'd heard anger in his words—or any other emotion—it might have lessened some of my dread. But all I register is coldness. And unflinching determination.

"Leave me alone, Rodney. Please. Just . . . go away. Leave me and my mom alone."

It takes him a second to reply. When he does, the

sharpness of his voice cuts through me like a blade. Like a bullet. "We'll talk again, Avery. You can bet your life on that."

He ends the call and I'm left standing there, stunned and shaking.

I know Rodney means what he says.

He's not going to leave me alone.

He's not going to stop calling.

Now that he's found me after all these years, he won't stop coming after me. Not until he gets whatever it is he thinks he's owed. Maybe not even then.

"Are you all right, miss?" One of the grocers calls to me from where he is restocking a basket of baked goods.

"Yes. I'm . . . " I shake my head, feeling dazed. Trapped.

Desperate to escape the trouble I knew would find me one day.

God, what am I going to do?

Abandoning my filled basket right where I stand, I hurry for the exit. I hear the store clerk calling after me in concern, but I don't stop. I don't slow my pace for an instant, not even once I'm outside in the bright afternoon sunlight.

As I hurry for the subway station a few blocks away, the traffic light stops me at the corner as cars rush by. At my feet is a large sewer grate, with vents wide enough to lose a heel.

Or a phone.

I glance down at my hand. My fingers are wrapped so tightly around my cell it's a wonder the device hasn't shattered.

I can't outrun my past. I know that.

But I'll be damned if I'm going to make it any easier

than I already have for my demons to catch me.

The traffic light changes to green.

I relax my grasp on my phone, then watch the grate swallow it before I step off the curb.

7

I'm too keyed up to return to the big, empty penthouse right away. My stepbrother's voice is on an endless loop in my head, his not-so-thinly-veiled threat looming over me like a dark ghost that I cannot shake.

Instead of taking the subway to the station closest to Nick's building, I get off a couple of stops earlier and detour on a short walk to Central Park. Seated beneath the trees, surrounded by nearly 850 acres of nature and the sounds of children's laughter drifting over to me from the nearby carousel, I can finally breathe again.

I hardly notice the time until the shadows start to lengthen and the packs of nannies and their young charges begin to thin out.

By the time I reach the Park Place building, it's nearly sundown.

I hear Nick's terse voice as soon as I step off the

elevator into the penthouse. He appears in the vestibule, his phone at his ear. He looks haggard, still in his suit pants and black oxfords, his white shirt untucked and loosened at the top, the sleeves rolled up on his forearms. His gaze sears me, stark with anger . . . and relief.

"Never mind, Tasha." When he speaks now, his voice is low. Unnervingly level. "No. She just walked in."

He ends the call, then, without saying a word to me, strides back into the sprawling apartment and sets his phone down on the kitchen island countertop. I notice an open bottle of whisky there. Beside it is a glass with nearly two fingers of amber liquid in it. Nick downs it in one swallow.

"Where've you been?"

The calmness of his voice belies the displeasure I sense in every hard line of his body. Although we're separated only by the open space of the large living room, I feel as if I'm still standing on the other side of the emotional wall he constructed between us this afternoon. I stare at the back of his dark head as I approach him.

"I had an appointment to look at an art studio sublet this afternoon."

"So I hear. Tasha told me her aunt left you in East Harlem three hours ago."

Had it been that long? "I decided to stop by the park for a while afterward."

I tell myself I have no reason to feel guilty for going, yet as Nick pivots to face me now, it's all I can do not to flinch. He is furious. I've only been at the receiving end of his anger once before—the night we nearly broke up because of my secrets. He had a similar look in his eyes then.

A look of suspicion.

Distrust.

"You just take off without saying anything? Jesus Christ, Avery. I didn't even know you were interested in looking for a studio."

My own temper flares now. "I didn't realize I was required to tell you my every move. Or is that also part of your terms for our relationship? Do we even have a relationship, Nick?"

I know that's unfair, even as I say it. But I'm still pissed at him too. I'm still hurt from the fact that he shut me out today. I don't wait for his answer. Turning, I head into the bedroom to drop my purse on the dresser and take off my shoes.

Nick follows me in. "What's going on? You're upset with me, obviously. This is how you deal—by ignoring my calls and texts? I've been trying to reach you for hours, Avery. Then I come home and you're not here. For fuck's sake, I thought something happened to you." He blows out a sharp breath. "I thought you left."

I look at him. There's no question he's pissed, but I'm only now seeing the concern on his face. His lips are flat, his jaw rigid. And behind the flashing anger in his eyes is real fear.

Fear for me.

Because he came home and found me gone.

Because he thought I had left him?

"I'm sorry." I shake my head, feeling shitty for making him worry. And I must be all kinds of awful, because that small admission that he might need me as much as I need him makes my heart begin to pound heavily in my breast. "I didn't know you were looking for me. I . . . lost my phone today." The lie feels sour on my tongue. "I guess I must've dropped it on the subway or something."

"You've been walking around the city without any way to reach me all this time?" He scowls, his face darkening. "That's one more reason I ought to bend you over my knee."

My breath catches and I feel my cheeks flame at that remark. "I'm not a child, Nick."

"No, you're not." He steps toward me. "And that's not what I meant."

God help me, that grim but unmistakably carnal curve of his mouth as he speaks should trigger a hundred different reactions in me. And it does, but next to shock the strongest of them is excitement. I glance away from him, unnerved by how easily this man can entice me.

His fingers are briefly under my chin, lifting my gaze back to his. "Fuck the phone. It can be replaced. As for a studio, if you want space to paint, all you had to do was say so. There's plenty of room for you to work here."

"Nick, you don't—"

"Yes, Avery, I do. If you have needs—any needs at all—I will take care of them. I have the means. I think we both know I'm capable."

I lick my lips, feeling the heat of that promise wrap around my senses. Somehow I manage to break free from the spell he's casting over me and shake my head. "I already put money down on the sublet. It's a shared studio with a few other artists. I need to be able to paint. Not here, but someplace of my own." I force myself to hold his penetrating stare. "I need some boundaries between you and me and reality."

"Reality." His face remains impassive, but there is a

flicker of surprise in his eyes. Displeasure in the way his hand slowly drops away from me. "This is because of what happened at lunch today?"

"Seeing someone you used to fuck didn't bother me as much as what happened afterward." It's the truth, even though I burn with suspicion over what Kathryn once meant to him. "You shut me out today. You made me feel unimportant to you."

As shaken as I still am over my conversation with Rodney Coyle, it's this current confrontation that has me trembling. I don't want to lose Nick. I don't want to lose what we have, elusive as it may be. Today I felt our connection slip, and it terrified me. I'm still afraid to keep my heart open to him when I have nothing solid to hold on to.

When I start to withdraw from him, Nick traces the backs of his knuckles against my cheek, halting my retreat. His other hand slides around to my back, bringing me closer than I was before.

"I told you once that I don't do relationships. Christ, I wouldn't know how if I tried. I'm too selfish, Avery. I fuck things up. I hurt people. I guess today is a good example of that."

He sounds remorseful, his words careful as he strokes the side of my face.

"You *are* important to me. This *is* reality." As he speaks, he takes my hand, pressing it to his chest. His heart pounds hard and heavy against my palm. We're standing so close now, I can also feel the heat and power of his body. His gaze is locked on mine, giving me no room to run. Nowhere to hide. "You feel pretty damn real to me."

The temptation to give in to him right then and there

overwhelming, but I need more.

Today of all days, with doubt clawing at me and my past resurrected and threatening to destroy me, I need something more from Nick than just this need for each other that neither of us can resist.

"Tell me about her. Tell me what she means to you."

"Kathryn Tremont means nothing to me. I've already told you that."

"But you haven't told me what happened between you two."

The few details he has shared—and only because I pressed him once before—have painted only the briefest sketch. I know she and Nick were lovers. According to him it was only for a short time soon after he first arrived in New York. I know there had been a time when his sexual needs ran considerably darker than they do now, but he's insisted that Kathryn was never part of that with him.

Since he has no reason to lie to me, I don't doubt any of the things he has divulged about his past. It's the things he hasn't shared that frighten me the most. After all, I am a master at that game too.

"Kathryn and I are ancient history, Avery. Not important—neither is she."

"Then why do you still hate her?"

"I don't hate her."

"Did you love her?" I have to know, even if he won't ever be able, or willing, to apply the word to me. Maybe especially because of that. "Were you ever in love with her?"

"No."

My relief leaks out of me on a pent-up breath.

"I cared for her, though. What's more, I trusted her."

His jaw seems tense, though whether in reluctance to speak about her or in memory of what happened between them, I can't be sure. "I trusted Kathryn at a time when I had nothing else to give. She betrayed me. I don't allow anyone the chance to do it twice."

There is a vulnerable quality to this admission, but I don't dare take it as weakness. Not when his eyes are cold and dark with meaning. As much as he is sharing a piece of himself with me, it is also a warning.

It's one I respect, because when it comes to trust and the penalty for breaking it, Nick and I are very much alike.

It's a struggle to hold his penetrating stare, especially when the weight of my own lies and evasions are pressing down upon me even more now. He blinks, and some of the edge is gone from his gaze.

"I shouldn't have left you at the curb the way I did. Seeing Kathryn made me unfit company. We'd had such a good day together up until then, I didn't want to ruin it by bringing my shitty attitude home with you. Instead, I worked off my aggression on some contract negotiations back at the office."

He caresses the side of my head, trailing his hand over my unbound hair. When his fingers spear into the loose strands to cup my nape, the feeling is so warm and possessive, I can't hold back my small, pleasured moan. "If you had come home with me, I doubt your shitty attitude would've lasted for long."

A faint smirk tugs at the corner of his sinful mouth. "Is that right?"

I nod, falling deeper under the spell of his touch. "Next time, talk to me. You could've worked off some of that aggression on me."

A low groan rumbles in his throat. The tension I feel in him shifts instantly into something deeper, something needful and hungry. He descends on my mouth. Fevered, starving, he kisses me as if we haven't been in each other's arms for days, not just a few hours.

When he finally breaks contact, I'm gasping and so turned on I can hardly see straight. His mouth trails over to the sensitive spot beneath my earlobe before moving down the side of my neck and into the curve of my shoulder.

I startle when he gives me a sharp nip.

"That's for not telling me where you were this afternoon." When he draws back to look at me, his handsome face is taut with demand—and desire. "Don't make me worry about your safety ever again. And never withhold your needs from me. Understood?"

I slide my hands under his untucked shirt. "Yes, sir."

Raw sexual energy pours off him as I stare up at him and murmur those words. We've only played at these games a few times, enough for me to know the power my submission holds for him. His erection is already rampant, but it surges even firmer, as rigid as a thick column of stone where it presses against my abdomen.

"Baby," he snarls, and then he takes my mouth again, his tongue thrusting as his hands move expediently to strip me of my blouse and bra. When my breasts are bared to him, he scoops them into his palms, kneading them harshly, his touch as primal as his kiss. His mouth is hot on mine, then savage on my breasts as he licks and suckles and fondles me into a state of near boneless arousal.

I fumble with the buttons on his dress shirt, but I'm too slow. My movements are impeded by the slick, hot need that's roaring through every fiber of my being. On a wordless sound of impatience, he rips the custom-made shirt off, sending buttons scattering.

My hands roam his smooth skin and firm musculature of his chest and abdomen. But it's his cock I need in my hands even more. I wrap my hand over the solid ridge beneath the zipper of his suit pants, moaning when I feel his shaft jerk against my palm. A deep tremor answers in my core, setting my blood on fire.

"Oh, God, Nick. Please . . . "

My jeans and panties come off in the next instant. His hand goes between my thighs, nudging them wider. I cry out when his fingers glide into the wet seam of my sex. He torments my clit, his fingertips rubbing and flicking, knowing precisely how to make me burn. Pleasure spirals through me, sharp and white, ready to explode. I squirm on his hand, shameless in my need. When he enters me with two fingers, then another, I clutch his shoulders, needing something to hold on to as my orgasm twists with the first inklings of release.

He makes a low noise, somewhere between a chuckle and a growl. "I shouldn't make it so easy for you."

I'm panting, on the verge of coming when he suddenly takes his touch away. He steps back a pace and looks at me with burning, hooded eyes.

"After the way you made me worry today, I should make you beg." His voice is edged with a dangerous, carnal authority.

My clit throbs as though on command.

"I will," I gasp, wholly unashamed. With him, I'm willing to do anything. And he knows it. "If that's what you want, I'll beg."

His fingers find my clit again, but this time he's only

playing with me. Teasing. Showing me just how completely he controls my pleasure. His touch sears me, but it's his eyes that consume me even more. Whether it's the hunger I see in his gaze that's drawn me to him from the start, or the darkness that lives behind it, I can't be sure.

"What do *you* want, baby?"

"You," I gasp as he takes me right to the edge again, then eases off. "I want you in my hands. In my mouth. Inside me, Nick . . . Please."

His fingers wrap around mine now, guiding both my hands to his belt buckle. It's all the permission I need. I can't free him fast enough, can't wait to feel the heavy length of his cock in my grasp, in my mouth.

I drop down in front of him and fasten my lips around the head of his penis. I want to make him come like I did this morning in his office, but he doesn't have that kind of patience this time. All too soon, he pulls me up, kissing me long and hard.

"Go to the window."

I glance over my shoulder at the large pane of floor-to-ceiling glass. Outside, the sun has just dipped below the skyline. The horizon is aglow in shades of peach, dark salmon, and lavender, while above Manhattan's blanket of twinkling lights, the sky glows impossibly blue. The same incredible hue of Nick's eyes.

Naked, I approach the glass and wait for him to either join me or command me to do something more. As much as I need the release he's teased me with, I know how delicious he can make the torment of waiting. My body is ready for anything he wants to give it.

A shiver races over my bare skin as I look out at the glittering city below and anticipate whatever pleasure that is to come. I hear the soft glide of a bureau drawer being opened inside his massive walk-in closet that's adjacent to the bedroom.

"Hands on the glass," he orders me as he steps out behind me a moment later. "Spread your legs. Wider. I want that beautiful pink pussy open and waiting for me when I'm ready to fuck it."

I hurry to obey. Anything to please him, especially when the reward is mine in the end.

I stand at the window, my palms pressed against the cold glass on either side of my head. My feet are spaced wider than my shoulders, making my hips cant forward and my ass jut up and out behind me. I feel exposed, vulnerable. At Nick's mercy in this position that doesn't permit me to shift without losing my balance.

I feel him approach, even though his steps are soundless on the rug-covered marble floor, his movements smooth and silent at my back. Yet each soft circulation of the air in the room rushes past my wet, swollen flesh like a kiss. I shudder at the sensation, desperate to turn around and look for him. I bite my lip to keep from asking where he is, what he intends.

His touch lights on my spine, fingers splayed between my shoulder blades before moving softly, tenderly, down to the small of my bowed back.

"You made me crazy with concern today," he says, his deep voice quiet, but firm. "What do you think I should do about that, Ms. Ross? Reward you? Or punish you?"

I swallow. He's teased me with this word before, too, but never after I've upset him. And never when I cannot see his face or his eyes to know if he is serious.

His tone seems to suggest that is.

When I feel the cool slide of long leather laces being draped gently against the curve of my ass, I have no doubt he's serious. Alarm spikes through me, along with something too hot to be fear. He moves the flogger's tails slowly over my skin, giving me a chance to get used to them, gauging my response.

"Do you know what this is?"

I nod, even though my knowledge is limited to photos and fiction.

"Have you ever felt one?"

"No."

He grunts. "Do you want to?"

"I don't know."

He leans in close, his words low and hot against my ear. "Yes, you do."

I suck in a sharp breath as the long leather tails slip into the seam of my ass. They brush against my pussy, still cool, but warming from the heat of my body. I shiver, though not out of fear.

Nothing close to fear.

Not when Nick is gentling me with one hand, while the other swings the flogger back, then snaps the tails against my bare backside. I flinch, even though the sting of the leather is less intense than I expect it to be.

"That's for the first hour, when I thought you were just trying to make a point by ignoring my texts and voice mails."

He cracks the flogger against my other cheek. The tips of the leather laces brush my swollen folds, and the cry I emit is anything but pained.

"That's for the second hour, after I left half a dozen messages on your damn phone, asking you to just call me back and let me know that you were all right."

His deep voice is level, controlled, but I can hear the raw edge in his words. I can hear the worry he's carrying, even now, when I'm standing here in front of him, safe and sound and vibrating with desire for him.

The flogger snaps against my ass again, and this time it does hurt. There's more power in this blow, even though Nick's voice drops to a tone that's as tight and raw as I've ever heard before.

"Damn you, Avery. That's for the third hour you were gone without a word—and for how fucking certain I was that I had lost you today."

"Nick—"

He doesn't give me a chance to say anything. Not to apologize nor to assure him that I have no intention of walking away from what we have together. Not willingly, anyway. Hell, I'm not even certain I could walk away if I were forced to.

I'm in too deep with him.

Today, more than ever before, I realize that he's in deep with me too.

I glance over my shoulder, just in time to see that he's thrown down the flogger. He's already wearing a condom, and when he comes in close behind me, he is vibrating with sexual heat. I need him inside me with a desperation that rocks me. My body is aching for him. Empty without him.

Guiding his cock into the center of my slick, wet folds he impales me on a hard and unforgiving thrust.

A low, guttural roar boils out of him as he pounds into me, his strokes rough and deep. I've tasted Nick's sexual fury before. I know what it is to be swamped by the ferocity of his need, his powerful, ruthless desire.

There is a torment in him, but it's never been more

evident than in this moment. I can't hold out against it. With my palms and forehead pressed against the glass, I cry his name as my body shatters, every nerve ending detonating with the incredible force of my orgasm.

Nick's not far behind me. His shout is guttural, animal. The sexiest sound I know. His big body shudders against me, his cock seated so deep inside me I can hardly tell where he ends and I begin.

"You feel that, baby?" His voice rasps beside my ear as his tempo finally slows. "This is *real*. You, me . . . us."

"Yes," I whisper, wanting so badly to believe it, my chest aches with the wish.

Our bodies continue to move together, pressed between the haven of our pretty cage in the sky and the rest of the world teeming and turning outside. The world where real monsters live—my own, and maybe his too—just waiting for the chance to tear us apart one day.

But not today.

8

I was starting to think I'd never see you again."

Lita flips her safety goggles up as I enter the studio later that week. Today she's got an old Godsmack CD in the boom box. While drums pound rhythmically and Sully Erna sings about snake bites and voodoo, Lita holds an industrial-size soldering iron in her hand, the metal tip still smoking from whatever she's working on.

She uses it to gesture at my small rollaway that contains my paints and brushes. "Where's the rest of your shit?"

"This is all of it." I wheel the box inside, careful not to jostle the large zippered portfolio that's slung over my shoulder and almost as big as I am.

"You didn't drag that here on the subway, I hope?"

I glance to the other side of the small studio, where a tall, lanky male artist with a mop of light brown hair has paused his work to stare at me as I come in. He's got a lean, boyish face and a friendly, open smile.

"No," I reply. "I, ah, took a car today." Limousine, actually, but I see no reason to mention that I have a billionaire boyfriend who insisted his driver take me to the studio.

"I'm Matt, by the way. You must be Avery." When I nod, he tilts his head in the direction of the live model he's painting—and quite expertly, at that. "This sexy beast is Travis."

I smile, trying not to gape at the nude, blond male who's mostly got his back to me, his muscular body twisted just enough to bring out the definition and the beauty of his masculine form.

He greets me without breaking his pose. "Hey, Avery."

"Hello, Travis. Hi, Matt."

Lita points to the empty easel behind Matt's workspace. "That's your spot. Feel free to use the tables and the cloths and anything else you find over there."

"Okay, thanks."

Matt pivots to look at me. "I used to split costs on chemicals with the other artist who worked here before you. If you want to go in halves with me on anything, just so you know, I'd be cool with that."

I nod, grateful for his warm welcome. "All right. That sounds good."

He and Lita both go back to their work while I unpack my things and try to get comfortable with the new work setting.

Once my paints and brushes are arranged the way I like them, I retrieve my portfolio and unzip the protective sleeve that holds my most recent work in progress.

The canvas is only partially painted. Just the initial strokes on a piece I was experimenting with before I ended up moving in with Nick. I haven't worked on it since. Now, as I take it out and set it on the easel, I can't resist tracing my fingers over the lines.

The memory of what inspired it tugs my mouth into a small, private smile.

"You into religious symbolism?" I glance up and find Lita staring at me from across the room. "Angels and demons, that kind of stuff?"

"What? Oh. No, this is something else." I look at the abstract image that's not quite realized on the canvas yet. Just the suggestion of sky and water and a large white wing with falling feathers, their tips singed and blackened with soot. "It's Icarus."

"Cool," Lita says, turning back to her own work.

This piece isn't anything like the other paintings I've done. My early work was comprised of cityscapes, architectural painting, even some portraiture—none of it particularly good. Nick was right when he said my work was inhibited, throttled before it had a chance to become something real on the canvas.

But this piece is different. It is my first step away from realism and toward the abstract, inspired by my getaway to the Florida Keys a couple of months ago on Nick's sailboat, the *Icarus*.

Even though my vision for this piece is far from finished, I like what I see.

I like the freedom it conveys. I like the passion this painting stirs in me when I look at it and think about everything Nick and I shared on that boat.

I mix some paint and prepare to get reacquainted

with my canvas, but don't know where to start. I'm afraid I'll mess it up.

Just like I'm afraid of messing things up with Nick.

When I sigh and set my brush down for the fourth or fifth time without touching the canvas, Matt slowly pivots on his stool to face me.

"How long has it been?"

"Since I painted?" I shrug. "A few weeks. But before then, it had been even longer."

He nods soberly, looking both innocent and wise. "My boyfriend died a year and a half ago. It was eight months before I picked up a paintbrush again. Took another three before I remembered how to move paint around on a canvas."

"God," I murmur, sympathy tight in my throat. "I'm so sorry, Matt."

His expression softens, then he gives me a faint shrug. "The point is, you show up at the canvas. And then you start again."

He motions for me to get up and follow him to the back corner of the studio. Leaning up against the wall is a stack of used canvases in assorted sizes. Whatever had been painted on them is now covered with a thick coat of primer. "This is my recycle pile. If you want to warm up on something else, help yourself to any of these."

"Thank you."

I select a rectangular one of medium size and bring it back to my easel, switching out Icarus for this fresh canvas. I have no idea what I should paint, so I tell myself to mix some new colors without any expectation and simply see where it takes me.

With the heavy bass and slow, sensual tempo of the song pouring out of the speakers across the room, my thoughts drift back to Nick. No surprise, considering how shamelessly he had me screaming in pleasure this morning. For the past two weeks, we've begun every day with an orgasm—or three—and today was no exception.

My sex is still tender from having him inside me, and each little shift I make on my stool creates a delicious friction that is equal parts pleasure and pain.

A shiver of arousal rushes through me, making me think of the other night with Nick. Of thin leather tails and blue velvet skies.

Swept up in the memories, I add more paint to my palette, turning the small swirl of azure into a darkening pool of fathomless blue and an indigo so deep it's almost black. When the colors feel right I dip my brush, then bring it to the canvas and give my hand free rein to move wherever and however it wants to.

It's liberating, exhilarating.

I'm entranced by the sensuality of my brush as it licks the pristine field of the canvas. Color explodes in the wake of each stroke, some of it dark and brutal, some of it sublime.

I'm so caught up in my work, I don't even realize I'm being observed until another song on the boom box ends and the studio plunges into silence for a moment.

I sit back on my stool and startle to find Lita standing behind me with Matt and Travis, who's now dressed in loose jeans and a white T-shirt that somehow makes him look even more gorgeous.

"Earth to the new girl. You didn't hear a damn word I said, did you?"

"Um . . ." I can't even pretend she hasn't just busted me, so I shake my head.

"It's noon, so we're all heading out for a bite to eat.

Wanna come?"

I glance at my canvas, reluctant to leave it.

"Never mind." Lita shakes her head. "You're in the zone, so don't break it. We'll bring lunch to you. You like turkey or roast beef?"

"Turkey, please." I hop down and pull out a twenty-dollar bill.

"Nah, forget it. Seeing how it's your first day and all, it'll be my treat."

"Really? That's so nice of you. Thanks."

She smirks. "Don't get used to it. We'll be back in forty-five."

After they're gone, I grab a bottle of water from my rollaway and sip it as I stand back and look at what's taking shape on my easel. A complicated riot of emotions tangle through me as I follow the lines and strokes that fill the canvas. It's not bad.

Hell, it might even be pretty good.

Looking at what I've created, I'm excited and hopeful.

I am happy for the first time in a very long time, not only because I am finally reunited with my art, but because for the past few weeks—the past four months—I've felt more alive than I have for most of my life.

There's only one part of me that's still missing, and in the solitude of the empty studio, my heart aches for the piece of me I've left behind in Pennsylvania.

Retrieving the new cell phone Nick bought me from out of my purse, I dial the prison infirmary and ask if my mom could have permission to take my call. I've already updated her doctors and public defender with my changed phone number, but I haven't spoken to my mother in several days.

They put me through this time, informing me that she's awake, but is due to get another dose of painkillers in about ten minutes. Her accident a couple of weeks ago left her with a pierced lung and multiple fractures, the worst of them being her broken femur.

At her age, recovery is expected to take time, but I can't curb my worry when I hear how small her voice sounds when she finally comes on the line.

"Avery, honey? Oh, I'm so happy you called. Are you back in town again?"

"No, Momma. I'm in New York." I don't miss her small exhale, or the disappointment in that wordless response. "I've been thinking about you. How are you feeling today?"

"Tired, mostly. They keep giving me pills and shots at all hours of the night. I wish they'd release me so I can go back home."

I wince, recognizing with more than a little regret that to my mother, home is the single-windowed cell she's been living in for these past nine years.

"The doctors are just trying to make you better," I tell her gently. "You got hurt pretty bad in that fall. It's going to take time for you to heal."

Talking about her accident makes the specter of my stepbrother's threats crowd in on me like a thunderhead. I can't prove that he had anything to do with her fall, but my gut feels certain.

"Do you remember anything about that day, Mom? Do you remember what happened before you fell?"

"Nothing I haven't already told you, honey. I was coming out of the laundry after my morning shift. I remember it was crowded near the stairs. Everything happened very quickly. I must've lost my balance somehow."

She goes quiet, and I know she can sense that I am pensive.

She knows me too well, even though we've been separated for nearly a decade.

She knows my heart better than anyone.

She's the one person who knows all of my secrets . . . just as I know hers.

Then again, maybe there is one other person who knows them too.

"Have you had any visitors lately, Momma? Anyone you haven't mentioned to me?"

Her silence nearly kills me. I can feel her wariness. Her worry.

"What's this about, honey? Has something happened?"

I can't tell her. Not on a prison phone. The lines are monitored, and it's too risky for me to so much as mention Rodney Coyle's name, let alone what he's demanding of me.

But even more than that, I don't want to burden my mother with the knowledge.

She's got enough to deal with.

She's carried too many burdens for me in her life already.

"Avery," she whispers. "Please tell me you're okay. Please tell me you're safe."

I close my eyes, feeling selfish for my call now. I needed to hear her voice, but now I've made her anxious. I'm scaring her, when that's the last thing I want to do.

"I'm okay, Momma. Everything's just fine." I force

a lightness into my voice that I don't really feel. "You just get better, all right? I'll talk to you again soon, I promise."

9

I take the subway home from the studio that afternoon, even though Nick seems less than enthused by the idea when I text him to tell him my plans. As appreciative as I am of his concern for me, I need him to understand that I also enjoy my freedom. And besides, the last thing I want to do is alienate my new friends by rolling in and out of the studio in a chauffeured sedan.

I know Nick doesn't like it, but he relents on the condition that I text him when I leave the studio, then call when I arrive back at Park Place.

As I wander through the empty penthouse, dropping my purse and stepping out of my shoes, I dial his cell. He picks up immediately.

"Right on time," he says by way of greeting. "Good girl."

My mouth curves at his maddeningly authoritative,

confident tone. "Satisfied, Mr. Baine?"

"Not yet, but let's work on that." His voice is dark with meaning, and I feel it all the way to my core. "I'm taking you out for dinner tonight. Can you be ready in an hour?"

"Sure. Where are we going?"

He hesitates a moment. "Someplace we haven't been before. I'll be waiting downstairs to pick you up in one hour."

"I can hardly wait."

In spite of the heaviness I'm still carrying with me after my brief conversation with my mom a few hours ago, I can't deny my excitement at the prospect of being with Nick. I shower and dress quickly, slipping into a simple black wrap dress that falls just above my knees and ties at the waist. Strappy black heels complete the look, then, on impulse, I go to the top drawer of the bureau in the bedroom and retrieve the long string of pearls that were a gift from Nick.

The creamy gems are cool within my cleavage, and so richly lustrous there is no need for any other jewelry. I can't wear them without recalling how wickedly Nick made use of them the night he gave them to me. Draped around my neck now, the long rope slides sensually against my skin with each step I take out of the apartment and down the elevator to the lobby.

As promised, Nick is waiting for me.

Standing just inside the building's entrance, he's talking with Manny as I cross the gleaming marble and head toward them. He's wearing the black suit he had on when he left for the office this morning, but his dark hair looks soft and slightly damp from a recent shower, and the hint of a beard that usually shadows his face by evening has been whisked away with a razor. He's so handsome and commanding, so profoundly male, my knees threaten to give out beneath me.

Nick sees my slight falter. He knows the effect he has on me and during our time together I've learned that it's pointless to try to pretend I'm not entirely taken with him. Even more powerful is the fact that he seems just as caught up in me. His expression is so wolfish, so unwavering, it's all I can do to keep my gait steady when his hot, appraising stare is licking fire through my senses and making the world tilt on its axis.

I nod at Manny, and he offers me a beaming smile. "Good evening, Miss Avery."

"Stunning," Nick says, looking at me as though Manny and the other dozen or so people in the lobby no longer exist. "Shall we?"

Manny gets the door for us and Nick leads me out to his black BMW M6 that's idling beneath the porte cochère. He waves off Manny's help at the car, smoothly opening the passenger door for me, then halting me so he can press a fleeting kiss to my cheek.

"The pearls were a perfect choice," he murmurs beside my ear. "I'll be envisioning you naked wearing nothing else but that strand all night."

I tremble at the suggestion, because now I'll be strung tight in anticipation, longing for the moment when Nick will make that vision a reality for us.

I'm half tempted to plead with him that we skip dinner and stay in instead, but his hand is firm and intent at the small of my back, so I climb into the car and wait as he closes the door then walks around to the driver's side.

"Busy day?" I ask, once he's seated and we're both

buckled in.

"Nonstop meetings," he says, navigating out to the boulevard with an easy command of both the vehicle and the hectic traffic that surrounds us. "I was just out of the last of them when you called to say you were home. How was the first day back at the easel?"

"It was good. Actually, it was great." When he glances my way, I can't resist telling him about my new piece. "I'm trying something different. Playing with colors and abstracts. Seeing where my brush takes me."

He nods, studying me for a moment. "Sounds interesting."

"It was. I can't explain it. The whole thing just kind of . . . poured out of me today. I finished the piece in a matter of hours. That's never happened before."

He grunts, his brows lifting as he watches the sea of illuminated tail lights at the intersection ahead of us. "You must've been inspired."

"I was." I slide my hand over to his thigh, reveling in the bunch and flex of his muscles as he brings the car to a stop at the traffic light. "You inspire me, Nick."

I see something flicker in his gaze as he stares out the windshield, but I'm not sure what to call it. There and gone in an instant, when he turns his head to look at me, all I see is hunger. His hand goes around the back of my neck and he pulls me close, capturing my lips in a deep, sensual kiss.

When the light changes, he punches the gas and we prowl past the taxis and other vehicles to the next corner. We turn left, heading down a couple of blocks before Nick slows to a stop in front of a tall, brown-brick and limestone trimmed building that's nestled within a street full of similar looking ones. Some are clearly office space, others appear to be multi-use buildings with retail shops and everything in between.

There is no signage on the one we've parked in front of, and only a few windows glow with light from inside, most of it coming from the top floor five stories up.

"I thought we were going to dinner?"

"We are." Nick's cryptic response only confuses me more as he gets out of the car and comes around to open my door. "Trust, Ms. Ross. Remember?"

Smiling, and so curious I'm about to burst, I take his hand and walk with him to the building's front door. It's locked, but he has the key in his jacket pocket.

"After you."

I step inside the dimly lit vestibule, surprised to see pretty Art Deco tile on the floors and polished dark wood millwork on the walls. There's an elevator immediately to our right. Nick pushes the call button and I watch the dial above the brass doors count down as the car descends to meet us.

"Is the restaurant on another floor or something?"

Nick doesn't answer me, just guides me into the elevator, then presses the number five. As we climb the short distance up, I finally catch a whiff of something delicious cooking. Garlic and grill smoke and fresh-baked bread, along with a host of fragrant spices I can't even begin to name. My mouth is watering as the doors open and Nick and I step out of the lift.

But there is no restaurant waiting here.

Just a single table in the center of a spacious loft with soaring beam ceilings and beautiful exposed brick walls. Candlelight glows softly from tall candelabras set up around the room, and from the fat pillar candle in the center of the table, which is cloaked in a white linen tablecloth with a diaphanous length of red silk draped across its center. A silver bucket of ice sits on a pedestal beside the table, a black-labeled bottle of Krug champagne chilling in the cubes.

I turn to Nick in question.

"I'm considering buying the property," he says, urging me forward. "I wanted to get an inside feel for it first. I wanted your opinion too."

My brows rise. "Do you evaluate all of your prospective properties with champagne and romantic candlelight dinner for two?"

"No. Just this one." A small grin quirks the edge of his lips as he takes off his suit jacket and nods toward the waiting table. "Come on, have a seat. We're celebrating."

He no sooner says it than a pair of waiters emerge from a doorway and enter the room with us. They're dressed in tuxedos and white gloves, their service both efficient and impeccable as they see to our comfort at the table, then proceed to serve us the champagne and a basket of warm French bread.

A plate of oysters arrives a moment later, carried in by a third server.

I'm gaping and there's nothing I can do about it. "How did you arrange all of this?"

Nick smiles and tips his flute toward mine. "I have my ways."

"You certainly do." I laugh as our glasses meet with a soft clink. "What are we celebrating tonight?"

"The rec center approvals came in today."

"Nick, that's wonderful!"

He nods, his pride plainly evident. "Took a long damn time, but we finally got clearance on the plans for construction."

"Congratulations." I raise my glass to him in another toast. "This is a big deal, Nick. I know how much the center means to you. You should be having a big celebration."

"I am. This dinner is costing me a small fortune," he says with a boyish smirk. He sets down his glass and reaches for my hand. "And it's worth it. There was only one person I wanted to share this news with outside of Beck and the rest of my staff."

He strokes the back of my hand, his gaze locked on mine with such intensity I've suddenly forgotten how to breathe. His smile breaks slowly, sinfully, and I can only wonder how he intends to continue our celebration once we leave here tonight.

My body is already way ahead of my imagination. Just the sensation of Nick's touch, the mesmerizing heat of his deep blue eyes, is enough to make me quiver with unabashed desire. If he asked me to leave with him right now, I wouldn't hesitate for a moment.

"I hope you like oysters."

I nod, watching him pick up a shell and loosen the tender flesh from its cradle. His fingers move so gracefully, so adeptly, it makes my mouth water just to observe his hands in motion. He has beautiful hands, even with the scars.

"Did you order oysters because you're planning a seduction, Mr. Baine?"

His answering grunt is rough, sexy. I lick my lips as he hands the oyster to me across the splash of red silk that separates us. Our fingers brush against each other, lingering.

"Will I need oysters in order to seduce you, Ms.

Ross?"

"What do you think?" I take the shell from him, but instead of putting the meat into my mouth, I dip my finger into the shallow cup of soft, slick flesh.

His groan is a raw sound, a deep rumble in the back of his throat. After I've tormented him for another moment, I lick my wet, salty finger, then tilt my head back and slide the oyster into my open mouth.

"Fuck," he utters hoarsely. "You're better at this game than you should be."

I smile and arch a brow, totally unrepentant. "I'm learning from a master."

We settle in, enjoying the appetizers and the champagne, which flows endlessly thanks to our attentive servers. It's amusing—definitely impressive— sitting in our private dining room at the top of a charming, if vacant, building just five minutes away from the luxury of Nick's penthouse.

As always with this man, he's managed to conjure magic for me.

For us.

We enjoy the rest of the oysters, and moments after we've eaten the last one, our waiter returns to clear the plates.

He nods politely to me, then addresses Nick. "Dinner will be served in a few minutes, sir."

With Nick's murmured thanks, we are once again left alone. "I hope you don't mind that I ordered for both of us tonight. Filet mignon a la Castille."

"Castille," I echo, my mouth going a bit slack. "You don't mean, as in, Gavin Castille?"

Nick nods, then takes a leisurely drink of his champagne.

I'm gaping. "Gavin Castille, one of the most recognized celebrity chefs in the country. That Gavin Castille?"

"That's the one. The one and only, I'm sure the arrogant Aussie would hasten to add."

"We had lunch at his restaurant earlier this week."

"Yes, we did." The only thing more incredible than having arguably the hottest chef of the moment catering a private dinner for us is Nick's self-satisfied grin as he watches me absorb the news. When he said this meal cost him a small fortune, I have no doubt about that now. He shrugs, oh-so-nonchalantly. "I told you I wanted to make up for the way our lunch ended. Consider this my version of a do-over."

"You're crazy." I bark out a laugh I couldn't hold back if I tried. Popping out of my chair, I lean across the table and yank him up for an impulsive kiss. "You're totally insane, you know that?"

He chuckles, even though his eyes are dark with arousal as I release him and slowly resume my seat across from him. "Gavin's a friend. He's also going to be part of the rec center. He's agreed to donate a chef's kitchen and personal cooking time with the kids every month, once the center opens. We're hoping it'll give the ones recovering from injuries or other trauma a creative outlet while also teaching them skills they'll need as adults."

"Cooking as therapy, huh?" I recall Nick mentioning to me once how he learned to cook because it helped him regain his dexterity and the use of his hand. That he's applying something so personal to his plans for the recreation center moves me. It amazes me, just as the man himself does.

"We'll have other programs in place too," he says. "I

plan on calling in a lot of markers to make the center a success."

"It sounds great, Nick. I'm excited for you. I'm excited for the kids you're going to help." He nods in acknowledgment, and I take the opportunity to reach over and brush my fingers along the back of his right hand—the one whose scars shine silvery in the low light of the candle. "Maybe you should do some of the cooking lessons too. I can personally vouch for your killer talent in the kitchen. Your breakfast repertoire alone is enough to give Gavin Castille a run for his money."

He smirks, turning his hand over to still my tracing of his scars, capturing my fingers in his warm, firm grasp. "Here I thought you loved me for my many other talents."

I laugh softly, but my pulse quickens and the center of my chest warms at hearing him acknowledge the depth of my feelings for him.

"Does it bother you that I told you how I feel about you?"

He studies me, his handsome face unreadable. "Why would it?"

"Because you've told me yourself that you don't do relationships." Because I've also seen the scorched earth remains of his other past lovers—beginning with my friend, Margot, who manages his gallery, Dominion. And, more recently, Kathryn.

I swallow now, uncertain I should be venturing down this path, especially when we're having such a good time tonight. When I don't answer right away, Nick does.

"And because I haven't said those words to you?"

I want to deny that it stings, that it confuses me how he can desire me so fiercely—take me so possessively—yet keep me at arm's length when it comes to his heart. We've only been together a few months. A blink of time.

But it's been long enough for me to know.

When he speaks now, his deep voice is gentle, as reflective as I've ever heard it. "I've never been relationship material, Avery. I had no delusions that I could be when I first laid eyes on you. I wasn't looking for this. I sure as fuck wasn't intending for things to go this far between us. I wasn't expecting . . . you."

I nod, because he's saying the same things I felt. Things I feel even now, except my regrets for how deeply I've become entangled with him are complicated by how much I care for him.

His thumb strokes the center of my palm. "Sometimes I wish I could start over with you, be someone better for you. Someone who isn't as fucked up. Someone who can love you properly . . . someone you deserve."

"Everyone's fucked up, Nick. And anyway, what makes you the best judge of what I deserve?" When his hand starts to edge away from mine, I hold fast. "I wasn't expecting you either. I wasn't looking to feel something like this. But then you look at me like you are right now . . . you take my hand, or you pull me down beneath you, and I think maybe I've been waiting for you—looking for you, for this, *for us*—all my life."

He doesn't say anything for a few seconds, and there is a part of me that worries I've said too much. Revealed more than I should have, more than he wants to deal with. He could shred me with a single word right now, with a single shuttered glance.

But he doesn't.

"Avery." My name is so soft and reverent on his tongue, it nearly makes me weep. His fingers close more intently around mine and he draws my hand to him. He brushes his lips over my fingertips, drawing one of the sensitive pads into his mouth in a sensual, yet heart-breakingly tender kiss.

My throat constricts with all the love I feel for this man, while inside me every nerve ending strums to life, yearning for the moment when I can be alone and naked with him again.

I've never been more conflicted than I am in that next instant when our waiters walk back into the room, interrupting us with a meal that looks and smells beyond divine.

Nick releases me as our plates are set in front of us and a bottle of red wine is opened beside our table. The food is amazing, everything cooked and seasoned to perfection.

We eat with abandon in the candlelight, the nighttime city glittering like a box of dark jewels outside. I feel like a princess in a fairy tale. Even better than that, because as Nick has promised me, this is real.

He smiles at me as I finish off the last bite of my steak. "What do you think?"

I take a sip of the smooth Cabernet, reveling in the slight buzz that's building inside me from the champagne and the wine and the food. The most intoxicating part of the evening is the gorgeous man seated across from me at the table, looking at me as if he cannot wait to devour me next.

"I think you're spoiling me beyond all reason. And I'm not just talking about tonight."

"Reason is overrated," he replies, his gaze dark on me. "The best things—the most pleasurable things— only exist on the other side of it."

"Is that so?"

He nods slowly, his gaze riveted on me as he brings his wine glass to his mouth, studying me over the rim. "I want to push you to the limits of everything that pleases you, Avery. I want to push you past those limits."

I swallow, heat rushing over my skin at his sensual promise. My breasts feel heavier under his hungry stare, my nipples peaking in anticipation of his touch, his kiss. The desire that's been smoldering inside me all evening intensifies now that I know it won't be long before I'm in Nick's arms, in his bed.

I want to ask him to take me there right now, before I combust with need, but at that same moment, our private waitstaff enters the room to clear our dishes and remove the empty wine bottle and glasses from the table. Nick seems in no hurry, and I can't deny that his patience is somewhat maddening, especially when I am practically itching with the urge to leap on him and tear his beautiful clothes off.

The muffled sound of wheels rolling over rustic hardwood turns my head in the direction of the door. A tall man in black pants and a white chef's tunic enters the room with us now, bringing in a silver cart of covered bowls and pedestaled plates with him.

Although I've only seen Gavin Castille on television and the Internet, his trademark dimpled grin and mane of beachy blond hair is unmistakable. The power of that grin, coupled with his pale green eyes, hits me like a tidal wave blast as he approaches Nick and me at the table. After cuffing Nick on the shoulder, Gavin looks at me.

"You must be Avery." He holds out his large hand, and my fingers are engulfed in his warm, firm grasp. "Everything to your liking tonight?"

"Yeah, um, yes," I stammer. "Everything was incredible."

"Glad to hear it. I don't make a lot of house calls, but my good buddy here said this one was special." He glances at Nick, giving him a crooked smile. "You weren't kidding, mate."

Nick's gaze is still searing me, but my senses are tempted by all of the intriguing goodies hidden beneath the polished steel domes on the dessert cart Gavin has brought. I smell warm chocolate, buttery cake, and fresh fruit. I can't see what awaits us, but I'm certain it's decadent.

"How did you manage all of this?"

"Aussie magic," Gavin replies with a wink. "And a portable, full kitchen in the truck we've got parked out back of the building."

"Castille on Wheels," Nick adds drolly.

"Hey, that's not bad."

"I'll have my assistant bill you for the marketing advice."

Gavin chuckles. "Yeah, you would, ya bastard."

As impressed as I am with Nick for his tremendous business success and his obvious erotic prowess, it is this other side of him I'm seeing now that makes me fall even further under his spell. I love his thoughtful generosity when it comes to the children he aims to help through his recreation center project. I love his unexpected romanticism with me tonight, and his easy camaraderie with his friend.

God, the truth is, I simply love . . . *him*.

"All right, you two," Gavin says, giving a clap of his hands. "We're cleaned up and ready to roll. I've sent my staff home and I'll be shoving off here in a minute myself."

Nick nods. "Lock up on your way out."

"You got it, chief." Gavin pivots to me and offers a slight bow. "My lady, a pleasure."

"Thank you, Gavin. Nice to meet you too." I glance at Nick in question as our handsome personal chef strides out of the room, cutting the lights as he goes, and leaving us alone under the candle light. "They're not going to serve the dessert?"

"No," Nick says, a dark glimmer in his eyes. "I am."

10

I watch, transfixed and anxious, as Nick slowly stands up, unfastening his tie. Draping it over the back of his chair where his jacket rests, he steps away from the table and walks toward me, casually rolling the sleeves of his white shirt up on his muscled forearms.

"Don't move, Avery."

Oh, God. I couldn't if I tried. His voice is so deep with carnal command, it roots me to my seat.

I'm not even certain I'm breathing as he approaches me on the other side of the table. He's so tall and powerful, so darkly masculine, everything female inside me responds with eager, wanton invitation.

"You look so beautiful tonight," he murmurs, reaching down to cup my face in the cradle of his broad palm. "Do you have any idea how hard it was for me not to send everyone away so I could touch you—so I could taste you—the way I've been dying to all damn night?"

His words make me shiver. They make the warm, wet knot of yearning between my legs twist even hotter, even wetter. His fingers slide beneath my chin, traveling along my jaw line toward my ear as he moves behind me now. I close my eyes when his hands come to rest lightly on my shoulders. The heat of his body at my back radiates so intensely it's a wonder I don't melt right where I sit.

"Jesus, these pearls," he says, moving his hands down onto the swells of my breasts, then into the tender valley between them where the long strand is nestled. He leans down, so close to my ear that his voice vibrates through me. "I can't see you in them without remembering how sexy you looked with them roped around your wrists while I fucked you."

"Yes." My words shudder out of me, my heart pounding rapidly. "That's all I think of when I'm wearing them too."

My sex clenches at the memory of his cock buried deep within me and his finger delving into the tight channel of my ass until I came in wave after wave of violent pleasure. For as long as I live, I know I'll never be able to see a string of pearls and not think of Nick and all of the dirty, wicked, delicious things we've done together.

He reaches for them, gathering the strand in his fingers. The gems click and slide against one another, sending another erotic shiver through my body. He lifts the necklace off me, over my head.

"Hands behind your back, baby."

As soon as I comply, I feel the cool pressure of the pearls being wrapped around my crossed wrists. He binds me just tight enough to hold my hands immobile without straining the delicate string of precious gems. I'm not going to test them. I'm not going to test him, because I know this is only the start of the pleasure he has in mind for me. With Nick, there is always more to come.

Once I'm bound, he takes hold of my chair and drags me back from the table. He steps in front of me, looking at me with a combination of approval and hot lust in his eyes.

"So beautiful." His fingers skim tenderly beneath my jaw, tilting my face up. "What would you like to try first for dessert?"

I watch as he reaches over to the cart and removes the polished dome lids from the bowls of ripe berries, decadent sauces, and a mound of fluffy whipped cream. I can't possibly choose, and besides my only true temptation is the man who's got me totally under his thrall.

"Surprise me."

His black brows arch in mild amusement. "You told me once that you didn't like surprises."

"I'm learning to like a lot of new things with you."

His mouth curves, and he leans down to reward me with a deep, unhurried kiss. I feel his body swiveling slightly as our lips and tongues tangle. He's reached for something on the cart. I'm not sure what it is until he brings it up to our joined mouths and I inhale its sweet fragrance.

He draws back, placing the strawberry between my lips. I bite down, moaning as flavor explodes on my tongue. After I chew and swallow the succulent fruit, Nick follows it up with a dollop of cream on the end of his finger.

I wrap my lips around the tip, our eyes locked as I suck him into my mouth and lick the cream away. Now he's the one breathing heavily and moaning, his body growing tense and rigid as I swirl my tongue over the tip of his finger, then suck it hard inside my mouth.

On a low snarl, he pulls free, only to grasp my face in both hands and hold my head steady as his mouth descends on mine. He licks past my lips, his kiss hungered, scorching.

"I love the taste of cream on your tongue," he rasps. "I loved watching you wrap this pretty mouth around my cock in the office the other day. Makes me so fucking hard to think about you sucking me dry like that."

I'm already half mad with need for him, but hearing his desire-roughened voice, hearing him describe the things we've done together, makes my arousal almost unbearable. But he's not ready to show me any relief just yet.

He draws back from me, a merciless glimmer in his eyes. "Open your mouth for me, baby. Tip your head back a little. That's it. Now let me see that pretty pink tongue."

I obey him, waiting with my hands secured behind me and my face tilted up to him like a supplicant at the altar. I hold my tongue out, watching as he lifts a small ladle of chocolate sauce and holds it an inch or two above my head. He pours it slowly, watching as I lap at the thick, rich stream, swallowing it down, sip after delicious sip.

It's difficult to catch every drop. Some of it dribbles onto my lips, onto my chin. Nick doesn't give me the chance to lick it up. He descends on me, kissing me deeply, his tongue erasing every errant drop.

I moan his name, unable to keep from shifting on my chair as my core floods with heat and longing. I want to reach for him, but the pearls restrict all but the most careful movement. My precious bonds are both a frustration and a titillation.

I'm panting when he breaks our kiss. My body feels electrified and throbbing with the need for relief. I can't hold back my hopeful sigh when he reaches down to unfasten the tie at my waist, the only thing holding my simple wrap dress together. The garment loosens, and Nick sweeps the black fabric off my shoulders, baring my chest and torso.

"You wore the new bra for me," he says, approval deep and dark in his thickened voice.

I can't curb my smile. I've got another surprise for him, but since he's taking so much pleasure tormenting me, I decide to keep the secret to myself for now.

He pets my breasts for a moment, clearly delighting in the way my nipples rise under his touch. Every nerve ending in my body belongs to him. Just as every gasp and sigh and pleasured sound I make is only for him too.

He removes my bra, unfastening the delicate front clasp and sliding the slackened straps down my biceps before his hands come back to me to knead and caress my naked breasts. He kisses my nipples, teasing them with his tongue and teeth until I'm writhing, desperate with stimulation.

Then he reaches for the ladle and scoops up another serving of chocolate sauce. His gaze scorching, he slowly pours the chocolate over my exposed breasts. Thin rivulets fall onto my skin, making my core tighten in reflexive response. I can hardly bear the erotic sensation of the warm spurts of chocolate raining down onto the swells of my flesh and the valley between them. He drizzles more onto the pebbled buds of my nipples, and I can see from the strained look on his handsome face that I'm not the only one being tormented and teetering at the edge of madness.

On a coarsely voiced curse, he sets the ladle aside and drops to his haunches to eat the chocolate off me. Licking, sucking, nipping with his teeth, he leaves me shuddering with desire.

"Not fair," I say when he draws away from me and rises to his feet. I shake my head. "I want to taste you too."

He doesn't argue. From the look on his face, I'm not sure he'd have the will to try.

Unfastening his belt and pants, he pushes the tailored trousers and boxer briefs down his muscled thighs, then hastily removes his shirt. His cock stands hard and heavy in front of my face, more tempting than any of the succulent treats I've had tonight.

I lean forward, greedy for him, yet determined to take my time. I tease the soft, broad head with the tip of my tongue, then trace the veined underside of his shaft in a long, slow sweep. When I finally work my way back up and take him fully into my mouth, Nick's curse is little more than a strangled groan from the bottom of his throat.

Gripping the edge of the table, he drops his head back for a moment, tendons jumping in the sides of his neck. I continue my unrushed exploration of his cock and balls, knowing it's got to be driving him beyond insane that he can't order me to put my hands on him now too.

His fingers spear into my unbound hair, fisting and flexing as I suck him deep into my mouth and tighten my cheeks around him, all the while holding his dark, hooded gaze.

Then he frees his hold on my hair, my name a harsh gasp as he reaches behind him for something on the table. The red silk runner. His eyes blaze with wicked intent as he brings the sash around in front of him, dangling the fringed edge of it over my bare shoulders.

Stroking the side of my face, he gently draws me away from his erect cock.

There is a question in his glittering eyes. I answer by holding still, allowing him to tie the silk around my head like a blindfold.

"You're not finished with dessert yet," he tells me, his voice my only anchor in my new molten-hued world.

I hear him move, followed by the soft clink of a spoon against a bowl. His fingers alight gently below my chin, guiding my mouth back to his cock and to whatever additional treat he intends to gift me with now. I know in that instant, when something sweet and sticky meets my tongue as I lick the crown of his penis.

Honey.

It slides down the sides of his thick shaft and I chase it with my tongue, with my lips, savoring the taste of him even more than the nectar that now coats his smooth, steely flesh.

"Mm," I hum as I lap and suckle my way along every hard inch of him. "Now you've got me craving cream."

His answering curse is profane, highly erotic. "I'm going to give you some, baby. Right after I sample the cream I'm craving."

He crouches down in front of me and roughly lifts

my skirt. I hear his sharp inhalation when he finds me bare beneath my dress. Bare and drenched and quivering for him.

"Jesus Christ. Your pussy's been naked and waiting for me this whole time." It hardly sounds like a complaint.

I can't see his face, but I'm pretty sure his gaze is beyond fevered now. "If I had told you, we never would've made it past the champagne."

"Baby, if you had told me, we never would've made it into the car."

He goes down on me without warning, pushing my thighs apart and burying his face in my sex. I have no hope of staving off the orgasm that's been on the verge of breaking ever since we began indulging in our decadent dessert. With his palms holding me aloft in my chair and keeping me steady against his wicked mouth, Nick makes me come in what seems like seconds.

I shudder against his tongue, pleasure arcing through me in wave after glorious wave.

I am boneless, still spiraling through my climax as he carefully lifts me from the chair, mindful of the pearls that still bind my hands behind my back.

With my blindfold in place, I have no choice but to surrender to him completely as he bends me over the table and spreads me open. I hear the soft rustle of the condom packet he retrieves from his pants pocket, and then I feel Nick's heat against me as he guides his cock to my body's entrance and pushes inside on a long, slow thrust.

"I want you to come for me again," he demands harshly. "I want to hear you scream for me."

And in those next moments, as he roars and bucks

with the onslaught of a staggering release, I tumble over the edge with him, his name torn from my throat like a prayer.

I can't deny him. My body and my will are both at his mercy.

And so is my heart.

11

I am sore in all the right places as I step out of the shower the next morning and towel off in the large master bathroom of the penthouse.

Nick is ahead of me by nearly an hour. His towel is damp on the heated chrome rack mounted on the wall where I now hang mine, and I can hear him talking to someone on Bluetooth as I slip into short silk kimono robe, then proceed to finger-comb and dry my hair. My makeup takes all of five minutes since I'm only going to the studio to work today and anything more than mascara and a little color on my lips is overkill around Lita and Matt.

I pad out of the bedroom barefoot and find Nick in the kitchen. "You let me oversleep."

"I thought you might appreciate the extra rest this morning."

To my surprise, I see that not only is he already

dressed for his day in a pearl gray shirt and black slacks, he has also had time to make breakfast. As I approach, he puts a fluffy poached egg on a bed of crab meat, tomato, and spinach, then spoons some creamy yellow hollandaise over the whole thing.

"Hungry?"

"I shouldn't be. But for one of your famous Benedicts? Always."

He arches a dark brow. "I felt the need to reestablish my dominance in the kitchen after that meal Gavin put on for us last night. I don't want you thinking about any other man today."

"Dinner was incredible," I admit. "But my body only knows one master." I go up onto my toes to kiss his sexy mouth. "My stomach—and the rest of me—is all yours."

He plates another serving and we carry our dishes to the table where he's already laid out place settings for us. I get coffee for both of us while he pours two glasses of juice. It's all very domestic and natural, and I can't deny the feeling of contentment that sweeps over me as we sit together and have breakfast like any other normal couple.

I can't deny how natural it feels to be with Nick, no matter what we're doing. Whether that's light bondage and food play or getting ready to start our daily routines together the morning after.

We settle into an easy rhythm at the table, enjoying our coffee and breakfast and making plans for the rest of the week. Nick's phone chimes repeatedly with incoming texts and phone calls, all of which he pointedly ignores.

"Shouldn't you answer?" I ask him over the rim of my coffee cup after we've both finished the last of our breakfast. "From what I've gathered, morning in this city doesn't officially start until Dominic Baine says so."

He gives me a wry smirk. "Careful, or you'll inflate my ego."

"I enjoy inflating your ego." I lick my lips, grinning now. "Along with other things."

He makes a low noise in the back of his throat, and for a moment I'm not sure if the dark, sensual glimmer in his eyes is a warning or a promise. Then he sets his napkin down beside his empty plate and gets up from the table.

I hold my breath as he walks over to me.

"Close your eyes."

Visions of last night send streaks of desire racing into my veins. I glance back at him when he moves behind me in untenable silence.

"Close them, Avery."

My lids drop and I wait, uncertain of his intentions and far too easily aroused by just the thought of what he might have in mind for me now.

Something silky brushes my cheek.

He's tying something loosely around my neck from behind me. Then . . . something cold and metallic settles between my naked breasts.

I look down and find a key on the end of a long red silk cord.

I recognize the key immediately. It was the same one he used to open the door of the building last night.

"Nick, what—" I pivot around to gape at him. "What is this?"

"A gift." He reaches down, touching the key that rests against my skin. "Your new private art studio."

My own studio? I'm so incredulous, for a moment I

can't speak. "You said you were thinking of buying the building. You meant buying it . . . for me? That's why you brought me there last night?"

He slowly shakes his head, sliding his palm around to my nape. I sigh against the warmth and comfort of his touch. "I also wanted to celebrate with you, like I said. So call it multitasking."

His smile is so full of pride and affection, I feel light-headed as I stare up at him. "Nick, you shouldn't have done this. I mean it."

"The building is a solid investment. Besides, there's no reason for you to spend your own money on shared space all the way across town when you can have your own private studio just five minutes from here."

I glance down at the key, astonished that he would do something so generous. Then again, I shouldn't be shocked. Nick may have earned a reputation as a cold, shrewd businessman—a heartless player in commerce and in life—but he's never been that with me. Not with the people I care about either. He stepped in with Vendange when Tasha needed help. He's even been pressing me lately to let him help with my mother's situation.

He has given me more kindnesses than I can ever hope to repay.

But that's not the entire reason I am hesitant now.

As much as I've dreamed of one day having my own space in which to work, I've never wanted the dream handed to me. My art is my own. It's always been the one thing that's belonged solely to me. My outlet. My haven.

The place I go when there is nowhere else I feel safe or understood.

I'm not ready to surrender that part of me.

Not even to Nick.

"Thank you for offering this to me," I murmur. "I love that you want to help. But you've already given me too much. More than I can ever hope to repay."

"Have I ever said anything about repaying me?" His voice takes on an edge as he looks at me now. "I want you to have it. You said yourself, you need somewhere to paint."

"I have somewhere, Nick." I pick up the silk cord and lift it over my head. "I hope you understand. When it comes to my art, I want to do it—I *need* to do it—on my own."

He doesn't move. Doesn't open his hand to take the key when I hold it out to him. I set it down on the table between us, next to his phone. Then I fold my hands in my lap and wait for him to say something. It takes a long time.

Finally, he blows out a heavy sigh. "If you're going to be making the trip to East Harlem on a regular basis, then do me the favor of allowing Patrick to take you and pick you up. I'd rather not spend most of the day wondering if you're safe or if you've lost your damn phone somewhere and can't reach me."

"Okay."

I nod, guessing this is about as decent a compromise as I can hope to win from him. He's brooding, not happy with my rejection of his gift, but at least he's talking to me.

When he caresses my cheek, his fingers are tender and affectionate against my face. "Your ride starts today. I'll go with you, then Patrick can take me to my office."

"All right."

As he leans in to kiss me, his phone chimes again. He glances down at it, frowning. Andrew Beckham's picture is on the display. Nick gives me a rueful look, then reaches over to swipes the screen lock.

"Yeah, Beck."

"Sorry to call you at home." The attorney's baritone voice carries through the speaker. "You got a second? It's about that condo project over in Brooklyn."

Nick exhales, already stepping away from me. "I have to take this."

"It's okay. I've got all of this."

I stand up and start clearing the dishes while he walks into the living room with his phone. I load the plates and silverware into the dishwasher, then wipe down the counter and table.

The key on its silken cord feels heavy and cold in my palm as I place it on the bar.

When I glance over at Nick, he's watching me. He moves the phone away from his mouth. "I need to head in now. How soon can you be ready?"

"Give me five minutes."

He nods, retrieving his suit jacket from where it's folded neatly over the back of the sofa. "I'll meet you downstairs. Patrick will have the car waiting out front."

"Is everything okay?"

"Just the usual schedule delays and contract bullshit. Nothing big, just things I need to take a look at personally."

"All right. I'll be right down."

He goes back to his call, heading out the door as he speaks, and I walk into the bedroom to get dressed. A few minutes later, wearing jeans and a layered camisole and gauzy tunic, I step off the elevator and into the lobby.

Nick isn't on the phone anymore. He's standing just outside the building entrance, talking with a beautiful strawberry-blonde. Although the tall, elegant woman has her back to me and I don't know her well, I would recognize her anywhere.

But I didn't realize that Nick knew her too.

They both turn my way as Manny opens the door for me and I step out of the building.

"Hi, Avery!" Claire Prentice beams at me, as vivacious and stylish as I remember her.

"Hello," I reply, as she draws me to her for an air kiss at the side of my face.

Four months ago we met for the first time at Vendange, after a friend who was supposed to housesit Claire's apartment here at Park Place stood her up at the last minute. On her way out of the country for an acting job for several months and left with no one to watch her place while she was gone, Claire convinced me to move in to her apartment instead.

Actually, it was her five thousand dollars in cash that convinced me.

On top of the fact that I desperately needed to find a place to live, since the crappy apartment building where I rented a tiny one-bedroom hole in the wall had been sold out from under me.

If not for Claire, I never would have had a reason to come to this building.

Nor would I have almost crashed headlong into Nick in the elevator that first night, when we both were hit with the intense attraction that drew us inexorably together—beginning with our chance encounter that night, followed by our explosive second meeting at his gallery, Dominion, which ended with the two of us in a hot, sweaty tangle in his bed.

It boggles my mind sometimes to think that I owe all of my current happiness to Claire's shitty friend.

I take in her glowing tan and chic designer sheath dress. She looks like she just walked out of a fashion ad, while in my BoHo casual outfit and sparsely made-up face, I feel like the barista who should be serving her a skinny latte.

It boosts my confidence immensely when Nick casually wraps his arm around my back as if to tell her and anyone else in the immediate vicinity that I'm with him.

"I haven't seen you around lately," I say to Claire. "How's the talk show going?"

She had been going to Japan to shoot the pilot when she hired me to housesit for her. Three and a half months later, she returned home and I filled her in on the basics of how I'd met Nick and was moving in with him.

She'd seemed excited for me, but I didn't get the sense that she and I were going to be much more than occasional neighbors. She seemed fairly private with her personal life, and God knows Nick and I are too.

"The show got cancelled, unfortunately. I was just telling Nick about it. They ran a bunch of audience tests on the pilot recently and the producers decided to kill it."

"Oh, I'm sorry."

Smiling, she gives me a dismissive wave of her bejeweled hand. "Ah, well. C'est la vie. Or whatever the Japanese equivalent is. There's plenty of other gigs out there."

"We should get going." Nick's hand urges me toward the idling limo where Patrick waits to open the door for us. "Claire, nice to see you."

"You too. I'll see you around, Avery."

I nod as Nick guides me to the car and we climb into the back.

I watch Claire Prentice step into the building, noting how Manny and every other male in the lobby can't take their eyes off the stunning woman. Hell, even I find it hard to tear my gaze away from her smooth stride and radiant sex appeal.

But Nick stares forward, almost deliberately so.

I can't deny the sudden, sharp stab of suspicion that needles me. With Patrick not yet inside the vehicle, I look at Nick. "I didn't realize you and Claire know each other."

He gives me a disinterested shrug. "I own the building. I'm acquainted to some extent with everyone who lives here."

"But you never mentioned it. Not even when I told you that first night at the gallery that I was housesitting for her." When I even went so far as to lie to him and tell him I was a friend of Claire's, he never acknowledged her. Not at any time in the past four months. "You never said you knew her."

"Didn't I?"

"No. You didn't."

Now he turns his head to look at me straight on. "Is there something you want to ask me, Avery?"

I sense the challenge in his tone, even though his gaze remains unflinching, unreadable.

Jealousy reduces my voice to a whisper. "Have you and Claire Prentice slept together?"

He reaches out, tenderly cupping my jaw. "No. We haven't."

"Never?"

"Never. I don't fuck anyone who lives in my building. Just as I don't fuck my employees. Those are two long-standing rules that I've abided by forever." He strokes my cheek, and the solemn look on his face obliterates all of my doubts. "There's only one woman who's tempted me to break my rules, and she's sitting right here."

He draws me toward him for a sweet, slow kiss as Patrick slides into the driver's seat. My heart is pounding heavily, my body quickening as Nick scoots me against him on the seat and drapes his arm possessively around my shoulders.

"East Harlem, please, Patrick. Take the slow way, so Ms. Ross and I can make out a little longer."

Patrick chuckles. "Yes, sir."

12

As the week nears its end, I've not only completed another painting but started on a third. Whether my burst of creativity has been inspired by my new work environment, the companionship of other artists I share the space with, Lita's ever-changing, eclectic taste in music, or a combination of all three, I can't be sure.

I have no doubt that Nick has inspired me too.

Like the first painting I did a few days ago, these other new pieces are abstract and moody, unmistakably sensual. Although I didn't paint any of them with the intention of producing something erotic, it's difficult not to see the powerful sexual suggestion in the combination of aggressive lines and bold brush strokes juxtaposed against sinuous curves and fluid, entangled shapes.

I stand back from my easel and tilt my head, assessing the progress of my current piece. Matt pauses beside me, having just returned from cleaning his brushes in the studio's small bathroom sink.

"I like what you did with the red in that one, Avery. Very hot."

"Thanks." I let my eye follow the twisting ribbon of scarlet that runs through the composition, binding the soft shapes that seem to glow in the foreground, lit by an unseen flame. In the background, pinpricks of light pierce a field of inky blackness.

"It's actually pretty damn good," Lita says, which, coming from her, is the height of praise. "My favorite so far is your other one, though."

She uses the end of a ball-peen hammer to point at the first painting I completed since coming to the studio. The one that still makes my heart race and the cheeks of my ass sting deliciously every time I look at it.

I try to curb my private smile as I murmur the title I've given it. *"Blue Hour, Black Leather."*

She nods. "You ever try to sell anything?"

"No," I reply. "Well, I tried for about a year, soon after I came to New York. Only one piece sold in all that time—one of the first things I ever painted. Nothing sold since, and I lost my spot at the gallery."

Lita purses her pierced lips, scrutinizing my work from across the room. "Were you painting like this back then?"

I glance back at my easel and the piece that reminds me of my candlelight dinner—and wicked dessert—with Nick a few nights ago. "No, this is something different for me."

Matt crosses his arms as he looks at my newest. "I've got a friend with a gallery down in SoHo. I'll bet I could get you some space there if I ask him."

"Oh, thanks, but I don't think so. I don't think I'm ready for that." And if I were, I would want to get the gallery spot on my own merits, not through favors or friendships.

"Speaking of galleries," Lita says to me, "some of my shit's going to be part of a multi-artist exhibition next week in Brooklyn. You wanna come?"

Matt nudges me. "Please, say yes. She's already twisted my arm to be there. It's at some chichi new gallery over in Greenpoint in the middle of the afternoon, for God's sake. If you don't come, I'll be forced to find a corner and day-drink all by my lonesome."

I smile, thinking that some time out with my new friends sounds like fun. "Okay, sure. I'll go."

As we settle on plans to meet up at the event, my phone chimes with an incoming text. There's no dimming my smile when I see Nick's message on the display.

Thinking about you all morning.

I sigh, catching my lip between my teeth in longing. He's been in Boston on business since yesterday afternoon, and not due back to the city until later this evening.

Been thinking about you too. I turn away from Lita and Matt, who've already moved on to another conversation without me anyway. *Missing you like crazy.*

Good. I like you hungry.

My eyes narrow as I tap my reply. *Not nice to tease.*

His response comes back immediately. *That's not what you said the other night.*

I'm grinning now, and wishing I wasn't in a room with two other people when he's making me think about all of the wicked things we did before he left town.

Are you hungry now, baby?

All right, Nick. Two can play this game. *For you? Always.*

That's my girl. There is a pause before his next text arrives. *How do you feel about lunch?*

I freeze, staring at his message for a second. Suspicion, along with a fluttery thrill of hope, sends me over to the window that looks out over the street below.

Nick's black BMW is idling at the curb.

"Oh, my God." When Lita and Matt swivel curious looks on me, a small burst of giddy laughter bubbles out of me. "My, um . . . my boyfriend's here."

Lita frowns. "You have a boyfriend?"

Matt grins. "What are you waiting for? Tell him to come up here so we can meet your man!"

Two minutes later, they're both gaping in disbelief as I introduce them to Dominic Baine and show him around the little studio.

He's not been up here yet, even though I've invited him to come check things out and meet my friends. I know he's busy, but part of me had been wondering if he was still brooding over the fact that I'm insisting on keeping this part of me separate from him for now. If the tables were turned, I doubt I would handle it much better than he has. Maybe a lot worse.

But if he's upset or resentful, it doesn't show as he talks easily with Matt and Lita, then follows me over to my work area while I fetch my purse and phone. I see his shrewd gaze travel over my canvases.

I can't deny that the urge to hide my work from him is strong. Nick knows art—good art—and he's made no secret of the fact that he found mine lacking. As much as it hurt to hear him say it, looking back, I know he was right.

But these new pieces are different. They are more a part of me than anything I've done before, and I'm terrified to see him look at them with disappointment.

"Ready?" he asks, his face adopting that unreadable mask that gives nothing away.

We say our goodbyes to my friends and Nick asks me to pick a restaurant I like in the neighborhood. I settle on an Italian hole in the wall that doesn't look very promising from the street, but serves the best lasagna I've had in all of New York City.

"You like it?" I ask Nick as we both dig into the cheesy, saucy goodness.

He nods enthusiastically, looking somewhat out of place seated at our rickety little table with its red-and-white checkerboard tablecloth in his crisp white custom-tailored shirt and charcoal gray tie. He's turned more than a few heads since we arrived. I'm sure it's not often that one of the wealthiest, most recognizable men in the country sits down to enjoy a ten-dollar plate of pasta in Spanish Harlem in the middle of a Thursday afternoon.

I try to ignore the surreptitious stares we're getting from the patrons and the restaurant staff alike. I don't doubt that a lot of the curious looks are directed at me, too, even though Nick has never tried to hide the fact that we're dating.

As for me, I'm just marveling at how he manages to avoid splashing marinara all over himself while I am eating under the constant threat of disaster.

"I knew you'd like it. Lita and Matt and I eat here at least twice a week because the food's not only cheap but awesome. If I'm not careful, pretty soon it's going to start showing on my hips."

Nick grins. "You're not going to hear me complaining. I love your curves."

Our eyes connect and the hungered look he gives me makes more than just my cheeks flood with heat. I clear my throat, shifting a bit on the black vinyl cushion of my chair. "How was the Boston meeting?"

"Promising. That technology company I invested in last year is ramping up to launch their first app very soon. It's got all the indicators of a real showstopper, some really innovative work and ideas."

"Nick, that's great."

"Yeah. There's a big international tech expo coming up in London. They'll be announcing the release to a packed house and media outlets around the world." He lifts the raffia-wrapped bottle of cheap red wine and pours me another glass. "I'd like you to be there with me."

"London?" I've never been outside the United States, and traveling to Europe has long been a dream of mine. But there is one slight problem. "I don't have a passport."

"I'll take care of that for you. I'll take care of everything you need." He reaches for my hand. "I want you with me, Avery."

I stare at him, mesmerized. Not only by his breathtaking handsomeness, but by his kindness. By the fact that in a few short months he's made me feel more important than anyone ever has in my life, aside from my mom.

He makes me feel content and safe and cherished—so incredibly alive.

He makes me feel loved.

There are times, like now, when he makes me feel as if the time we're sharing will go on forever. He makes me wish it could.

"Okay, Nick." I turn my hand around beneath his and lace our fingers together. "I'm ready to go anywhere you want to lead me."

His phone chimes and he curses under his breath. "That's Beck again."

"Go ahead and take it. I need to find the restroom, anyway."

Taking my purse along with me, I wade through the tightly arranged tables, making my way to the back corridor of the gloomy little restaurant. The restrooms are hidden around a corner near the rear door of the place. To my amazement, the ladies' room is unoccupied.

I push the battered white door open and step inside—

And before I can shut it and turn the lock on the tarnished knob, the door explodes inward. The force of it throws me back on my heels. I open my mouth to shout my outrage at the clod who barged in on me, but my voice evaporates on my tongue.

I stare up at the face I prayed I'd never see again, least of all here and now.

"Surprise, surprise, baby girl. I told ya you'd be hearin' from me again."

Rodney Coyle's face is older than I remember, and taut with menace as he locks the door behind him, sealing us inside the small bathroom together.

13

I lunge for the door, but Rodney blocks me. The rangy teenager who'd drifted in and out of my past during the horror of my mother's marriage to his father has since put on pounds and muscle. I try to shove my way past him, but I can neither get around him nor through him.

Fear streaks into my marrow. A scream lodges in my throat and it's all I can do to stifle it. I can't let it loose. Not when the last thing I want to do is draw attention to us.

Not when Nick is sitting in the restaurant outside.

Rodney knows this. I can see that confidence glittering in his close-set, dark eyes.

"You changed your phone number." He tauntingly wags his finger at me. "Now, is that any kinda way to treat your long-lost brother?"

He was never my brother, not by any stretch of the

imagination. Two years older than me, kicked out of his father's house long before my mom and I moved in, Rodney was habitually wasted and chronically unemployed. A loser I hardly knew, let alone considered family.

Now, I see an opportunist in front of me. A dangerous one.

"Here I thought we were just gettin' back on friendly terms. What was I supposed to think when all of a sudden you just cut me off like that?"

I back up as he advances on me. "W-what are you doing here?"

"I always did wanna come to New York. Figured it was as good a time as any to make the trip. Check in on you and see how well you're livin'." He clicks his tongue. "Livin' pretty fuckin' good, baby girl. I'm impressed."

"How did you find me? How did you know where I was today?"

He chuckles. "I've been tailing you for days, you dumb bitch. Waited for you outside your boyfriend's fancy-ass place on Park Ave, then had a taxi follow you in your chauffeured limo to the shithole building just up the street from here. Since you seem to eat at this place on a regular basis, I figured it'd be my best shot at catching you. And whattaya know, here you are, *caught*."

I wince inwardly at my stupidity that led him straight to me. I never imagined he'd come all this way. I'm afraid to guess what it will take for him to go now that he's here. Now that he's seen firsthand what my life is currently like with Nick.

He takes another step toward me. I take another retreating step, only to be stopped by the sink mounted to the wall at my back.

Even though I'm terrified, I hike up my chin and muster all the defiance I can into my voice. "Leave us alone, Rodney. My mom and me both. If you or any of the fucking lowlifes I'm sure you hang with even think of laying another finger on her, I swear to God I'll—"

His thin chuckle interrupts my threat. "Relax. I'm not interested in that old cunt anymore. I just needed her so I could get your attention. I had to let you know I was serious."

My hatred for him ratchets even higher to hear him admit that he had my mother injured in order to get to me. "Well, you have my attention. So what do you want from me? Money?"

"We can start there," he says, grinning now. "We can start with ten grand, how's that sound?"

"Ten thousand dollars?" I practically choke on the demand. "You're out of your mind. I don't have that kind of money."

"Oh, come on, now. You're smarter than that. And so am I. You can find a way to make this work. Guy like the one waiting for you out there, he's so fuckin' rich he won't even notice the money's missing."

"You think I'd steal from him? Never. Fuck you for even suggesting I would."

"Then I'm gonna need to have a talk with him." Rodney's mouth flattens with the threat. "Maybe I'll have a talk with some reporters while I'm in town too. Bet I could make some serious bank off what I know about Dominic Baine's girlfriend. Bet the gossip rags would eat that shit up. He ain't gonna be too happy, though."

How much does Rodney know? Surely not all of it. No one knows that much. My mother made certain of that.

Still, dread settles cold in my stomach as I stare into his narrowed, predatory eyes—eyes that are so like Martin Coyle's I cannot curb the shudder that wracks me. "If you're talking about the fact that your father repeatedly abused me and eventually raped me, save your breath. Nick already knows."

The news catches him by surprise, but it doesn't move him. No, that vulture's stare refuses to let me go. "That's all he knows, though, right? There's something nobody knows about you."

He's not asking a question. I can see from the satisfied look on Rodney's face that he's been confident in his knowledge for a very long time.

From the beginning, if I had to guess.

He confirms it with a chilling smile.

"I saw your car parked outside the house that afternoon, Avery. Me and some buddies were coming back from an all-nighter and just by chance we drove past the old man's place. There was that piece of shit Honda of yours sittin' in the driveway."

I don't say anything. Dear God, I can hardly draw a breath as he continues to describe the day that's branded into my memory.

"Now, maybe I wouldn't've thought nothin' of it. Prolly a good chance I would've plain forgot, but later on, after the news broke all over town that the sonofabitch was killed and your mom confessed, I remember thinking how odd it was that she made a point of telling everyone she was alone when she popped the old man. That you were gone all day."

"I was at my grandparents' house," I murmur, repeating the story my mother made me tell following the killing. "I was sick that day and I stayed home from school. Mom sent me to Gran's that morning, then she and Martin started fighting . . ."

Rodney chuckles even before I finish reciting the lie. "Yeah, I know that's what she told the cops. But you and me, baby girl, we know different. Ain't that right?"

I stare at him, realizing with cold certainty that he is a problem I cannot outrun. Not now.

"If you're so sure you have something over me, why wait until now to speak up?"

He shrugs. "My old man got what was comin' to him. I sure as shit didn't shed any tears when I heard the asshole was dead. And I didn't give a fuck why your mother did it. Nothing for me to gain by stirring shit up back then. You two bitches were poor as fuck. What did you have that I could possibly want?" His grin flattens into a leer. "I mean, don't get me wrong, you and me, baby girl, we coulda made things interesting. But the way the old man used to look at you, I figured he'd already been all over that fine little ass and I don't take sloppy seconds."

As he talks, bile rises up the back of my throat. To think he knew what his father intended for me and never bothered to speak out or to help me? It sickens me. Enrages me. My fingers curl into fists, my fingernails digging into my palms.

He steps closer to me. "I'd about forgotten what I saw that morning . . . until a couple months ago, I ran across a picture on the Internet. Picture of you all fancied up, hanging off the arm of some rich dude who owns half of New York by the looks of it. Hot piece of tail like you, guess it shouldn't surprise me that you're using it to snag a rich fuck like Dominic Baine."

His crudeness grates, but even worse, I hate that he knows Nick's name. I hate that I have brought this vile part of my past into my life with Nick. I have no one to blame—not even Rodney. This is all my fault, and I need to make it better. I need to make it go away.

The problem is, I can't give Rodney what he's demanding.

"I don't have the kind of money you want. And I won't take it from him—not for any reason."

"Then you got a big problem coming down the pike real soon. I came here to collect on a debt you've owed me for a long time, and if I don't get it, there's no telling what I'll be forced to do."

"Rodney, you have to believe me—"

"No, baby girl. You have to believe *me*. I want that money. You've got the next seven days to make it happen." He reaches out, snatching my purse off the floor and grabbing my phone from inside it. He punches in a number and his phone rings. Then he silences both devices, tossing mine at me. "I expect to hear from you once you've got the money. Don't be stupid enough to test me, Avery."

With a sneer, he leaves me to sag against the hard porcelain of the sink as he pivots toward the restroom door. Unlocking it as if he had every right to be inside with me, he blithely strides out.

Oh, God. My breath rushes from my lungs in a heaving gasp. My legs feel weak, unstable beneath me. I'm not sure how long I stand there, suspended between misery and terror. My hands are shaking so hard, they are all but useless to me as I stare into the mirror and try to gather my composure.

Nick will be wondering about me soon, if he isn't

already. With Rodney outside the restroom now, I have no idea what he might do and I don't dare delay in here any longer. Forcing myself to calm, I run some cold water over a paper towel and press the coolness to my ashen cheeks and brow.

It helps a little. I look better, even if inside I'm nauseous with dread and worry. After a few moments, I finally emerge from the restroom and head back into the restaurant dining area. Nick is no longer on the phone, and I see that he's paid our bill.

"Everything okay?" he asks as I approach our table. "You've been gone awhile."

"Yeah. I'm fine." I shrug, finding it hard to meet his eyes. "There's always a line for the ladies' room."

My non-answer seems to satisfy him, but I notice his shrewd gaze looking past me, as if his instincts alone are telling him something is off. I barely resist the urge to glance over my shoulder, especially when the hairs at the back of my neck begin to prickle.

I don't know how I manage to sound calm when I am desperate to get out of the place. "Ready to go?"

Nick nods. "Sure. We can leave anytime."

At that same moment, to my horror, I catch Rodney in my peripheral vision. He swaggers through the restaurant, walking almost directly past our table on his way out. As he heads for the front door, I hold my breath, praying he'll keep going. Outside, he turns left on the sidewalk, finally disappearing from view.

I know Nick saw him, even if there is no reason for him to think anything of the man in the beer logo T-shirt and jeans who looks like any other patron in the place.

"Do you want me to take you back to the studio?"

"No." I shake my head, forcing myself to snap out

of my anxious distractedness. "I, um . . . I'm feeling kind of out of it. Maybe I had too much wine or something. Can we please just go home instead?"

"Of course."

Nick wraps his arm around my shoulders as he guides me away from the table.

As we get into his car at the curb, I'm relieved to see no trace of Rodney anywhere. But I know he's watching. I know he's waiting.

After today, I realize he's been watching and waiting for a long time.

Since the day I pulled the trigger and shot his father.

14

Rodney's threat hangs over me, cold and dank and inescapable. I'm not sure how I make it through the weekend and into the next week with the dread of the situation pressing down on me like the dead weight of a corpse.

Like Martin Coyle's bloodied, bullet-riddled corpse.

Ironic that I have him and the abuse I suffered at his hands to thank for my current ability to pretend everything is normal, no matter what I'm dealing with on the inside.

Being with Nick helps too.

He is my safe harbor, even if he doesn't know how badly I need his shelter now. He's so passionate and protective, so solid and strong, I can almost convince myself that none of the ugliness is happening. That Rodney doesn't know anything about that awful day. That he's not here in New York, making me afraid to leave the building for fear that I'll run into him—with or without Nick beside me.

I can almost believe, for brief stretches of time, that Martin Coyle never existed.

And that my mother isn't serving a life sentence purely out of love for me.

Of all my secrets, shames, and sins, it is this one that's been the hardest to bear.

"Where are you, baby?" Nick's deep voice draws me back to him as we lie in a tangle together in bed on Tuesday morning. Propping himself on one elbow, he strokes my cheek, his touch infinitely gentle after a vigorous couple of hours of intense, mind-blowing sex. As tender as his touch is, his gaze is dark with concern. "Something's been bothering you for days. What is it?"

I shake my head as I look up into his stormy blue eyes, hating that he can read me so well. Loving him for it too. Of all the people in my life, he's the only one who understands me so intimately that he can gauge my emotions even when my self-protective walls are at their highest.

But I can't let those walls down, not now.

Not even with him.

God, right now, especially not with him.

"I'm fine. I'm just . . . thinking."

As I murmur the lame explanation I turn my head away from him, because the care in his eyes is too much for me to take. If I look too long, I'll be tempted to bare my soul and that's a burden I won't place on him.

My problems are my own. I made them. I will be the one to fix them, if I can.

And if I can't fix them, then I have to be prepared to walk away from Nick before my past brushes any closer

146

to him and his world.

I've already let it come too damn close.

I close my eyes, summoning an evenness to my voice that I don't feel. "What I'm thinking is I'm a mess and I need to take a shower."

As I start to roll away from him, his hand clamps down on my wrist. He's not playing. There is no give in his grasp. My retreat stalled, I have no choice but to turn back to him.

"Tell me, Avery."

"Tell you what?"

His stare is hard, his grip on my arm unyielding. "What's going on with you? You've been different . . . distant. Something's got you upset."

I swallow past the knot of fear that's resided in my throat since my confrontation with Rodney.

I don't want to lie to Nick. I can't betray his trust when he's given me no reason to feel unsafe with him. But I can't tell him what I'm going through.

I can't tell him what I've done.

No one can know. That was the promise I gave my mother nine years ago.

If I could go back in time now and undo it, I would.

I would give anything to go back and convince my mother to let me stay at her side instead of leaving her to clean up my mess.

Everything I have—my life, my freedom, this amazing man and the love I feel for him—is a gift I wouldn't have if not for my mother's sacrifice.

I would undo all of it, even knowing it would mean I'd never have met Nick.

"I've just . . ." I force a casual shrug. "I've got a lot on my mind, that's all."

"So, tell me about it." I should know better than to try to dodge him. He only studies me closer, his sharp gaze narrowing. "When is the last time you spoke to her?"

I must look surprised, maybe even shocked. When I can't summon words, Nick lets go of my wrist but brings his hand up to cradle the side of my face.

"Don't say you haven't been worried about your mother, Avery. You've been avoiding talking about her for days. And it's not like you were very forthcoming before then." His gaze searches mine. "We should go see her. I want to talk to her about her legal representation and start putting that ball in motion."

Panic crawls up my spine. "Nick, you don't have to—"

"I know I don't." His thumb caresses my cheek. "I want to do it. For you, and for her. I've already got Beck working on a few contacts. We should have a new defense team put together in a couple of weeks."

"What?" I can't control the sharpness of my reply. I'm shocked. More than that, I'm alarmed and gripped with a new kind of dread. "You didn't tell me anything about this."

"Actually, I did. I mentioned what I wanted to do at lunch that day at Gavin's restaurant."

I remember the conversation, of course. I'd been just as opposed to the idea then, and he'd said nothing about giving his attorney orders to begin the process. My mother won't want this, and he has no idea what he'll be stirring up if her case were to be reopened.

"You didn't even ask me, Nick." I pull away from him, sliding to the edge of the bed. "You have no right to insert yourself into my life like this!"

His expression stills, then hardens. "That's funny. I thought I already was inserted into your life."

"That's not what I mean."

"Then what do you mean?" He pivots to the other side of the mattress and stands to face me, naked and formidable. His hands are fisted loosely at his sides, and I can see from his rigid stance that he is furious. "What the fuck is going on, Avery?"

I stare at him across the wide expanse of his king-size bed. It feels like more than a mile is separating us in this moment, but I don't dare reach across it. In some sense, the physical distance gives me strength. I'd rather have him angry and shutting me out than see him drawn any deeper into the mess I've created.

I'd rather have him hate me now than face his disappointment if he ever learns the worst of my lies.

"I didn't ask for your help with my mom's situation, Nick."

"No, you didn't." Clipped words. A tendon pulses in his jaw as he looks at me. "I thought we were well past the point where you'd need to ask me. Am I wrong about that?"

I could push him away with a careless reply. I feel the volatility of this moment and I know I could end things between us right here and now.

Part of me knows I should. Without Nick's wealth and status in the equation, Rodney's threat to expose me carries no weight. I'm not afraid of facing the consequences for what I've done. In many ways, it would be a relief. What I cannot bear is the thought of Rodney using my sins against Nick and everything he's built.

"Am I wrong about us, Avery?"

"No." I slowly shake my head, unable to deny him or what he means to me. "You're not wrong about us."

"Then tell me what this is really about."

I want to. God, how I want to blurt everything out to him and hope, *pray*, that he'll understand. He's forgiven me for lying to him when we first met, but how can I expect him to forgive the rest of the lies that still hang between us? Lies of omission and half-truths. Lies that have protected me for half my life.

He demanded trust and honesty from me—things I promised to give him freely.

Things I have never dared to give anyone before him.

"Tell me what's really bothering you, Avery." His voice is steady and calm, but firm with command. He walks around the bed, closing the distance between us. "You're afraid of something. If it's not me, then what is it?"

I feel the weight of my promise to him as I hold his penetrating gaze. I owe him my trust. He's earned it, after all.

But the words stall in my throat.

"You just . . . You caught me off guard, that's all." I reach out to him and find his jaw like granite against my fingertips. "I'm sorry I overreacted."

His eyes study me too closely. He is not a man who is fooled easily, and I'm not naive enough to assume he believes me now.

But he doesn't push me to deepen my lie.

"I'll tell Beck to hold off on those calls." Reaching up for my hand, he draws it from his face. "I have meetings at the office all day. I need to clean up and get out of here."

He steps away from me without another touch or another word.

I watch him go, feeling the coldness of his withdrawal like a chill that's opened up in my chest. I want to follow after him, but my feet stay rooted to the floor. Guilt and regret sit like acid on my tongue, but they are nothing compared to the bitter taste of my cowardice.

As the sound of the running shower drifts out from the large master bathroom, my phone rings on the nightstand with an incoming call.

I reach for it, half expecting I'll find Rodney waiting for me on the other end of the line. For one perversely self-destructive moment, I actually hope it's him, at the same time imagining Nick coming back out of the bathroom to catch me talking with my stepbrother and leave me no choice but to confess everything I'm holding in.

But it's not Rodney.

"Hi, Matt."

"Hey." Matt's cheery voice jolts me back to the here and now. "So, we still on for Lita's thing this afternoon?"

It takes my brain a second to catch up. "Um. That's today?"

"At one o'clock in Greenpoint. Oh, shit. Please don't tell me you're going to cancel."

The excuse that's perched at the tip of my tongue dissolves when I hear the disappointment in his voice.

"No. No, it's all good," I assure him. "Of course, I'll be there."

He exhales dramatically. "Oh, thank God. Lita's already called and texted me five times this morning about one neurotic thing or another. I swear there's not enough cheap Chardonnay in all of Greenpoint to get me through an entire afternoon of her angsting."

I laugh, even though I don't really feel it. We make arrangements to meet up at the gallery, and although an exhibition forty-five minutes away in Brooklyn is the last thing I feel like doing today, I don't want to let my new friends down. I also know I can't cower in the penthouse any longer, wishing my problems would just go away.

Sooner than later, I need to figure out how I'm going to deal with Rodney.

And if I can't deal with him, I need to figure out how I'm going to find the strength to walk away from Nick.

15

I set out for Lita's exhibition in Brooklyn a little past noon, using the long subway ride and the crush of people all around me to drown out the noise in my head. It's not so easy to drown my remorse. My guilt for how I left things with Nick this morning clings to me as I get off at the station in Greenpoint.

It's been months since I've been back to my old neighborhood, but today it feels like years. Some of the shops on Nassau Avenue have changed or closed down. Others are sporting new paint jobs and rehabbed interiors. Even my old apartment building—the mid-century brick eyesore where I rented a tiny one-bedroom unit—is undergoing a dramatic renovation.

I'm so close to the narrow side street off Nassau, I can't resist detouring past it for a quick look on my way to the gallery. Construction scaffolding climbs the sides of the building and on the wire fencing surrounds the property, vinyl banners advertise the modern new condominiums that will be opening for occupation later in the year.

Once the renovations are complete, there will be little left of the old building. Would I even recognize it? In many ways, my life has been just as profoundly altered since I left this neighborhood a few months ago.

How different everything would be if I had never met Claire Prentice.

I had considered her housesitting offer a miracle at the time—a life line I desperately needed.

If not for that opportunity from Claire, serendipitous as it was, I would have never have met Nick. Without him, my stepbrother would have nothing to gain from me. I would still be working behind the bar at Vendange and Rodney might never have reentered my life.

But there's no turning the clock back now, no more than I can turn it back and change what happened nine years ago.

Fate never forgives.

It never forgets.

I realize that now, even if I've been too foolish—too selfish—to truly understand that before.

As I head back up the main street to the gallery, I am relieved to find Matt waiting for me as soon as I enter the place.

"There you are!" He's got a half-empty glass of wine in his hand as he hooks his arm through mine and leads me into the center of the gathering. He turns a serious look on me and lowers his voice. "We have a situation."

I frown, confused. "You mean with Lita?"

"Our girl's on the verge of a meltdown. She's been hiding in the restroom for twenty minutes and won't come out."

"Seriously?" I hurry along with him to the back of the gallery, cutting through the throng as discreetly as possible. There is one small unisex bathroom, and we find the door locked. I rap quietly on the panel and call Lita's name.

"Leave me alone." Her reply is muted, miserable-sounding. "Just . . . go away, you guys. I can't do this."

Matt and I exchange a glance. "What do you mean, you can't do this? Lita, open the door."

All I get is silence. Followed by the sound of a toilet paper roll rattling and then Lita blowing her nose.

"Come on, honey. Talk to us. Open the door." I slide my gaze to Matt and lower my voice to a whisper. "Is this normal for her?"

He shrugs. "I dunno. This is the first exhibition of hers I've been to. Like I told you on the phone this morning, she's been neurotic about this showing all day."

"I can totally hear you two." Abruptly, the lock on the door clicks free and Lita opens the door. "If you're going to talk about me, you might as well do it in here."

I know I'm gaping, but I can't help it.

Instead of her usual goth-meets-grunge style, Lita is wearing a 1940s vintage royal blue dress with a fitted bodice and a sweetheart neckline that work together to emphasize all of her killer curves. The A-line skirt falls from her cinched waist in long, loose pleats that end at her knees. Gone are Lita's favored combat boots, and in their place is a pair of high-heeled black patent leather Mary Janes.

With her multi-hued pixie haircut and extensive body art juxtaposed with her romantic outfit and flawless makeup, she looks edgy and feminine. More than that, she's an absolute knockout.

"Lita," I gasp, my eyes wide. "You look amazing!"

"I look fucking ridiculous. Who the hell am I trying to impress, right?" She frowns down at herself before looking back at Matt and me with terror in her eyes. "Did you see how many people are out there? Oh, God. I think I'm going to be sick."

Clutching her stomach, she pivots back into the bathroom. Matt and I follow her inside, closing the door behind us.

"You've got to pull yourself together, girl." Matt holds his wineglass out to her. "Here, drink some of this."

She takes the glass from him, draining it. To my surprise—and relief—instead of worsening the situation, the wine seems to calm her. She leans against the tile wall and presses the cool glass to her forehead.

"Do either of you have any idea who's out there in that room right now?" Before we can even attempt to guess, she answers her own question. "Forgetting the other artists in the exhibit—whose shit is, like, a hundred times better than mine—there are no less than three critics from the biggest art publications in the country and a couple of museum curators out there. Not to mention all of the private collectors milling around sipping martinis and champagne and shit."

I tilt my head at her. "Okay. And that's a problem, because . . . ?"

"Because I'm not ready for all of . . . *this*."

"Yes, you are," Matt says. "But you're not going to know that unless you get out of this bathroom."

She moans and hands the wineglass back to him. "I

think I'm going to need more wine before I'm ready for that. God, I'm pretty sure I even saw the CEO of that hot new tech firm over in Brooklyn Heights out there— you know, the dude who used to be in that rock band a few years ago?"

Matt nods, but I don't think he's really listening. He holds the empty glass up. "I'm going to get you another one of these. Avery, will you make sure she doesn't try to drown herself in the toilet bowl before I get back?"

I nod, holding back my grin as he leaves me alone with Lita. She eyes me sullenly, one perfectly defined brow arched. "Guess I'm not as tough as I look, huh?"

I shrug. "Most people aren't."

She snorts, pushing away from the wall and shuffling over to the toilet. She drops the lid, then plops down onto it. "Fuck. What am I doing here, Avery? Did you see the other art out there? The paintings, the photography, the pottery." She shakes her head, huffing out a gust of air. "It's all traditional, beautiful shit—even the other sculptures in this exhibit are refined. They're fucking lovely. Mine's not like any of that. It's harsh. It's jagged and disturbing. It's—"

"Unique?" I suggest. "Lita, your art is special. It's a reflection of you, and it is beautiful. It's surprising and unusual and totally unforgettable. Just like the artist who created it."

Her ruby-red lips twist in a skeptical line. "What if I get shredded by those critics out there? What if everyone laughs their asses off at my work?"

"What if they don't?"

She looks at me as if she had never considered the alternative possibility. For a long moment, she simply stares at me in silence. Then she swallows. "This is a big deal. And I'm scared, Avery."

"Of course you are. Three art critics, a couple of museum curators plus a former rock-star-turned-CEO? Anyone who's not afraid of that crowd would have to be seriously fucked up."

A laugh bubbles out of her, then she rolls her eyes. "You think I'm being an idiot."

"No. I think you're being human."

Saying nothing, she stares at me, and I wonder not for the first time about the caution I see in her eyes. She is guarded, self-protective. She is wounded, and so vulnerable from the pain of what's inside her it's all I can do not to pull her into a hug and tell her that I understand those feelings too.

We hardly know each other, and despite her irascibility, I sense a kindred spirit in Lita Frasier. I sense the start of a friendship I didn't expect with her.

"Incoming." Matt's voice carries through the door before he enters the bathroom with a bottle of water in one hand and a glass of wine in the other. "Pick your poison, sweetheart."

"Water," Lita murmurs. "I'll save the wine for after this thing is over."

Matt shoots me a look of surprise. "Wine for you?"

"Thanks. Don't mind if I do."

While I sip the wine, Lita chugs the bottle of water, then crushes the empty container and pitches it into the recycle bin across the room. "Thanks, you guys. For just . . . being here."

I smile, glad to see her rebounded. "Anytime."

"So, you're good now?" Matt asks.

She nods. "Yeah. I'm good."

"Then, what're you waiting for?" He fists his hands

on his hips, then jerks his head in the direction of the door. "Get out there and slay, girl!"

"Okay, yeah. Dammit, I'm going to." She stands up, smoothing her blue dress. Then, with her spine straight and shoulders squared, she marches out ahead of us.

Thank you, Matt mouths silently to me. "Join me at the bar?"

I lift my glass in salute. "Lead the way."

We wend through the clusters of people, and I notice Lita approaching her sculpture display, where a small throng is gathered to look at her art. There is little trace of the anxious woman I consoled in the bathroom. She looks poised and confident and uniquely captivating. I don't miss the fact that one of the gallery patrons—a hot twenty-something guy wearing jeans and a black oxford with the sleeves rolled up over his tattooed, muscular arms—has taken notice of her too.

With his rugged good looks, shaggy mane of silky dark hair, and bad boy swagger, he's got former rock star written all over him. The numerous awestruck side glances and whispers he leaves in his wake as he approaches my friend leave no doubt. To Lita's credit, the smile she turns on him as he holds out his hand to her in greeting is cool and unaffected.

I shoot her a wink when she briefly looks my way.

Yeah, she's going to be just fine.

The exhibit has brought an impressive variety of artists and patrons together, and the energy in the room is invigorating. As we head to the bar, Matt and I duck around a little throng of attendees listening indulgently to a young photographer waxing poetic about his love of painted doors as subject matter. Nearby, I hear a textile artist explaining how her sabbatical to Africa inspired the intricate beadwork and woven threads she has incorporated into her work. In another area of the gallery, painters chat up spectators, several of whom I see tapping on tablets and speaking quietly into handheld recorders.

The buzz of conversation and intermittent laughter fills the air—so much so, I hardly register the familiarity of the female voice ordering a very dry martini at the bar as Matt and I break through the crowd.

But Kathryn Tremont's slender, willowy figure is unmistakable.

I freeze, but it's too late to avoid her notice.

She turns her head toward me, and her brows lift in surprise over her dark eyes. "Oh. Hello . . . Avery, right?"

"Hi, Kathryn."

I feel Matt pause beside me in question, but he must sense my unease. Instead of waiting for an introduction, he discreetly moves off to order a drink.

Kathryn's gaze flicks past me for a second, almost undetectably. "Are you here with Dominic?"

"No. I'm here with friends."

Am I imagining the subtle shift in her expression when she learns he's not with me? I know Nick makes her uncomfortable. I saw that the day she bumped into us at lunch. As much as I'm certain he'll be displeased to know I'm talking to her now, I can't deny my curiosity about this woman from his past.

The bartender hands Kathryn the martini she ordered, and she leaves a twenty on the bar before turning to give me her full attention. "Quite an interesting exhibition. I wasn't expecting much when I came here today, but I have to say, I'm intrigued."

The way she scrutinizes me as she says it makes me

wonder if she's only talking about art. "One of my friends is a mixed media sculptor. Lita Frasier," I add, gesturing toward the healthy crowd of people assembled near her art. "I came out to support her."

Kathryn nods, then takes a sip of her cocktail. "Have you got some of your work on exhibit today too?"

The question takes me aback. "No. How do you know I—"

"Jared," she explains breezily. "He mentioned you a few months ago, after meeting you at Dominic's gallery."

She tosses out Jared Rush's name casually, as if she assumes I'm aware that she and the much younger, successful artist are intimates. I am aware that Kathryn and he share some kind of connection, but the fact that Jared has spoken to her about me is more than a little surprising.

"I understand you paint."

"A little," I admit. "I'm still getting started, really."

"Hm." She studies me over the rim of her glass. "I'd be interested to see your work."

"Why?"

Her chin lifts. "Because I enjoy art, of course."

I take a drink of my wine, searching for courage. I know I have no right to pry, but of all the questions I have about Nick, this woman is the mystery that troubles me the most.

"What happened between you and him?"

"He hasn't told you?" She doesn't pretend to misunderstand. Her shrewd eyes bore into me, searching for truth the same way I am. She tilts her head. "No. He hasn't told you anything, has he?"

I'm not expecting those words. I'm not prepared for the chill they send through me. Or the questions—the uncertainty—that suddenly begins to flood my heart.

What does she mean?

Aside from Kathryn, how much more don't I know? Is she only trying to shake me up, knock me off balance? If so, it's working.

"You betrayed him." I blurt the accusation. It's a hollow one, since Nick hasn't elaborated beyond the basics of his falling out with Kathryn. But I see how it hits her. She flinches as if I've struck her. "He trusted you, Kathryn. Now he hates you because you betrayed him."

"Dear girl," she says, and that cultured voice of hers falters just a bit. "Dominic hates me because I loved him."

I'm still processing the weight of that statement when Lita comes toward us, practically bouncing with excitement.

"Avery, oh my God! You're not going to believe it." She grabs my arm in both hands, her eyes wide and her grin beaming. "Derek Kingston just invited me to propose a sculpture design for Dektech's lobby!"

It's impossible not to share in her enthusiasm, no matter how distracted I am by my conversation with Kathryn. "Lita, congratulations. That's great."

"I know, right? And I'm talking about Derek-fucking-Kingston besides." Belatedly, she glances away from me to look at Kathryn. "Gah, sorry. I'm totally interrupting."

"Not at all," Kathryn replies smoothly. She glances at me. "I'll let you get back to your friends, Avery. But I meant it when I said I'd love to see some of your work. I'm always looking for new pieces to add to my collection." She opens her small handbag and withdraws an ecru card with elegant script lettering. "If you're interested in talking some more, get in touch."

I take the card from her impeccably manicured fingers. Even though I'm tempted to tear up her contact information as soon as Kathryn dissolves into the crowd, I can't bring myself to do it.

Slipping the card into the inside pocket of my purse, I look up at Lita and return her giddy smile. "We should go find Matt and celebrate your good news."

She beams. "I approve of that plan. First round of champagne is on me!"

16

The penthouse is empty when I return later that
evening.

Nick texted me around three o'clock to let me
know his business meetings had run long, and that he'd
made commitments with Andrew Beckham to take a
couple of prospects out to dinner. Rather than come
home and eat alone, I joined Lita and Matt for
celebratory burgers and beer following her successful
exhibition.

The time out with friends was fun, but it didn't make
me forget about Rodney. It didn't make me forget about
Kathryn or the fact that answers about Nick's past—
and, hell, possibly even my best shot at making some
money off my new art—is just a phone call away.

Kathryn's card has been a temptation ever since I
slipped it into my purse.

I should have torn it up. I probably still should. But

I have to admit I was more than tempted by her offer. I am even now, as I sink into a tub full of sudsy, warm water in the penthouse's master bathroom. Nick has come right out and demanded that I stay away from her. But why single her out? He's had other discarded lovers—Margot Chan-Levine from his gallery, Dominion, to name just one. He hasn't forbade me to talk to her.

Only Kathryn.

Kathryn, who had been as close as family to Nick at one time, according to Jared Rush.

Her remark about Nick—that he hates her because she loved him—has played through my mind repeatedly today.

I'm aware of his pattern of cutting people out of his life when they get too close. But with Kathryn I sense something different, something deeper.

I sense a secret that Nick will do anything to protect.

A secret that either begins or ends with Kathryn Tremont.

Maybe both.

Margot told me months ago to be careful or I'll get hurt, that Nick is cold and unfeeling. Is Kathryn the reason? What the hell happened between them? What could she have done to earn the kind of scorn he obviously feels toward her?

My mind churns on all of the things I clearly don't know about the man I've fallen in love with. All of the things he doesn't know about me crowd into my thoughts, too, until my head feels on the verge of exploding.

On a moan, I shift in the bath and reach for the glass of Malbec that's perched on the wide marble edge of the sunken tub next to a trio of stout pillar candles providing the only light in the room. Outside the window that frames the oversized tub, Manhattan glitters like diamonds scattered against the deep indigo backdrop of twilight.

Taking a drink of the smooth red wine, I tap the volume on the song pouring in through my earbuds until Adele's contralto crooning is the only thing I hear. My eyes close and I let myself drift into the music, into the peace of the fragrant water lapping all around me.

Suspended in an artificial, yet welcome, state of calm, I don't know how long I stay there. Long enough that one song on my playlist blends into another, then another. Long enough that my bones feel weightless and all of the tension has finally leached from my limbs.

Long enough that I begin to imagine Nick is in the room with me. I can smell the light trace of his cologne and the warm, spicy scent that belongs solely to him. I feel a charge in the air behind me, a heat that awakens me on a cellular, instinctual level.

It *is* him.

Not my imagination.

I exhale slowly, a shiver of arousal traveling through me. My senses recognize Nick's presence with me even before his fingers gently brush the sides of my face from behind. He removes my earbuds and crouches down at the side of the tub, his voice a low rumble against my temple.

"Don't move." His lips brush my skin in a tender command. "I want you right where you are."

Fabric rasps, a swift, satiny whisper. A moment later, something sleek and silky covers my eyes. His tie. His body heat still lingers on it, along with his intoxicating scent. I breathe it in as he fastens the tie around my head, securing it with a knot beneath the messy bun of my upswept hair.

I feel the shift in the air as he stands up, then I hear him undress. His shirt is unbuttoned, then tugged from the waistband of his bespoke suit pants. I hear it drop to the tiles, and I frown at my inability to open my eyes and watch the magnificence of Nick's body being unveiled. My mind paints the picture from memory.

Behind my closed lids, I see his broad shoulders and strong arms. I see his smooth skin, his muscled chest and abdomen, all of the ridges and planes that I've explored with my mouth and hands. Places I'm hungry to explore again now. The anticipation alone is enough to ignite the bloom of wet heat that's kindling in the center of my being.

His belt jangles as he unbuckles it, then unzips his slacks. I lick my lips, knowing that any second now, he'll be completely naked. He's already fully aroused. I don't need to see his jutting cock to know he's as hungry for me as I am for him. I can hear it in the jagged tempo of his breathing. I can feel it in the electricity that crackles through my veins as he approaches me in the tub.

His fingers alight under my chin. Without a word, he draws me around until I am facing him, until I have risen up on my knees in the water.

The hand cupping my chin falls away, only to reach down and guide my fingers to him. His big cock fills my palms, thick and heavy and gloriously erect. "I've wanted your hands on me all day," he utters gruffly. "Stroke me now."

I hardly need the instruction, but it sets my fingers in motion instantly. I caress every rigid inch from the root to the tip, reveling in the strength of him, so much power wrapped in the velvet of his skin. Veins rope the length of his shaft, and I trace each one with my fingertip, eager to do the same with my tongue. A bead of slick, hot wetness leaks out as I stroke my palm over the head of his erection, and I moan with the need to taste him.

Holding him in both hands, I lean forward to find him with my lips.

"Not yet." He's got the tails of the tie in his hand now. He winds them tighter around his fist, physically holding me back from doing what I want. "Not until I say you can."

I don't move, struck by the sharp denial. In spite of the blindfold, I didn't realize we were playing a game. Then again, his curt order sounds anything but playful. Is he still pissed from what happened between us this morning? Or is this just what he craves from me tonight?

I can't see his face to know for sure. The only thing I am certain of right now is that he is in control here.

He is in command of my body and my pleasure.

And he is waiting to hear me tell him that I understand. That I agree.

That I submit.

"Yes, sir."

My reward is the low, wordless sound of approval that rumbles in the back of his throat. Then the tension on my blindfold increases, slowly tipping my head back on my shoulders. Nick's mouth descends on mine, his tongue licking at the seam of my lips before pushing inside. I moan at the sensual invasion, feeling the erotic heat of it in my core.

"Touch me," he growls against my parted lips. "Pump my cock. Use your hands to show me how much you want me."

I stroke him as he continues to kiss me. His tongue thrusts into my mouth in time with the pumping of his hips as I slide my hands all over him, caressing him, milking him.

Worshiping him.

I want to make him come like this, with only my hands. I want to breach the chasm that opened up between us this morning and let him know that no matter what, in spite of everything that might yet destroy us, this is real.

We are real.

I need him to know that.

I need him to feel my love, even at the risk that he'll hate me for it one day.

He grinds out a fevered growl, breaking our kiss as my hands and fingers work his shaft. My strokes are fervent, determined, pleading.

"Yes," he snarls. "Fuck, baby. Yeah. Just like that."

His fist is still gripped around the ends of the tie, keeping my head tilted up to him. I feel his shaft grow harder in my grasp, the friction of my hands made slick and silky by the fluid dripping from the broad crown of his cock.

A groan rips out of him, raw and primal. I answer it with a soft whimper I cannot bite back. As good as he feels in my hands, I need more. I want to taste him. I want him inside me.

"Please." My voice is a threadbare whisper, but I don't care how needy I sound. I don't care about the game of control we're playing, or the fact that he might deny me just for breaking the rules. I lick my lips, which are still wet and swollen from his kiss. "Nick, please. Let me have you."

He doesn't answer, but his hold on my blindfold loosens just enough for me to tip my head back down. It's all the permission I need. My mouth seeks him out in urgent hunger. I close my lips around the head of his cock and suck him deep.

He draws in a sharp breath. "Christ."

He wrenches tightly in my grasp, his thighs bunching. His palm moves restlessly on the back of my head, holding me to him as I begin to fuck him with my mouth. I tongue his length, reveling in the sheer masculine power that pulses through him. The head of his cock is slick with his juices and I lavish attention there now, too, greedily lapping up every drop that spills out of him as his climax builds toward the breaking point.

He's close. I can feel the tremor of mounting pressure that shudders through his body as he pistons and thrusts in time with my relentless caress and the questing, demanding urgency of my mouth.

He grunts, bringing both hands to the back of my head. My hair falls free from its loose bun, dropping around my shoulders as I rise up farther out of the water to take him deeper, faster, harder into my mouth.

I feel the clench of his muscles the instant before the first hot burst of semen explodes onto my tongue. He convulses, gritting my name out like a curse as he comes. I swallow another jetting stream, then draw him out of my mouth to nestle my face against his pulsing shaft.

A hard tremor tears through him with his continued release, wetting my cheek with the musky hotness of his seed.

"I love the taste of you," I confess. "I love the feel

of you on my tongue, inside me . . . all over me."

Cradling his cock in my palms, I guide him to the tops of my breasts, milking him until he is finally spent. His body jerks, spurting the last scorching streams onto my skin.

I reach up to touch his chest, but he moves away on a harsh curse. Have I displeased him? I need to know. I lift my hands to remove my blindfold, but Nick's hands come down firmly atop mine.

"Just because I let you have your way, don't think I'm finished with you yet."

The erotic promise chases fire through my veins and straight to my sex. The water sloshes as Nick steps into the tub with me. Sinking down at the opposite end, he drags me toward him through the fragrant suds. Water laps around my stomach as he places my legs on either side of him.

"I'm the one in control tonight, Ms. Ross, remember?"

"Yes." The word slips off my tongue like the surrender it is. "You are in control. I have none when it comes to you."

"Good answer," he murmurs darkly. "Let's see if you mean it."

His strong fingers caress my cheek before trailing down to the tops of my breasts. I catch my lip but I can't hold back my moan as he begins to massage the earthy slickness of his ejaculate into my skin. When he traces his thumb over my parted lips, I greedily lick at him, savoring his flavor.

He groans as if he disapproves of my defiance, but I can hear the heat in that wordless sound. Without warning, he reaches down into the water and between my spread thighs. His finger invades me, pushing deep into the tightness of my channel. I'm wet and ready, but the sudden pressure of one finger, then another, wrings a gasp from my throat.

His thumb circles my clit, making me writhe and dance on his hand. I can't help the wanton movements of my body. I can't curb the jagged little cries that spill out of my mouth as he drives me wild with his touch. I am lost to it, blissfully at his mercy—my favorite state of being.

Behind the blindfold covering my eyes, my vision spins as an intense orgasm begins to swell. I am transported, surrendered. Utterly at his mercy.

"You like that," he rasps thickly. "You like my fingers taking you to the edge."

"Yes." I squirm in his grasp, trying to work him deeper, harder. "God, Nick . . . don't you know? I'm at the edge every time you touch me."

"Good." His free hand catches my nape and he pulls me to him for a long, slow kiss. "Tonight I'm taking you all the way over the edge."

I don't know what he means until I feel his touch readjust between my legs, his fingers moving from the slick folds of my sex to the cleft of my ass. He kisses me again, and as I melt under the passion of his mouth and tongue on mine, his finger pushes into the tight entrance of my anus.

I gasp at the sensation of being stretched open for him. His thumb teases my clit as he seats me even deeper, making me pant and shiver with the ferocity of the pleasure he's giving me. He fucks my ass with his finger, each thrusting penetration rocking me, every brush of my swollen clit driving me higher, leaving me shaking with the need for release.

It's too much for me to bear. My eyes water with the intensity of sensation and I come violently, shuddering and quaking, crying his name.

As soon as I do, Nick hauls me against him. He pulls off my blindfold and stares into my tear-filled gaze. "No barriers between us, Avery. That's what you promised me. That's what I demanded of you from the beginning."

I nod, unable to form words when every fiber of my being is still vibrating with pleasure and the need for more. When it comes to Nick, I need everything. I want it all.

His big cock is gloriously erect, jutting up between us in the water. I've been on the pill since I had my first period at fifteen. And after four months together, I know we're both clean and healthy.

I reach up to stroke his handsome face. "No barriers tonight, Nick."

As I say it, I lower my hand and take his shaft into my grasp. He glances at me in question but doesn't stop me when I guide him between my legs and settle the head of his penis at my body's entrance. I press down on him, taking him inside me inch by inch.

As incredible as our sex has been from the start, nothing has prepared me for the sensation of having Nick enter me like this, skin on skin, flesh to flesh.

"Jesus," he hisses, letting out a deep, jagged sigh as I seat myself onto him all the way to the root. "You're scorching hot inside. So fucking tight. So wet."

Despite all of the times I've had him inside me, this is the most intimate of all. His gaze locked on mine, nothing to separate us. No barriers in this moment. No bounds to our passion.

"Avery . . ." He tilts his head back as if the pleasure is too much. "Ah, Christ."

His hands clamp down on my hips as I begin to move slowly atop him, my small muscles gripping the naked hardness of his cock. He is large and thick, almost more than I can bear at this angle, but I revel in how completely he fills me. I want even more.

His gaze comes back to me now, stormy with desire. "Take me deeper, baby," he coaxes, his voice like gravel and dark as sin. "Take it all. Your pussy makes me so fucking hard."

His pelvis bucks beneath me as I ride him, an involuntary thrust that betrays the threadbare state of his control. I love that I can do this to him. It's only fair, considering how easily he can strip away mine.

Holding on to his shoulders, I rock up and down on his erection. Each slick friction of our bodies makes the coil of need in me twist tighter. Nick's hands move up my sides, skimming over my ribs and onto my bare breasts. I moan as he kneads the sensitive mounds. When he rolls my nipples between his fingers, then bends to take one of them roughly into his mouth, I cry out, feeling the erotic suction all the way to my core.

Quivering, undulating on his hips, I increase my tempo in time with my need. I want to prolong the feeling, stave off the climax that's rolling up on me too quickly as the head of his cock touches somewhere deeper than he's ever been before. My inner walls stretch to accommodate even more of him as his shaft grows thicker, harder with each driving clash of our bodies.

"Oh, God, Nick!"

He lifts his head from my breasts, his face taut and

intense. "I know, baby. Let it go. I want to feel you break apart on me, all around me. I want to feel you come now."

I shake my head, desperate to make it last. But Nick shows me no mercy. As if to prove to me that my pleasure is his to control, his thrusts deepen, filling me to the limit . . . then ruthlessly, deliciously past it.

His hands clutch my backside, moving me on his cock to the rhythm he has determined. He owns my body, just as he owns my heart. I surrender both to him as he powers into me. As I rise up to take the full measure of his plunging thrusts, his hands part the cheeks of my ass. His slick, soapy fingers slide into the valley between, stroking my anus, teasing the tight entrance.

"Yes," I gasp, knowing it will do me in if he touches me there again, yet craving the possession. "I want you, Nick. I want you to take it. I want you to take all of me."

Dark heat flares in his eyes. He leans back, lowering himself into the water and dragging me onto him. Then he drives home with deep thrusts that have me gasping, whimpering in need. His finger enters my ass, and it's almost too much for me to hold back. I moan at the sensual invasion, while the bliss of his naked cock sliding in and out me builds to an ecstasy too intense, too powerful to be contained.

I feel him swelling to even greater girth inside me, each hard stroke taking both of us to the razor's edge of release. I'm the one who tumbles first. My sex constricts around him and a wave of sensation ripples through every fiber of my being. I cry his name, shattering, just as he intended.

"Fuck," he growls through clenched teeth. His cock

LARA ADRIAN

pistons with each strong thrust of his hips, and behind
me, his finger pushes deeper into my ass. "God, Avery .
. . I'm going to come so fucking hard."

And then he does. His big body tenses. On a roar,
he drives so deep it makes me cry out. Then I feel the
sudden, hot blast of his seed erupting inside me.

"Nick . . . " I can't manage any more than that. I'm
too awash in pleasure, too astonished by the feeling of
his cock filling me, coming inside me, while his finger
continues to stroke tenderly within the sensitive sheath
of my ass.

I want more, even though I can't articulate the depth
of my need for him. Tonight I want nothing between us.
Tonight I want to give him everything.

As if he knows all of the things I can't say, he swiftly
slides us into a new position, turning me around on his
lap so that I am facing away from him, my hands braced
on the edge of the tub.

"You're mine, Avery." His deep voice is ragged
behind me. His palms slide down the line of my spine
and onto my rear.

I moan in protest as he withdraws from inside me,
but my complaint soon turns into a breathless entreaty
when I feel the hot slickness of his seed spurting into the
seam of my body. He rubs the last of his orgasm over
me with his fingers, and with the blunt crest of his
erection.

"Tell me you're mine, baby. Whenever and however
I want you."

"I am. You know I am." I gasp the words, arching
shamelessly into the slick heat of his probing touch, his
ready cock. "Show me that you believe me, Nick. Take
me."

His answering growl is pure animal, so primal I nearly come from just the sound of it. With one hand gripped on my hip to steady me, he slides the head of his shaft through the silky lubricant of his release.

"You've never had anyone here before," he says as he primes me. It's not a question because he's asked me once before. "I'll try to go slow for you, but it's not going to be easy. Christ, you get me hot. You've obsessed me, Ms. Ross."

"Good." I don't even try to mask my satisfaction. Nor can I curb my soft mewl of longing when he presses the tip of his cock into the ring of my anus. "You've obsessed me too. You've ruined me for anyone else."

"Baby, I'm so hard for you," he utters softly, and at the same time he gives a gradual, yet firm thrust of his hips. "Push against me a little. Open for me."

I obey his commands, trusting him completely. Needing him desperately. My body gives as his takes, breath by breath, inch by erotic inch. He is gentle, but strong. Patient, but determined.

I don't know how he manages to break me in so tenderly when each fraction that he sinks into me seems to test every ounce of his control.

"Tell me if this is okay." His voice sounds strained behind me. "Are you all right?"

I nod, more than all right. I'm on the verge of breaking, overwhelmed by sensation and the even greater arousal that comes from feeling his care with me. One hand guiding his cock, he reaches around me with the other to stroke my clit. Pleasure throbs across all of my nerve endings. As soon as I start to come, Nick pushes inside my ass.

And, oh, God, it feels good.

He's barely begun, and yet my orgasm slams into me in wave after wave, electricity pulsing through my veins, into my limbs, into the marrow of my bones. The fullness is intense, commanding all of my attention even as my body splinters in a hard release.

"Avery." Nick starts to move, his thrusts slow and shallow, giving me all the time I need to adjust to this new sensation, this darkly erotic new pleasure. His breath saws out of him. He is trembling beneath me, his iron control clearly at war with his body's own needs.

"Fuck, baby . . . what you do to me."

I moan in response, grinding against his touch, spurred on by the low sounds of arousal he makes as we continue to move together. His cock swells within me. His tempo tightens, quickens.

When he comes an instant later, he roars with the violence of his release.

"I love you," I whisper, unable to hold it back. I'm too vulnerable in this moment, laid bare for him in every way. "I love you so much it hurts."

He shudders deeply, murmuring my name as his orgasm slowly subsides. He pulls out, only to shift his body until he's covering me from behind. His strong arm snakes around my waist, holding me against him as he sinks his teeth into the soft flesh of my shoulder, claiming me.

Marking me as his.

I tell myself it's enough.

This passion we share. This insatiable need for each other that neither of us has known with anyone else.

I tell myself this is the way that he shows me I mean something to him, that he cares about me.

Maybe even that he loves me a little bit too.

It's not much to cling to.

But tonight, with my hideous past looming and the troubling words of Nick's former lover still echoing in my ears, what I have with him here and now is enough.

17

When we step into the elevator together that next morning, Nick's hand rests possessively on the curve of my backside. He's dressed for the office in an impeccably tailored dark gray suit and tie, while I'm headed for the studio wearing a loose white T-shirt and faded, torn jeans cuffed over lace-up summer flats.

As the doors slide shut and we descend toward the lobby, he draws me against him, sealing his mouth over mine in a bone-melting kiss.

"I want to take you to dinner tonight," he murmurs against my lips. "And then I want to bring you back home and devour you. From this wicked mouth to your sweet, greedy little pussy and your very delectable, very fuckable ass."

I smile up at him. "Why, Mr. Baine, you're making me blush."

His gaze smolders. "And you're making me hard, Ms. Ross."

"After last night and again this morning, I don't know how you could be."

He smirks. "When I find something I enjoy, I give it my all. And making you come is most certainly something I enjoy," he says, slipping both hands into my back pockets and pulling me into the firm ridge of his erection.

I laugh, but it dissolves into a moan as Nick squeezes my ass and licks his tongue into my mouth with deep strokes that leave me breathless. Like him, I am far from sated, even though our passion reached erotic new heights last night. If anything, I only want him more. I want him in every way, with a need that is only deepening every moment we're together.

I would let him take me right here, right now. There's a wanton, reckless part of me that's tempted to beg him to, but in that same moment the soft chime of the elevator announces that we've reached the lobby. On a low, predatory growl, Nick releases me and we step out together.

Manny stands at the building entrance, assisting one of the residents inside. He smiles and nods to us in friendly greeting as we approach. Patrick waits beside the car, which idles beneath the glass overhang outside.

"Glorious day today, isn't it, Miss Avery, Mr. Baine?"

"That it is," Nick replies, guiding me out to the car ahead of him.

Manny gets the back door for us and I slide in, making room for Nick beside me. As we settle in, Patrick gets seated behind the wheel, smiling at me in the rearview mirror as he bids us a good morning. Nick gives him instructions to drop me at the studio first, lacing his fingers through mine as he speaks.

As we begin to pull out of the porte cochère, I don't know what draws my attention to the other side of the street—not at first, anyway.

But the instant I see Rodney, my blood freezes.

He's standing on the other side of Park Avenue, leaning casually against a building and smoking a cigarette. I feel his dark gaze on me like the steely point of a dagger. A shudder races through me, leaving me cold and unmoving with alarm.

He wants me to feel this chill.

He wants me to know that he's this close to me and that he's not going away. Not until he gets what he came for.

Patrick turns out onto the avenue and we make our way across the traffic to change direction and head the opposite way. Our new course takes us directly past Rodney. My lungs seize. I know he can't touch me, but that doesn't stop my heart from banging like a caged bird in my chest.

As the limo rolls past the spot where he stands, I force myself to look anywhere but at him. I feign interest as Patrick jokes with Nick about the score of last night's baseball game, but I'm hardly listening. All I can hear is the heavy drum of my pulse as the hairs on the back of my neck prickle with dread.

"They'd do a hell of a lot better if they had a pitcher who was less of a prima donna," Nick says, his thumb stroking the back of my hand where it rests on his thigh.

He's chuckling at something Patrick says when his phone begins to ring in his jacket pocket. He fishes it out with one hand and swipes the screen to answer the call.

"Nick Baine. What?" His voice goes terse with impatience. "Try again. You've got the wrong number."

Shaking his head, he glances at me as he slides the phone back into his pocket. "Some jackass calling to see if my piece of shit Honda is still in the shop."

I blanch. The odd reference cannot possibly be coincidence.

No. Far from it.

That call was no wrong number; it was Rodney. There is not a shred of doubt in my mind.

Oh, my God.

I feel suddenly sick. My throat is parched, my skin clammy.

Fortunately, Nick is distracted just a moment later with another call, this time from his assistant, Lily. As he runs through his morning's schedule with her, I turn to stare out the window, seeing nothing but the gray haze of my barely contained panic.

I have to get rid of Rodney.

I have to find a way to pay his price.

Nick draws my hand up to his mouth, startling me out of my dark thoughts. His lips are warm and tender on my knuckles. The car is stopped now, parked at the curb on Lexington outside the studio building.

"I'll call you later," Nick says. "Any preference on where we go tonight?"

I blink, trying to wrestle my focus back to him and me, not the threat that lurks just a few miles behind us.

"Dinner," he prompts when I stare at him blankly. "Where would you like me to take you?"

I shake my head. "Um. Surprise me."

His answering grin is positively sinful. "Careful, Ms. Ross. That could become one of my favorite things to do."

As heavy as my misery is right now, his smile and the heat of his low-voiced promise has the power to kindle true joy inside me. Framing my face in his palms, he leans forward and tenderly kisses me.

"I'll see you tonight, sweetheart."

"Okay." I nod, my heart so full of affection for him it reduces my reply to a whisper. "I miss you already."

He climbs out of the car, helping me alight behind him. I manage a smile as I leave him, waving to both him and Patrick as I enter the building.

As soon as the limo drives off a few moments later, I reach into my purse and pull out Kathryn Tremont's card.

I don't know if she's the answer to my problems with Rodney.

I don't know if she's the answer to my questions about Nick, either.

Right now, all I do know is that she's the only hope I've got.

My fingers tremble as I call her number. I'm surprised that she answers personally. She sounds tired, slightly distracted, but I forge on.

"Hello, Kathryn. It's Avery . . . Avery Ross. Are you still interested in seeing my art?"

18

Not even an hour later, I am being shown in to Kathryn Tremont's Fifth Avenue apartment. Although calling the massive, richly appointed residence in one of the loveliest pre-war historic brick and limestone buildings a mere apartment is tantamount to calling St. Patrick's Cathedral a simple church.

I have my large zippered portfolio in my hand as I enter the elegant vestibule, following the handsome blond male attendant who greeted me at the door.

"Kathryn's in the drawing room," he says, walking ahead of me.

He is young—probably younger than my twenty-five years—and he carries himself with the smooth fluidity and vague aloofness of a model. Or an escort. It wouldn't surprise me if he is both. At least when he isn't playing doorman for the lady of this grand house.

He leads me off the main hallway where I find

Kathryn seated in the middle of a large room with soaring ceilings and windows that must be twelve feet tall. The long draperies are drawn, dimming the room to a state of near darkness.

Ornately framed art graces the silk-covered walls. Beautiful antique sofas and chairs upholstered in gleaming velvets and rich satins are arranged in intimate groupings within the formal sitting room, but Kathryn isn't using any of them.

Dressed in black silk pajamas and robe, she lies on an overstuffed modern recliner, her bare feet elevated on the raised footrest. A nurse is seated on a stool beside her, monitoring the portable machine and tubes that are hooked up to Kathryn's body. One of the tubes is attached to a taped port affixed to her chest.

She glances up as her male attendant parks me in the open doorway, then struts away without a word. "Ah, Avery. You're a bit earlier than I expected."

"I'm sorry." I feel awkward and intrusive. I had no idea she wasn't well. No wonder she sounded weary when she answered the phone. "I didn't mean to interrupt your day. I, um . . . I should come back some other time."

"Don't be silly." She waves her hand faintly, motioning me in. "We're just wrapping up."

I take a hesitant step inside the room, marveling at the enormous collection of fine art on display all around me. Everything from masters to unknowns, all of it awe-inspiring. And then I see it—a full portrait of Kathryn at a younger age, when her hair wasn't steely gray but rich, dark brown. She is lean and vibrant, her gaze tenacious yet vulnerable.

Arresting and . . . *familiar.*

"Beauty," I murmur, glancing back at her in surprise. "It's you. Jared Rush's painting on display at Dominion. You're *Beauty*."

And now that I'm looking at Kathryn, I don't know how I didn't realize it either of the times I saw her in person. The haunting nude portrait of a defiant, beautiful woman taking pleasure in her body despite the disease that was ravaging it had mesmerized me when I saw it at Nick's gallery. It had disturbed me, even aroused me.

"That painting was done several years ago," she confirms. "It was meant to be a celebration. A declaration of war. It was my way of telling cancer to fuck off." She gestures to the medical apparatus sprouting from her body. "Jared's the only one who knows it's come back. They already took my ovaries and uterus. Now it's in my bones."

"I'm sorry."

"For me? Don't be." She scoffs, her lips curved in a tenacious smile as the nurse begins to carefully remove the chemotherapy tubes and equipment. "I've never backed down without a fight. I have no intention of starting now."

I say nothing as she is attended to, then given instructions for her medicines and reminded of her next appointment. I don't know Kathryn well enough to be standing here now, but there is a part of me that feels closer to her than any other woman in the world.

After all, we both love Dominic Baine.

Kathryn's love for him might not be the same passionate, all-consuming kind that I feel for him, but I have no doubt that she still cares about him. And in that sense alone, we are connected.

"I was surprised to hear from you," she says, once her nurse has departed the room. "I didn't think you'd call."

"I didn't want to," I admit. I'm still uncomfortable with the whole idea. Coming here like this. Keeping it from Nick. "I haven't told him that we met. He doesn't know I'm here."

She nods, understanding without me telling her that Nick's feelings about her may never warm. "Of course, he doesn't know you came. He would never permit it."

"Permit it?" No matter how guilty I feel for keeping this from Nick, the implication that I should need his permission to do anything grates on me. "He doesn't control where I go or who I see. He doesn't own me, if that's what you think."

"No," she says. "It's not what I think. But you love him. And so I'm trying to decide why you would risk coming here, knowing he won't approve."

I hold her shrewd stare. "I had to come."

"Because you want me to buy some of your art? Or because you think I can help you understand him?"

"Both."

"All right," she says, lowering the recliner's footrest, then slowly easing herself out of the chair. "We can begin with your work."

I set down my padded portfolio and unzip it as Kathryn slides her feet into Chanel logo scuffs, then walks gingerly to the windows to open the drapes. I've unpacked all three paintings and leaned them against the wall, waiting in silence as she returns to me.

I can't read her pensive expression. The long moments of silence seem endless as she looks from one piece to the next, then, finally, to the next.

"How long have you been painting?"

"Ever since I can remember. I started painting with my fingers when I was a kid. Once I picked up a brush, I never looked back."

"Hm."

That wordless response is neither a comment nor a critique, yet I see her shrewd gaze narrowing slightly as she studies each of my pieces. She tilts her head as if looking for meaning in the dark, abstract compositions. Does she see their sensual nature, the eroticism that inspired them? Maybe she does, and the images are offensive to her more conventional tastes.

I clear my throat, feeling the need to fill the lengthening quiet. "Until recently, I painted mostly architecture and still life. Portraiture here and there. I'm trying new things now."

"I have no doubt about that, dear." Kathryn's slender brows quirk almost imperceptibly, the first crack her implacable veneer has allowed. "Has Dominic ever given you his opinion of your art before?"

"Yes. He has." I swallow, glancing away from her. As much as I hope she'll like my art enough to offer for one of my paintings, I can't stand here and pretend I'm better than I truly am. "Some of my earlier work was on display at Dominion a few months ago. Nick didn't think I was a good fit for his gallery."

"Is that right?" There's no masking her curiosity. She doesn't even pretend that she's anything but avidly intrigued. "What, precisely, did he say about your work?"

"That it was self-conscious." There was a time when I might have recited Nick's criticism with embarrassment, even shame. But the sting is gone as I recount his words now. "He said my art was dishonest, fearful. He said I wasn't letting the truth take shape on the canvas, that I was hiding from it."

Kathryn exhales a slow, thoughtful sigh. "Harsh judgment. And so classically him."

"He was right," I admit. "He made me better by telling me that. He's made me a braver artist, a better one."

She considers me for a moment, something cryptic flickering in her weary eyes. Something that looks very much like sorrow, like unbearable regret. "Dominic has unerring instincts when it comes to art," she murmurs quietly. "The only thing more extraordinary than his eye was the depth of his own gift."

"His—wait. Are you saying," I stammer, mentally tripping over what I just heard. "Are you saying Nick is an artist too?"

"Was," she replies. "One of the most talented painters I've ever seen. His work was breathtaking, raw and unrestrained. Heartbreakingly sensitive. It was astonishing."

I realize I'm gaping at her, but I can't help it. Nick, a painter? I'm not surprised to hear that he possesses this other talent among all of the other things he seems to have mastered so expertly, but why has he never mentioned it to me? Am I the only one who doesn't know this?

"Even to this day, I've seen few who compare to him," Kathryn adds. "But that was before, of course."

"Before?" The word hits me even harder than her first revelation. It hits me like a body blow, knocking the wind from my breast. "You mean, before the accident that ruined his hand."

"Accident." She slowly shakes her head. "Is that

what he told you?"

"He told me he got into a fight with a drunk when he was eighteen. Things escalated, and the man sent him through a plate glass window."

I recall how Nick told me about the incident over dinner on our first getaway together. I remember how he had relayed the details—scant as they were—in that nonchalant way of his, which neither invites questions nor offers any answers beyond what he is willing to share.

"What really happened to him, Kathryn?"

"Yes, there was a fight," she says, "but it wasn't an accident that stole his ability to paint. Dominic was nearly killed that night. And the drunk who pushed him through the glass was his father."

All of the breath in my lungs seems to evaporate as I absorb the truth of what really happened. Nick's pain must have been tremendous. Dear God, how he must have suffered, not only through the healing of his injuries, but with the realization of what he'd lost.

And by whom.

"I . . . I wasn't aware." I shake my head lamely, hoping I don't look as wounded as I feel by all of these unexpected discoveries. "Apparently, he didn't think it was important to mention any of this to me."

"My dear," Kathryn says gently. "That part of him died years ago. Unfortunately, I am also to blame for that."

She turns away from my paintings and walks back to one of the velvet sofas.

"Please tell me." I follow her over and take a seat beside her. "Please tell me what happened between you and him. Please tell me everything, Kathryn."

LARA ADRIAN

At first, I don't think she'll comply. She has no reason to divulge details about her past personal life with Nick, after all. I'm prying, and there is no excuse for it. Nothing except my love for him and the ache I have for everything he's been through.

"His hand was already destroyed when I met him," she murmurs, toying with the lace edge on the sleeve of her silk pajama tunic. Her fingers look frail and aged against the collection of diamonds and gleaming platinum rings on them. Only her beautiful, cosmetically preserved face belies the true state of her physical health.

"Dominic was young—barely twenty, as I would later find out—and he'd only been in New York for a few months. He was earning his living parking cars at the Four Seasons when I first noticed him." She shakes her head faintly, a faraway look coming into her gaze. "I was attending an art auction event and there he was, the handsome, dark-haired young man who'd parked my companion's Jaguar, standing at the back of the room utterly absorbed in one of the auction house programs."

My mind conjures the scene as she describes it, my heart squeezing at the notion of twenty-year-old Nick, freshly arrived in the city and completely unaware of the golden future and staggering fortune that awaits him.

It breaks a little, too, realizing only now that his success in business was born out of the ashes of his forfeited art ability.

"I've always enjoyed the company of beautiful younger men," Kathryn confesses, glancing at me now, her expression utterly lacking in remorse. "They make me feel younger too. They make me forget that I'm mortal." She shrugs. "I struck up a conversation with Dominic. His intensity was magnetic, even then. And he

192

impressed me when I realized there was something more to him than just that remarkable face and those blue eyes that could drown a woman if she's not careful."

I nod, because I know exactly what she means. I've swam in his fathomless gaze often enough to feel the tidal pull that comes with being the focus of Nick's stare. I succumbed to his powerful allure from the start, never able to resist him.

If he had been simply a gorgeous face and a body to match, maybe I could have walked away after having that first taste. But Kathryn is right. There is far more to Dominic Baine than just his amazing good looks and seductive persona.

It was his contradictions that did me in. The paradox of the cold, intensely private loner and the complicated, sensual man who stripped away all of my defenses.

It is these secret layers that I'm peeling back only now that make me love him even more.

Kathryn presses her fingers to her brow. "I'm feeling a bit flushed. Would you mind fetching those pills from the side table and pouring me some water?"

"I don't mind at all." I get up and bring her what she asked for, waiting as she takes a couple of fever reducers and washes them down with a cut-crystal glass of water. When she's finished, I return the pill bottle and glass to the table, then rejoin her on the sofa.

She closes her eyes for a moment, then continues where she left off. "When I saw that he seemed to have more than a passing appreciation for art, on a lark I asked Dominic to accompany me to another event the following week. I was shocked when he agreed. And thrilled. Things between us . . . progressed from there."

I try not to hear the wistfulness in her voice when

she talks about her time with my man. Except he wasn't mine then. As much as I want to think he is now, I can't pretend it doesn't wound me to realize how little I truly know about him, his past.

And maybe it serves me right, considering all of the secrets I hope I never have to share with him.

I swallow past the guilt that seems ever-present in my throat. "How long were you and he together?"

"A few months, perhaps close to a year." She shrugs vaguely, but by the regretful look in her eyes, I'm certain she could tell me the precise dates if I pressed her. She chases the expression away with a light wave of her hand. "I brought Dominic to parties with me and social events. He didn't seem to mind so much. Aside from being ridiculously good looking, he was also intelligent. Shrewdly so. I'm sure there were many who disregarded him as just another pretty, dull-headed piece of arm candy, but Dominic wasn't like that. He paid close attention to the conversations going on around him. Powerful, wealthy men discussing investments and business ventures. He made no secret of the fact that he wanted something more out of life, and I could see that he was capable of accomplishing anything he put his mind to."

I recall that Nick made his first million in real estate investments by the time he was twenty-two. And he's told me that in three more years' time, his net worth had reached a half a billion dollars. But what I didn't know is where he got the initial nest egg to make that first purchase. Now, I think I do.

"One day, Dominic came to me with a painting he'd done a few years before—the only piece of his work he said he had left. He asked if I would be interested in buying it. I was amazed at his talent. The piece was exquisite, one of the finest modern expressionist works I'd ever seen. Of course, I had to have it. After I bought it, he then invested that money into some real estate stocks he'd had his eye on. The rest, as you know, is history."

"Do you still have his painting?"

"Sadly, no. I don't."

"He told you it was the only one he had left. If he painted others, where are they?"

She blinks and looks away from me for a moment. "None of his work exists anymore. There were four others—pieces he brought with him to New York, along with the one he sold to me. I'd discovered he had sold the earlier ones to another collector. I made it my private mission to try to track each one down and buy it back."

From her somber tone, I realize this story does not end well. "Were you able to recover any of them?"

"Oh, yes. I found them all." She smiles sadly. "Each one was more stunning than the next. I was so proud of him. I believed in him so much, I wanted the world to recognize how gifted he was. I decided to host a party at my summer house in the Hamptons. Everyone I knew from the art world was there—critics, curators, collectors, other important artists. They'd all come with the promise of meeting this undiscovered new talent I had found. I hadn't told Dominic what I was planning. He had no idea that the party was intended to be anything more than one of my seasonal soirées."

"Did he know you'd found his other paintings?"

She shakes her head. "I wanted it to be a surprise. I thought he would be thrilled to see that I'd bought them all back for him. On the day of the party, only moments

LARA ADRIAN

before anyone arrived, Dominic figured out that I was keeping a secret from him. He found the paintings. When he realized I intended to show them publicly, he flew into a rage. He took them all down . . . then he destroyed every one."

I gasp, horrified. "Oh, Kathryn. He didn't."

"I'd never seen him so furious. He saw it as a betrayal. I hadn't realized how deeply it had wounded him to lose his ability to paint until that moment. Of course, by then it was much too late. He accused me of using him—of wanting to destroy him—when in fact harming him was the very last thing I ever wanted to do." She releases a deep, rattling sigh. "God . . . I loved him so hopelessly I would've done anything to make him happy. I truly thought I was. Instead, everything blew up in my face. He left, and we've hardly spoken since."

I feel for her, and for the pain she's reliving by sharing this memory with me. We were strangers when I walked into her house, but not now. I reach over and cover her hand with mine. Instead of pulling away, she glances at me in mild surprise before nodding silently, understanding the unlikely bond we'll share after today.

"I'm so sorry," I tell her. "For you, and for him."

I'm sorry for the tragic, irreplaceable loss of Nick's art, something I'll never see for myself.

No one will, which was apparently his intent when he destroyed it all.

She begins to cough and I let go of her hand. She's tired from her medical treatments, and talking with me isn't helping. I don't want to add to her burdens, especially when I've come here today for admittedly selfish reasons.

I get up and pour her another glass of water. She

takes it from me with a weak smile and dark, shadowed eyes. As she drinks, I walk over to my paintings and begin to replace them back into my portfolio. I doubt she has any interest in them, aside from the curiosity that spurred her to invite me to come in the first place.

"Do you despise me now too?" Her voice drifts across the room, thin and quiet. "Is that why you're running away so quickly?"

"What? No." I shake my head, frowning. "Of course, I don't despise you. Not at all. I just thought . . . You're obviously not interested in buying my paintings, and I've stayed too long already. I don't want to bother you—"

"You're wrong, Avery. I am very interested in your art." When I pause, she goes on. "These three pieces are very good. Better than good. But what I really want to know is why you want to sell them to me."

Her blunt question takes me aback, but I realize directness is just her way. I appreciate that about her here today, and I feel that I owe her some of the same respect now.

"To be honest, Kathryn, I need the money. I'm . . . I'm in some trouble and I need to find a way out."

She regards me in silence for a moment. "Trouble that Dominic can't help you with?"

I shake my head. "I can't ask him to. I won't. I have to find a way through this on my own."

"I see." She sets the glass down on the side table next to the sofa. "How much money will it take to make your trouble go away?"

"Ten thousand dollars."

One fine brow lifts above her fatigued, but erudite gaze. "Your paintings will be worth much more than that one day, my dear. But I will be glad to have them for the price you need." She stands up and smooths her black silk robe. "I trust a personal check will suffice?"

"Yes. Of course." My breath rushes out of me on a heavy sigh, gratitude nearly overwhelming me. "Kathryn, I don't know how to thank you."

"Yes, you do. Be good to him, my dear. Love him for me, even if he doesn't make it easy for you." Her smile is beautiful, if broken. "Love him especially then."

19

I call for Patrick to pick me up a while later, knowing Nick always prefers that I use his driver instead of taking the subway. Today I feel safer in the limo too. I cashed Kathryn's check after leaving her apartment, and the knowledge that I'm walking around the city with ten grand in large bills tucked into my purse has left me nervous as hell.

Even more so than the reason I need the money in the first place.

Once I'm in the backseat of the sleek black car, I send Nick a quick text. *Would you be disappointed if we stay in for dinner tonight?*

His reply comes back almost instantly. *Staying in with you is never a disappointment. Shall I bring dinner home with me?*

I stare at his message—at the mention of home, and the implication that the word belongs to both of us. On any other day, with anyone else, that word might mean nothing. Just a casual reference chosen for convenience more than anything else.

But Nick does nothing without deliberation. He is as careful with his words as he is with his feelings. And right now, he is telling me that I belong with him.

I'm already emotional from my meeting with Kathryn. Now, tears prick the backs of my eyes and it's all I can do to hold them at bay as I type my response to his text. *Just come home when you're ready. I'll take care of dinner.*

His answer is immediate. *A surprise, then? I can hardly wait.*

Me too, I reply, then slip my phone back into my purse and lean back against the soft leather seat with my eyes closed so Patrick won't see that I'm on the verge of breaking down.

As the car rolls through the midafternoon traffic, I try to reassure myself that everything will be better once I've given Rodney what he wants and he's out of my life again. I can only pray the money will be enough to get rid of him for good.

After he's gone, I'll find some way to make things right with Nick.

I'm terrified of what he'll think of me if he knows the truth. I'm even more afraid to let my secrets fester between us indefinitely. But I won't let Rodney control how Nick finds out. And I damn sure won't let him hurt Nick or the life he's worked so hard to build.

I can barely contain my relief to see no sign of my stepbrother anywhere near the Park Place building as we approach. I'll have to see Rodney soon enough as it is. He gave me only seven days to get in touch to arrange for him to collect his money. That means tomorrow.

The bundle of a hundred one-hundred dollar bills feels like a stone in the bottom of my purse. As glad as I'll be to get rid of it, I can't stomach even the thought of Rodney while my head and heart are still reeling from the time I spent with Kathryn.

I need Nick first. I need to feel his warmth and strength in order to find my own in preparation for facing my past again in what I can only pray is the last time.

"Thanks again for coming to get me on short notice," I tell Patrick as the limo slows to a stop at the front entrance.

He nods. "Anytime, Ms. Ross."

Manny opens the backseat door for me, greeting me with his friendly hello and smile brightens my day as usual. Even so, it's difficult to make small talk right now, and I simply go through the motions as I head for the elevators and step into the empty car. I don't relax until I am finally alone inside the penthouse and able to sag against the closed door, exhaling the ragged sob that's been clawing to get out all day.

Being tasked with cooking helps to calm me, particularly since I undertake it with a large glass of wine in hand. I peruse the refrigerator and walk-in pantry for dinner ideas, knowing that if I were cooking for myself in a place of my own, the options would be far more limited. Fortunately, Nick's idea of staples means I can make virtually anything I'm capable of putting together.

I settle on lasagna, my mom's family recipe and one of the few dishes I can make with reasonable competence. Once the pan of cheesy, saucy goodness is in the oven to bake and the kitchen is cleaned up, I grab a shower and change into something more suitable for dinner than my jeans and T-shirt.

By the time Nick arrives about an hour later, I meet him at the door in a simple, sleeveless black dress and heels, with the long string of pearls roped loosely around my neck. Soft jazz music flows over the sound system. Inside the apartment, the lights are dimmed and warm orange flames dance in the glass-fronted gas fireplace in the living room.

"Hi," I say, stepping aside to let him in.

"Hi yourself." He pauses just inside the foyer and closes the door, then reaches out to catch me around my nape for a hot, unrushed kiss. When we part, his gaze is dark and appraising. "If this is your idea of dinner in, I'm never making reservations anywhere ever again."

I smile, needing his touch more than he can possibly know. I turn my face into his palm as his caress drifts around to my cheek. I feel the scars on his fingers, and in the warm cradle of his hand. Scars that have an entirely new meaning to me now.

Sorrow for what he suffered—during and after his violent altercation with his own father—stabs me with fresh pain as he tenderly holds my face in his savaged hand. I kiss him there, my throat tightening with emotion again.

"Hey," he says quietly. "You okay?"

"Yeah." I nod, reaching up to place my hand atop his. "I'm more than okay now that you're here. Now that you're home with me."

He bends to brush his lips against mine again, gentle licks and nips that make my senses tingle with awakening desire. He releases me on a groan, then shrugs out of his suit jacket and folds it over the back of a chair in the living room as we walk deeper into the penthouse together.

He glances at the dining room, which is set for dinner with fine china and crystal, everything glimmering beneath the flickering light of the pillar candles burning at the center of the large, dark wood table.

"Everything looks and smells amazing." He looks back at me, amusement glittering in his eyes. "What did I do to earn all of this?"

I smile up at him. "Who says you've already earned it?"

His dark brows rise as he strokes his fingers over the length of pearls that plunges all the way to my abdomen. "You plan on putting me to work or something, Ms. Ross?"

"Or something." I grin, taking a step away from him. "You can start by pouring us some wine while I plate the salads and serve dinner."

"Whatever you say, boss."

I try not to be distracted, feeling his gaze studying me—and, yes, undressing me—while I make everything right with our meal and join him at the table. I don't know if I'll ever be able to look at this man and not melt under the heat of my want for him, and tonight is no exception.

No, tonight everything is intensified, including the love I feel for him.

As we eat and drink our wine, he tells me about the deals he's working on this week, including the mobile app launch that's coming up in London early next month.

"Lily sent me home with your passport application," he says, setting down his wineglass. "I'll have you sign it in the morning and then we can go and get your photo taken to complete the submission."

"Tomorrow?"

"Do you have other plans?"

"No. Nothing special." I take a sip of my wine and try not to think about Rodney or the money, and the fact that I need to contact him tomorrow and put this whole mess out of my life. "I don't have firm plans for anything, but I just . . . I had hoped to spend the day in the studio."

Nick nods. "That's no problem. I'll drive, and when we're finished I'll take you to East Harlem."

My smile feels thin. "All right."

"You never told me how it went the other day." He polishes off the last bite of lasagna on his plate, then glances up at me. "Lita's exhibition. How did she do?"

"Oh. She did great." Even though the exhibition happened only yesterday, it feels like a week after everything that's happened since. "It was an amazing event, and aside from some pre-show jitters, Lita really shined. She's even got an invitation from the head of some hot new technology firm to propose a piece for their building in Brooklyn Heights. I'm not sure what she was more excited about—trying to win the spot, or getting to spend time with the former rock star who owns the company."

Nick grunts. "Derek Kingston's a decent guy. Unfortunately, he's still carrying around a lot of his rock star ego. But who could blame him? That kind of lifestyle leaves a mark."

"You know him?"

Nick gives me a look. "At our net worth and both of us being under thirty-five, he and I belong to a relatively small club in this city. I also happen to own a fair amount of Dektech stock. I invested before it went public and the company really exploded."

I tilt my head, astonished, and yet not surprised at all. "Is there anything you touch that *doesn't* turn to gold?"

He reaches across the table to rest his fingers atop mine, then shrugs. "Huh. Guess so. Still flesh and blood, warm and sexy woman. Thank God."

"I'm being serious," I say, unable to curb my smile.

"So am I. Tell your friend to refuse Kingston's first offer, no matter what it is."

"What if his first offer doesn't have anything to do with her art?"

Nick smirks. "Then she should definitely refuse whatever he proposes right out of the gate. I've seen him in action—at the bargaining table and away from it. Derek doesn't respect anyone who folds too soon."

Even though he's offering this insight with a sense of humor, I know him well enough to understand that he doesn't dole out idle advice. "Thanks. I'll let Lita know you said so."

"This lasagna is incredible, by the way." He takes a second helping, offering to serve me some, too, but I decline. Instead of digging in, he picks up his wine and leans back in his seat to look at me. "What about you, Avery?"

"What do you mean?"

"How's the studio working out for you?"

"Good. Matt and Lita are great."

He nods. "They seem great. I'm talking about your art, though."

"Oh." I shrug. "It's going well, I suppose."

"I'd say so," he agrees, watching me intently. "I saw that last week, when I came to the studio to take you to lunch. I'm sure you saw me looking at your paintings, Avery. You still haven't asked what I thought of them."

I swallow. "No."

"Why not? Don't you want to know?"

"Of course, I do." Even as I say it, I wonder if I sound as unconvincing to him as I do to myself.

There was a time, months ago, when Nick's less than glowing opinion of my work had made me question everything about my ability and my passion. That was before I knew he was an artist. Before I knew about the extraordinary gift he lost.

Now, I'm terrified to hear him tell me that I still don't measure up in his view.

Not even Kathryn's praise or the generous price she paid for my three pieces will be enough to combat Nick's rejection of my art now.

I reach for my wineglass, not realizing it's empty until I bring it to my lips. Nick is right there in an instant, gently taking it from my grasp. Instead of refilling it, he sets the glass aside, giving me no choice but to meet his searching, solemn gaze.

"I haven't been fair to you, Avery. Especially when it comes to your art." He scowls, his sensual lips flattening for a moment as if he's uncertain of the impact his words will have on me. "I've made you question yourself. I've made you doubt. That was never my intention."

"Nick, you don't have to—"

"You have a gift, Avery. I saw it in you from the beginning." He reaches out to me, stroking the back of his scarred hand along my bare arm. "You remember I told you that it wasn't a matter of you lacking talent, only that it needed to be let free?"

I nod. There's not a thing he's said in the time we've been together that isn't still emblazoned in my mind. "You said I was the one throttling my art, holding it back before the truth reached the canvas."

"That's not what I saw in the studio last week."

"It isn't?"

"No. What I saw in those three paintings was you. Maybe for the first time." His touch trails down onto my wrist, then into the center of my open palm. "When I looked at the passionate lines and the raw, unrestrained images on your canvases, I saw things that move you and make you feel alive, things that scare you, even appall you. I saw things that make you weep, and the things that make you wet."

I blink rapidly, feeling a sudden rush of emotion building behind my eyes. I didn't realize how much I craved his acceptance until this moment. I didn't realize how much I needed it.

That he sees so much good in my art is enough to break me open. Especially tonight, knowing the paintings no longer belong to me, and why.

But it's the affection I see in his eyes that lays me low and leaves me trembling under the weight of my feelings for him.

"Nick," I whisper, my voice ragged. I get up from my chair and go to him, seating myself on his lap. I wrap my arms around him, holding him close, my face nestled into the warm strength of his shoulder. "Nick, I love you so much."

He envelops me in his embrace, his hands moving slowly on my back, stroking me. Gentling me.

"Hey," he says, his deep voice vibrating against me. "Baby, what is this? Are you . . . Jesus, are you crying?"

LARA ADRIAN

Drawing me away from him slightly, he searches my tear-streaked face and welled-up eyes.

"Talk to me, sweetheart. What's wrong?" Concern etches his handsome face, furrowing his brows. "Have I done this? Have I . . . have I hurt you somehow, Avery?"

"No."

"Then what—"

"I don't want to talk," I tell him abruptly, my tears already starting to subside. "Not tonight, okay? I just want you to hold me."

He doesn't look happy at my dodge, but he doesn't argue. He understands me too well, knows me almost better than I know myself sometimes. And right now, he can see that the only thing I need is him.

Us.

Taking my chin on the edge of his fingertips, he leads my mouth to his. We kiss, slow and deep and tenderly. When our lips part a long while later, I reach down to lift the string of pearls.

"Tonight, I just want to be with you, Nick." I loop the other end over his head, linking us together by the delicate rope of precious gems. "The only way we separate is if you pull away from me."

"Baby," he murmurs, reaching up to stroke his thumb over my lips. "I'm exactly where I want to be."

He stands up, lifting me with him. Our long pearl shackle slides against my skin as he holds me aloft in his arms. Then he takes my mouth in another kiss, this one hot and commanding, filled with desire.

"Make love to me," I beg him.

"All night if you want me to," he promises.

Then he carries me away from the table and past the twisting flames in the fireplace, not pausing until he lays

208

me down on his bed—our bed—and proceeds to make good on that vow.

20

We shower together in the morning, taking our time because neither of us seems eager to let go of the perfect night we shared. Nick makes love to me again, a slow mating beneath the spray of warm water, our hands and bodies slick with soap and sliding together deliciously in pleasure.

I'd love to stay cocooned with him all day in the penthouse. In truth, I'd love to stay here with him forever, shutting out the world and the unpleasant business that I have to finish today with my stepbrother.

God, I hope it will all be finished once Rodney gets the money he's demanded.

Nick startles me out of troubling thoughts and horrid memories with a kiss to the top of my head as I sit in front of the vanity mirror in the large bathroom robotically applying a little makeup while my mind is a thousand miles away.

"I put the passport application on the dresser for you to sign," he tells me, his gaze holding mine in our shared reflection in the glass.

He is shirtless and barefoot, wearing just a pair of black suit pants. Half-dressed like this, he looks the part of both the corporate conqueror and the sensual master. I can't help admiring what I see, no more than I can help the current of arousal that licks through my senses every time I look at my man.

"Lily's already got a copy of your birth certificate on order," he tells me, grinning with unabashed awareness of my desire for him. "We'll need to send her a scan of your driver's license before we leave to get your photo taken."

"Okay. It's in my purse in the bedroom."

He nods. "I can get it for—"

"No. I'll do it." My reply is too sharp, and so is my abrupt rise from the vanity chair. I realize that as soon as I pivot to face him and see his questioning look.

I try to cover my blunder with a smile and a quick peck at his mouth, but Nick is watching me too closely now. "What's wrong?"

"Nothing." I smile again, but it feels tight. "I'll go get that for you."

He follows me out to the bedroom. My purse is sitting on the dresser beside the form he's left for me. I unzip my bag, feeling his eyes on me the whole time. My fingers are shaking, despite my best effort to calm my nerves. I hate lying to Nick, and as desperate as I am to pretend nothing is wrong, my body seems determined to betray me.

I fumble to retrieve my wallet. It catches on the coiled shoulder strap, and before I can prevent the disaster from happening, my purse tumbles to the floor. I drop down to retrieve it, but there's no correcting the mistake.

Some of the contents spill out onto the rug, including the fat bundle of cash.

Nick pins me with a stunned look when I swivel my head to glance up at him. "Where did all of that come from?"

"I . . . I sold my paintings."

He frowns. "When?"

"Yesterday." I start to stuff the money back into my purse, but there's really no point in it now. I stand up and face him, guilt and dread raking me.

"You sold them." He sounds confused, almost disbelieving. He's still staring at the stack of hundred-dollar bills, and I know he doesn't need me to tell him how much I'm holding in my trembling hands. "Avery. What the hell are you talking about? Sold them to whom?"

"Kathryn."

His head snaps back as if I've slapped him. His tone is deceptively level. "What?"

I swallow, unable to tear my attention away from the thunderhead of fury that's beginning to gather in his narrowing gaze. "I bumped into her at Lita's exhibition. I had no idea she'd be there, Nick. We ended up talking for a little while. She gave me her card and said she wanted to see my work."

"Kathryn Tremont." A curse boils off his tongue. His eyes are flashing with outrage as he rakes his hand over the top of his head. "You talked to her two days ago and this is the first I'm hearing about it? Jesus Christ, Avery. Are you telling me you took money from her?"

"I didn't take anything," I point out. "Kathryn liked my paintings and she bought them."

"It's the same fucking thing!" His sudden explosion of anger makes me flinch. I've never seen him this upset. His powerful chest is heaving with every breath. His handsome face is flushed and ruddy with furious color. "I can't believe you would do this. You know how I feel about her and yet—"

"No, Nick. I didn't know how you felt about her." As terrified as I am that this breach of his trust could be irreparable, I cannot cower. "I didn't know anything about what happened between you and Kathryn, because you refused to tell me."

"I told you to stay away from her. God damn it, that should've been enough!" Sharp, controlling words.

There was a time when I would have bristled at such an arrogant assumption of authority, even bucked against it with vitriol of my own. But right now I hear Nick's harsh outburst for what I know it truly is.

Shock.

Pain.

Even fear.

For all of the secrets and shames I'm still protecting, Nick had tried to bury his with Kathryn. The grief over the gift he had lost. The anguish of having that special part of him ripped away by his own father's careless actions. Worse than careless, if what Kathryn said is true—that Nick's father had nearly killed him that day.

Nick had wanted to shut all of that out of his life when he destroyed his art then turned his back on Kathryn and her desire to help him, to heal him.

He thought he *had* shut it all out.

Until this very moment, when he stares at me and his

213

gaze lights with dawning understanding.

"She's not well, Nick." I swallow and shake my head. "Her cancer is back. I think she may be dying."

A tendon pulses in his jaw. "Kathryn's health isn't my concern. You are."

His right hand flexes at his side, unclenching the fist he'd been holding almost subconsciously. He glances down at the scars that twine around his forearm and down onto his fingers. A rueful smile twists his mouth.

"She told you."

"I wish you had." My voice is quiet, uncertainty making every fiber in my body ache with the dread of losing him, here and now. "I didn't go there to dig into your past, Nick. I wasn't trying to hurt you, or make things harder for you in any way."

"Then why?" He takes a step toward me finally, instead of continuing to pull away. His hands clamp around my biceps and I can feel the tension in him. He's still vibrating with anger and struggling to keep it under control. "Why her, of all people? Why now?"

"Because I didn't see any other choice." I press my lips together, stifling the raw sob that's lodged in my throat. "I went to her because I needed the money."

Emotion flashes in his taut face—outrage, confusion, insult. "If you needed money all you had to do was ask me for it. You know that. Have I ever denied you anything?"

"No, you haven't. You've given me so much, Nick. More than I deserve."

"Then why?" He shakes me slightly, as if I've pushed him to the very edge of his reason. "Why go behind my back when all I ever asked from you was honesty? God damn it, Avery. I trusted you. I—" He bites off the thought with a low, muttered curse. "Just tell me why."

The tears I've been fighting spill over now, streaming down my cheeks. "I did something terrible, Nick. Something I haven't told you."

I feel him go still as he holds me in that penetrating, inescapable gaze of his. "Something recently?"

"No. A long time ago. Nine years ago."

His grip remains firm on my arms, but some of his combustibility fades as he searches my face. "Nine years ago. You're talking about your stepfather . . . "

He doesn't finish the statement. We both know the reference well enough. The day of my rape at sixteen. The day my mother shot and killed her abusive husband in retaliation for what he'd done to both of us over the years, but specifically, finally, for what he'd done to me that day.

"I haven't been honest with you, Nick." My voice falters over the words. "I haven't told you everything. I haven't told you what I did that day."

His reply is flat. Remote. "Tell me now."

His deep blue eyes take on a guardedness, impenetrable steel replacing the fathomless oceans that have always drawn me in like the tide. It hurts to see his walls going up in front of me, ready to seal me out. I won't be able to bear it if I've ruined everything with this stupid mistake, with my secrets and lies.

Even if he turns away from me in disgust after hearing how selfish and cowardly I've been all this time, I owe him the truth.

All of it.

"The day Martin Coyle raped me was a Monday, August twenty-first. I had a math test in the morning, but I accidentally slept past my alarm. Martin was on disability leave from his job at the school in the neighboring town, so to make some extra money, my mom had just started working the third shift at the big factory in Scranton. Usually she got home around seven—about an hour before I left for school—but on that day she called home to let us know she had a flat tire and would be home late because she was waiting for a tow to the shop."

I swallow, pushing past the bile that rises up my throat as I recall the events of that awful morning.

I can still see my stepfather sitting in his recliner in front of the television, wearing a T-shirt and sweatpants, drinking a can of beer at seven in the morning. Watching me with too much interest as I wolfed down a piece of toast over the sink, then cleaned up the mess of dirty breakfast dishes and the ashtray full of cigarette butts he'd left for my mom on the kitchen counter.

"I hated being alone in the house with him. For a while before that day, he'd been making me uncomfortable with his staring and his persistent attempts to cozy up to me. He'd offer me liquor and cigarettes, neither of which I accepted. He'd volunteer to take me out for fast food or runs to the mall. I never said yes. He'd try to touch my hair or put his arm around me, even though I asked him not to. I made a point of avoiding him whenever I could, and that worked for a while. But that morning everything seemed different. I felt it instinctively. Something had changed, turned dangerous. I was too stupid to act on it before it was too late."

"You were only sixteen," Nick says, his voice low and tight. "Don't ever blame yourself for this. You were just a kid, for crissake."

I nod, some part of me acknowledging that he's right—I was a child, not yet equipped to deal with the very adult, very real problem of my stepfather.

Unfortunately, I wouldn't learn how to deal with him until after the assault had occurred.

"I was just out of the shower and getting dressed for school when he came into my bedroom. My door was locked, but he somehow picked it. All I had on was my bra and underwear. He stood there, leering at me. He accused me of trying to turn him on. He said he was tired of me teasing him then running away." I close my eyes, struggling to push the rest of the story out. "He said . . . he said he wanted me to suck his dick or he was going to give my mom a black eye when she got home. I knew he meant it. He'd hit her more than a few times by then. But she always made excuses for him. She didn't want to leave him. She didn't want us to be alone again."

"Baby, I'm sorry." Nick frowns as he reaches up to wipe a tear from my chin. A dark kind of rage smolders in his eyes. "You don't have to tell me any more. You don't have to relive that bastard's abuse just to make me understand it."

"Yes, I do." I draw in a fortifying breath. As much as his compassion touches me, I do have to tell him everything. "You need to understand, Nick. And I need to let this go, even if you never look at me the same way ever again."

His face stills, then he gives me the faintest nod. "All right."

"He lunged for me. He overpowered me so easily. I thought I was strong, but I couldn't break out of his hold. I couldn't move his heavy weight when he knocked me to the floor on my stomach. I don't know how he managed to get his pants down so quickly. He ripped my panties off from behind me. And then he pushed inside me. It hurt. God, how it hurt." My voice is threadbare now. "I was a virgin. He stole that from me. He shoved inside me and he pumped and grunted and groaned until he came, splattering my back with his foulness."

Nick's face is a study in animal fury now. His lips are peeled back in a grimace, his nostrils flaring as he listens in barely restrained silence.

"I don't know how long I lay there. He had gone back to the TV. I could hear it in the background as I got up and cleaned myself off with a tissue. I don't remember getting dressed, but I walked out of my room sometime later in my clothes for school. But I didn't leave for school. I went downstairs to the basement, to the gun cabinet he never bothered to lock. Then I came back up and put a bullet in his chest."

Nick doesn't say a word. He doesn't so much as blink.

"I shot him," I confess—at last, finally. "I shot him and then I sat across from him and watched him bleed. I don't know why I didn't shoot him again. Shock, I guess. I remember looking at him as he slumped out of his chair and onto the floor, wheezing and sputtering, trying to drag himself toward me. I moved across the room and I just . . . watched him. I waited for him to die, but he didn't."

"What happened with your mom?"

"She came home a while later. Martin was still alive, but barely." I exhale, picturing the whole incident as if I were looking in from outside myself. "She didn't scream. She didn't cry. She didn't ask me what happened. She knew. Just by looking at me . . . she knew what he'd done."

Nick draws me against him, holding me close.

"She walked right past him on the blood-soaked floor to carefully take the gun out of my hands and set it aside. Then she wrapped me in her arms and told me to go take a shower. She told me she would clean up the mess and that I should go to my grandparents' house down the street. She told me that she would take of everything."

"The second gunshot wound," Nick says. "The police reports and court evidence stated that it wasn't the first bullet that killed him. It was the second one, fired sometime between one to two hours afterward."

He's obviously been reading up on the case, since these are details I haven't yet shared with him. No doubt, he and his lawyer, Andrew Beckham, have been poring over all of the documents in my mother's case in preparation of securing that new legal team Nick has mentioned.

"According to the file, you weren't home that morning," he points out. "Your mother told police that you were at your grandparents' house all day, that you stayed home sick from school. Your grandmother corroborated the story."

I nod, finding it strange to hear Nick recite the old lie that Mom and Gran had drilled into me for weeks after the killing. I feel lighter now that it's out in the open.

But he isn't the only one who knows the truth now.

"My mother lied to protect me. She told the police she and Martin argued and she shot him twice. She told the story as if she had been the one to watch him suffer during the time between the first shot and the fatal one.

She killed for me, Nick. And for the past nine years, she's been living in a cell in order to keep me out of one."

Nick takes a step back from me now, scrubbing his hand over his jaw. "It was self-defense, Avery. For fuck's sake, what you did—it was justified. Any reasonable judge would've agreed with that. Any competent lawyer would've made sure you never served a day behind bars."

I can't say his logic is weak, or that I haven't thought the same things myself these past nine years. But at sixteen, I was just a terrified, traumatized girl. And it wasn't as if my mother gave me the choice in any of this.

"She didn't want to take that chance, Nick. She didn't want me going to trial, even as a minor. She said she blamed herself for letting Martin get anywhere near me, and refused to let me speak up for her." My heart aches to think of all my mother endured for me. And what she continues to endure. "If I could change places with her now, I would."

"No." His reply is adamant. "I won't stand for that. Don't even think it, Avery." He studies me, frowning. "Is your mother the reason you needed that money?"

I shake my head. "No. Not the way you're thinking."

"Then what?"

"Someone knows what really happened, Nick. Martin Coyle's son. My stepbrother, Rodney. He saw my car outside the house that day."

I tell him about the phone calls and texts, about Rodney's threat to expose my lie to Nick, and, eventually, to the press and anyone else he might be able to profit from.

I tell Nick how Rodney tracked me down from our photo that went viral on the Internet a few months ago, how he somehow arranged for my mother's accident as a means of getting my attention and ensuring my cooperation with him. I tell him how Rodney's harassment had recently escalated to an in-person confrontation here in the city.

"That son of a bitch is in Manhattan?" he growls. "When did you see him? Where was I, and how did he manage to get close to you?"

"It happened last week, at that Italian restaurant in East Harlem."

Nick's expression hardens. "We were together there."

"Not when I went to ladies' room."

He considers for a moment, then a sharp curse explodes off his tongue. "The smug asshole who strutted past our table as we were leaving. He got near you, alone, and you didn't tell me?"

"I couldn't. Please understand, Nick. I was so scared. I still am."

"Of your stepbrother? Give me five minutes with the fucker and there'll be nothing left of him to be afraid of."

Although he's vibrating with rage, I brave a touch anyway. Reaching out to cradle his hard jaw in my hand, I hold his simmering gaze. "I'm more afraid of losing you than anything Rodney thinks he can do to me."

"Nothing you've told me changes how I feel about you." Even still, he gently takes my hand away from his face and brings it down to my side. "Where is your stepbrother now?"

"I'm not sure. The last time I saw him was yesterday morning, across the street from this building. You remember that wrong number call that came in on your cell when we were in the limo? I'm certain it was him sending me a message that he's serious about this." At Nick's virulent curse, I add, "Rodney told me I have to be in touch with him by today to pay him ten thousand dollars for his silence."

"That won't be enough." Nick gives me a hard look. "Scum like that smell blood in the water and they'll keep coming back for more. I won't have it. Your stepbrother needs to go away permanently."

I'm not sure I want to know what he means. Without offering me an explanation, he presses a kiss to my forehead then walks into his home office and closes the door.

21

Central Park is unusually quiet, thanks most likely to a recent drizzle that's kept all but the most determined visitors indoors this afternoon. Only a handful of joggers and a few straggling tourists have passed me in the fifteen minutes I've been waiting. Not far from the bench I am sitting on, cheerful calliope music drifts out of the beige and red brick octagon that houses the park's carousel, which is apparently closed for maintenance today.

It is here that Rodney instructed me to meet him when I called to tell him I had the money.

I try not to look anxious as I check the time on my phone and see that he is nearly ten minutes late. I just want this done. I want him gone from my life.

I feel that wish intensify when I spot him sauntering up the sidewalk, heading my way. As he approaches the bench, he flicks his spent cigarette butt into the wet grass, exhaled smoke streaming out of his mouth and nostrils like dragon's breath.

I stand up, my skin crawling at the smug, satisfied look he gives me as he nears me. He's wearing baggy jeans with a denim jacket over an "I Love New York" T-shirt today. He smooths his palms over the big red heart as he glances at me. "Never thought I'd be the city type, but I gotta say, baby girl, New York is growin' on me. How do you like my souvenir?"

"She doesn't." Nick's deep voice sounds from behind Rodney.

My stepbrother swivels his head, watching Nick stroll up to where we stand. To keep Rodney from panicking or canceling the meeting, I didn't tell him that I wouldn't be alone today. As far as Nick was concerned, my coming here without him wasn't even an option.

He'd been adamant about that, even though he had said little else to me about his feelings in the time since my secrets all came spilling out today and this unwanted, unwelcome rendezvous with Martin Coyle's son.

Rodney is unable to hide his surprised expression, even if his gravelly voice is low with disrespect. "Well, well. The famous Dominic Baine in the flesh. Avery didn't mention I'd have the honor of meetin' you today."

"She didn't mention you either until very recently." Nick's reply is low, level. More lethal than Rodney realizes. "From what I understand, she's not happy to see you. Neither am I, for that matter."

"Now, ain't that an unfriendly way to greet me," he replies, his lips thinning in a sneer. "Didn't my sister tell you that you oughta be real nice to me?"

"Don't call me that," I snap, unable to stomach anything about him. "You and your father are nothing to me."

Rodney chuckles now, but his predator's gaze stays rooted on Nick. "Sharp tongue on this bitch, eh? 'Course, maybe that's how you like 'em. Maybe you rich fucks like your pussy with teeth and claws, that it?"

Nick's big body vibrates with menace beside me, but he stands utterly still. "Did you come here to get your ass kicked, or do you want to tell me what it's going to take to make you go away?"

"Get my ass kicked?" Rodney scoffs. "You're not gonna touch me, Baine. If you do, it's only gonna cost you more. See, I'm a businessman like you."

Nick doesn't even blink. "Is that what you call this? Stalking Avery. Threatening her. Putting her mother in the prison hospital."

Rodney gives him a thin smile. "I'll never admit to any of that."

"Then why am I standing here with ten grand in my pocket?"

Rodney pauses. He glances at me only briefly, then his tongue snakes out to lick his lips. "Let me see it."

"Not until we get some things straight," Nick says. "This stops right here. The second I put the cash in your hands, you stop, Rodney. You go away, and you don't come back."

His chin lifts. His eyes narrow on Nick as a sneer twists his mouth. "You think I'm stupid? You think I'm some dumb jackass who don't know my worth?"

I swallow anxiously as Rodney's voice rises. This is exactly what Nick predicted would happen—my stepbrother's arrogance and greed being fed by the promise of easy money.

"I don't know your worth," Nick says, his tone

clipped but calm. "You say you're a businessman. All right. Convince me. What do you think you're worth?"

"More than ten measly grand," he bites off sharply. "Ten grand is only a down payment. What I know about her is worth a helluva lot more than that. Think about it, Baine. I go to the press with what I know? They'll feed off the headlines for weeks. Dominic Baine's girlfriend, a white trash slut who got away with murder."

I close my eyes at the grating, ugly words—all of them close enough to the truth that it won't matter what Nick or I say to try to lessen their power. The damaging publicity for Nick will be inescapable. Unbearable.

He seethes beside me, his body radiating a palpable and growing violence. "If Avery had been the one to kill your child rapist of a father, he'd have had it coming."

Rodney grins now. "Struck a nerve, did I, Baine? The old man always did have an eye for prime tail. And with her tits and ass, 'specially back then, who could blame him for wanting a piece of that?"

"Fucking bastard." Nick takes a menacing step forward.

"No. Nick, don't!"

He stops abruptly, though not because of my sharp cry.

It's the gun in Rodney's hand that freezes Nick in place. He's pulled it from the back of his waistband, and now brandishes it in front of Nick's face.

"Oh, my God!" My voice reduces to a strangled whisper, terror arrowing through me to my marrow. "Rodney . . . please. Don't do this."

I don't miss how Nick gradually moves me behind him, inserting himself directly between my body and the barrel of the loaded weapon. I want to shout for help, but the park is so empty, I'm not sure anyone would hear me. And there is no way I'll risk Nick's life by pissing Rodney off any more than he already is.

"You smug asshole," he snarls. "You think you own the fucking world, don't ya? You got all the money, but I got this."

"Easy now, Rodney." Nick slowly raises his hands, palms open in cautious surrender. "You're right. This is your show now. You're the one holding all of the cards here."

"Damn straight."

"So, tell me what you want. You know I can make it happen."

Raw fear grips my heart as the seconds tick by in agonizing slowness. I don't know how Nick can sound so calm and collected when I am trembling from head to toe, terrified of what my stepbrother will do.

That I am the cause of this whole, awful situation makes me want to retch.

It makes me want to scream.

But Nick's strength grounds me. Right now, it's the only thing I have to cling to as Rodney continues to hold the pistol on him.

"This isn't the way you want to resolve this, Rodney. You're here to do business, so let's get it done. What's it going to take to satisfy you?"

"Helluva lot more than ten thousand dollars."

"Okay. So, what number do you have in mind?" Nick asks, his tone so rational anyone would think he was sitting in a boardroom, not standing at the killing end of a deadly weapon. "But let's be clear. I'm talking about no more contact. No more stalking or threats against Avery. No more so-called accidents at the prison.

What's it going to take for you to leave Avery and her mother alone, Rodney?"

"A hundred grand."

Nick nods slowly. "A hundred thousand dollars. If I pay you that much, it'll keep you away from us for good?"

"Maybe," Rodney replies after a moment. "Maybe not."

Nick slowly lowers his hands. "I'm willing to bet it will be."

"Yeah?" he scoffs. "And how can you be so fucking sure?"

"Take a look behind you."

Rodney swivels a glance over his shoulder, to where a group of no less than six armed police officers emerge from behind the carousel building and the surrounding trees.

I gape, just as much in shock as he is.

Well, maybe not quite as much.

One of the officers orders him to drop his weapon and get down on the ground as the rest of the cops move in en masse with weapons trained on him, ready to fire. I watch in astonishment and relief as they take him down and handcuff him.

Only Nick seems less than surprised to see the police reinforcements.

"You knew," I say as he wraps me in his arms and holds me close. "You arranged this?"

"I had a little help." He nods toward the walkway, where Andrew Beckham is striding toward us.

The tall, darkly handsome lawyer offers me a nod as he approaches us. "Everybody okay?"

"Yeah, we're fine," Nick replies. "Thanks for the

assist on short notice."

"What are friends for?" Beck shrugs, but his expression is full of relief. "This whole thing almost went sideways when Coyle pulled out that gun."

Nick grunts. "It was a surprise to me too. But now he's got a weapons charge on top of all the rest of them." He reaches into the front pocket of his pants and withdraws his phone. He hands it to Beck. "I trust the recording will give you everything you and the police need."

Beck nods. "Consider it done."

Now that the business of dealing with Rodney is handed over to his attorney and the police, Nick turns the full power of his attention onto me. As strong and confident and formidable as he is, I feel the faint tremor in his hands as he cups my face in his palms and draws me to him for a kiss.

Wordlessly, he gathers me against him, holding me tight for one long, desperately intimate moment.

"It's over now, baby," he murmurs softly into my hair. "Let's get out of here."

22

We don't speak during the short drive back to the penthouse. Neither of us seems to have the words or the breath to make them.

Nick holds my hand as he navigates the BMW down to the garage below the Park Place building. He only lets go long enough to meet me at the passenger door and help me out of the car, then his fingers find mine again, linking us together as if he understands how deeply I crave our connection right now.

Maybe he needs it too.

We could have lost hold of each other any number of ways in the time we've been together, but none more permanent than at the killing end of Rodney's gun.

The shock of what we've just been through doesn't fully settle on me until we've entered the apartment. Then the images swarm in front of me all over again. The terror and the pain. The anguishing, very real possibility that my past sins could have cost Nick his life today.

The weight of that realization makes my legs go weak beneath me. I shudder, my steps faltering. But Nick's strong hands don't let me fall.

"Hey," he says, drawing my shivering body against him. "Jesus, you're freezing cold, Avery."

"No." I shake my head weakly. "I'm afraid, Nick. God, I've never been so terrified in my life. You might have been killed today. Because of me. I might have lost you."

"I'm right here, baby." He pulls me away from him slightly, his fathomless blue eyes intense, solemn. "I'm not going anywhere."

"Nick." My voice quivers, but there's no helping it. My heart is too raw. The fear inside me is still too real, too consuming. My guilt for what I put him through today is even more crippling.

"Come with me," he says, brushing a kiss over my trembling lips.

Threading his fingers through mine again, he brings me into the spacious master bathroom, parking me on the edge of the tub as he walks over and starts the shower. With the water hissing behind him and silvery clouds of steam beginning to roil up toward the vaulted ceiling, he walks back and settles into a crouch before me.

"Nick, you don't have to take care of me," I murmur as he slips my feet out of my flats and sets the shoes aside.

He ignores my protests, standing up to lift my shirt off me then unzipping my jeans and pushing the dark denim off my hips along with my panties. My bra comes off last, and as he removes the lacy cups, he pauses to caress me in his warm hands. Hands that move with an artist's grace over the creamy swells of my breasts and the taut pink buds that crown them.

His dark head lowers, and as his mouth closes over one nipple, then the other, I moan with the pure pleasure of it. As wrung out as I am from the trauma of everything that's happened to us today, Nick is a force of strength and calm.

He is my rock, my anchor . . . and my wings.

I urge him up, tunneling my fingers into the silkiness of his ebony hair as I pull him to me for a slow kiss. I am aroused and needful of him, but right now I just need to feel him in my arms. I need him naked with me, if only to feel him warm and strong and alive against me.

I undress him with the same care he showed me, allowing my hands to worship every firm, muscled inch of him. His cock is fully erect, his gaze blazing with desire as he tenderly leads me into the shower and under the hot spray.

Yet instead of taking me with the kind of animal need that's radiating off him, he begins to wash me with utmost care. I do the same for him, my lathered hands sliding over his skin in worship, in relief, in unabashed devotion.

"Thank you," I whisper, once the heat of the water and the comfort of Nick's hands have chased away the bone-deep chill that had been with me since we left the park. "Thank you for everything you did for me today, Nick."

"There's no need to thank me." He strokes his palms down the sides of my arms, water sluicing from us as we hold each other under the soothing spray. "I wanted him gone too. Just knowing the bastard had threatened you was more than I could stand. If I didn't get rid of him like this, through legal channels, my other solution would have been far less merciful."

I swallow, acknowledging the danger in his steady, but lethal gaze. He would have killed for me. He still would. His solemn expression leaves no room for doubt.

"When you shut me out of your office today, I worried that I was losing you. You didn't tell me what you were thinking."

He smooths a wet tendril of hair away from my eyes. "Beck and I didn't have much time to put wheels in motion. Once we had our plan, I couldn't risk bringing you in on it. I needed to provoke Rodney, and that meant your reactions had to be natural. They had to be real. We had to make him show his true intentions in order to give the police plenty to use against him."

I nod, knowing he's right. Rodney would have seen through me if I'd been anything but terrified. He would never have let Nick steer him into the trap of his own damning words if there was any doubt that the meeting was his to control.

"What happens now?" I caress my hand over the muscled slab of Nick's chest, feeling his heart throb beneath my fingertips. As relieved as I am that Rodney can't harm Nick and I, we aren't the only ones he was willing to hurt in order to satisfy his greed. "What about my mom? Rodney must have friends inside the prison. What if they retaliate when they hear he's been arrested?"

"Beck and the police are already on top of it. We contacted the prison this afternoon to explain the situation. They've assigned your mother extra security and they're also going to be looking more closely at the report of her accident to see what they missed." He cups my cheek in his hand. "She's going to be okay, Avery. I'll see to that."

Gratitude overwhelms me at his earnest promise. But I feel ashamed too. "I'm sorry I kept all of this from you, Nick. I'm sorry for my lies. I should have trusted you with the truth."

"Yes," he says. "You should have. If I had known everything you'd been through, I would have been gentler with you from the beginning. God, Avery . . . everything would've been different."

I smile sadly, seeing the softness in his eyes. The regret. "If I had told you everything in the beginning, we wouldn't be together now, would we?"

He doesn't answer. I see him gauging the weight of my question, and his careful silence puts my heart in a vise.

When I can't take it any longer, I answer for him instead. "No, we wouldn't. Because you would have looked at me with pity in your eyes, the way you are now."

"Pity?" The word rushes out of him, a harsh denial. "What I feel when I look at you is astonishment. It's respect. Jesus, it's more than you can possibly know." His touch still lingers on my face. I feel the vibration of his deep voice against my skin and all around me. I see the ferocity of his emotion in his darkening scowl and the penetrating heat of his eyes. "You came through fire, Avery. The last thing I feel when I look at you is pity. You're stronger than I ever imagined. You suffered so much at the hands of someone you should've been able to trust, but you survived."

"So did you," I remind him gently. We've both come through fire. We've both had to find a way to survive. To not let our pasts destroy us. I reach for his hands, kissing the pristine one first, then the other. "Why didn't you tell me about your art? Or that the man who stole it from you was your father?"

"Nobody knows that."

"Kathryn does."

He scoffs, drawing out of my loose hold. "And she couldn't wait to use it against me, to try to humiliate me in front of a house full of rich, useless snobs."

"Is that what you think?" I slowly shake my head. "Nick, she loved you. She was proud of your work. She told me so. She wanted to share your gift with people who would appreciate it as much as she did."

"And then they could all cluck their tongues and shake their heads in dismay over the poor, mutilated artist as they speculated on what kind of lowlife monster would shove his own son through a window just to make him shut up."

His answer is so full of anger, so sharp with pain, it takes me a moment to find the courage to speak. "Is that what happened? With your father, I mean."

"Who knows." He raises his hands to his head, scraping his fingers over his scalp on a heavy sigh. "Who the fuck knows why my old man hated me so much. He was drunk half the time anyway. Let's forget it, all right?"

He pivots around and shuts off the water.

"Nick—"

"Drop it, Avery." The curt reply sends my pulse hammering with concern. The only thing worse is his long, agonized pause, and the tight whisper that follows. "Just . . . enough, okay?"

"Okay, Nick. We don't have to talk about him anymore."

I move in close, skimming my hand over the tense planes of his back. His muscles twitch at the contact. I don't know what I've said that's upset him the most, but the last thing I want, especially right now, is to put distance between us.

I press my lips to his shoulder blade, relieved when he doesn't pull away. "We don't have to talk at all."

I turn him around to face me. He's still hard and erect. His chest is heaving, his handsome face taut with rage and arousal and something darker that I'm afraid to name.

His neck feels like a column of steel when I wrap my hand around his nape and pull him toward me for my kiss. He doesn't resist. He moans as our mouths join, his tongue spearing past my parted lips and teeth.

There is fury in his kiss. And need.

So much need.

I slide one hand down the front of him, over the firm ridges of his abdomen and into the crisp hair at the base of his shaft. He groans thickly at the first stroke of my fingers along his length. When I close them around his cock and begin a slow but steady rhythm, his breath leaves him on a ragged sigh.

I break our kiss, my eyes hot on his as I sink down before him and take him into my mouth.

"Avery," he utters, his voice low. His expression is tender, tormented. "Ah, Christ."

I work his cock with my mouth and tongue and hands, swallowing him deep, then licking the plush crown, all the while never releasing his gaze.

I want to make him feel as safe with me as I do with

him. I want to make him unravel, make him lose that consummate control of his. I want to make him remember what is real.

Me.

Us.

He holds my head as I increase my suction and my tempo, my tongue searching for the spot that will take him to the edge. He closes his eyes on a curse gritted between his teeth. When his lids drag open a second later, there is nothing but heat in his eyes.

His fingers curl into my wet hair, clutching tight. His hips move in time with my mouth now, his thighs spread and braced. His stance is so carnal, so primal and male, as he thrusts into my demanding mouth.

I moan, losing myself to the power of his pleasure too. My sex throbs with each plunge and pull. I'm wet and aching, barely able to resist sliding my fingers into my folds to relieve some of the delicious pressure that's building between my legs as I suck and fondle and lick him.

"Fuck," he rasps sharply, his big body convulsing when I take him deep enough to knock the back of my throat. His eyes are hot with warning, with an unspoken plea. "Baby . . . I'm going to come."

"Mm," I hum as I swallow him again, opening my throat to take him nearly to the root.

His shout ricochets off the tile and glass of the shower. A jet of thick, hot semen floods my mouth. He shudders and bucks as I continue to work him, drinking everything he's got.

"Ah, God. Avery." He hauls me up with little gentleness, then claims my mouth in a feverish, possessive kiss. I'm still sticky with his juices, my lips and chin coated with him, but he doesn't seem to care.

Pressing my back against the marble tiles for support, he lifts one of my legs around his hips and drives into me on a harsh groan. My body arches into him as he fills me, yielding to him completely. He starts to thrust hard and deep, his scarred hand clamped around my hip, his other one splayed on the wall above my shoulder as he moves in and out of my body.

His eyes never leave mine, not for a moment.

We move together, our bodies and gazes bound, our desire for each other entwined.

When my orgasm chases through me a few moments later, Nick studies every nuance on my face. I cannot hide from him, not anymore.

There is no need.

The realization washes over me like a wave. I belong to him now, wholly, completely.

And he is mine.

His raw gaze tells me that, even if he can't give me the words.

He shouts my name as he comes again, inside me this time, his seed jetting forcefully against my core. He drops his head onto the curve of my shoulder. A hard shudder rocks him as a further burst of heat spills into me.

"Avery," he rasps, caressing me as he releases my leg from around his hips. "What have you done to me?"

I smile, sifting my fingers through his damp, silky hair. "I should ask you the same thing."

"I never imagined how deep I was going to get with you." He draws back now, his face sober. Almost apologetic. "Today brought everything home to me. When I saw that gun. When I thought about the fact that if things had been different today, you might have gone alone. You might've gotten hurt . . . or worse."

"I didn't. I'm okay. Because of you, I'm okay."

"Ah, God, Avery." He shakes his head. "I . . . need you."

"You have me." I hold his tormented gaze. "Nick, I love you."

The words seem to wound him more than soothe him. A scowl knits his brow. "I wish we could start over. Both of us do this right."

"We can. We *are* starting over, right now." I loop my arms around his neck, pressing a tender kiss to the edge of his jaw. "I don't have any more secrets, Nick. You know them all now. No more lies. No barriers between us, not anymore."

He studies my face, frowning as he strokes my temple. "Baby . . . "

I forge on, determined to reach him. "I want to make a new agreement with you. Let's start the clock all over again. This time, we both make the rules. We both decide on the terms. No limits. No more hiding who we are or what we need from each other."

"And what is it that you need?"

There is a hollowness to his voice that makes my heart skip a beat. Have I said too much? Have I fallen into the trap that I've been warned to avoid—allowing myself to get too close?

Part of me senses the danger. But another part of me knows that what Nick and I share is unlike anything either of us have had with anyone before. I trust in that knowledge.

I trust him.

"I need you, Nick." I stare up into his haunted eyes.

"Don't you know? That's where all of my wants and needs begin and end . . . with you."

"Avery." He whispers my name, claiming my mouth on a hushed curse.

I surrender to him, to the passion neither of us can deny, and to what I hope is the promise of our new beginning.

23

The following week, I am seated across from Tasha at Vendange just after noon, sipping a glass of wine and catching her up on everything that's happened since we last spoke. She's on break at the restaurant, and the back booth we've commandeered affords us privacy from the rest of the staff and the activity in the main dining area and bar.

Her mouth is agape, her soft brown eyes wide as I recount my stepbrother's threats and harassment, culminating in his arrest.

"Holy shit, Ave." She reaches for my hand across the table and gives it a tender squeeze. "Thank God you and Nick are all right."

Of course, I couldn't tell her about Rodney without first explaining my role in the whole ordeal. She had listened without judgment, without condemnation, as I quietly confided in her about my rape, and my actions in the time that followed.

That I'd been able to recount the details with dry eyes and a steady voice was a surprise to me. A revelation, really. Much of my emotional burden had lifted after I shared the story with Nick. He's been helping me to carry it ever since, giving me his strength when I need to lean on it, and a soft place to land whenever I fall.

I've never felt so safe and protected—so at peace— before in my life.

Nick has given me all of that and more.

For the first time in nearly a decade, I'm not dreading tomorrow's upcoming anniversary of that horrible day. Maybe someday August twenty-first will come and go without shredding me from the inside out.

"How's your mom doing through all of this?" Tasha asks. "Have you been able to talk to her?"

I nod, aware that I am grateful to Nick for yet another kindness too. "We just got back yesterday from visiting her at the prison. She's doing much better. The bone is finally healing, and they've even got her walking a little bit at the infirmary."

She smiles. "You must be so relieved."

"Yes, I am. It could've been so much worse. I'm still sick when I think about what Rodney did. Fortunately, the woman he was seeing who worked in the prison laundry cracked as soon as she heard he'd been arrested. She told the police everything—how he coerced her into pushing Mom down the stairs to get my attention and didn't care how badly she got hurt. According to Rodney's girlfriend, he'd gone to New York determined to collect as much as he could from Nick and me, even if he had to kill one or both of us to get it."

Tasha swears under her breath. "A point he demonstrated quite plainly when he pulled out that gun. My God, Avery. You and Nick are lucky to be alive. Your mom too."

"I know." I take a long drink of my wine, all too aware that my secrets might have taken the two people I care about most if Rodney hadn't been stopped. "Nick saved both of us that day. I have no doubt about that. I owe him so much, Tasha. I owe him . . . everything."

She gives me a warm, understanding smile. "Pretty sure that man is counting his blessings that he's got you too. He loves you, you know."

"He hasn't said it," I admit, tracing my finger along the rim of my wineglass.

She waves her hand dismissively. "I couldn't get Tony to say the words out loud for six months after we started dating. But I knew. I'll bet where Nick is concerned, you know too."

I shrug, wanting to believe she's right. In my heart, I know I'm the only woman Nick wants.

From the beginning, he's been nothing if not single-mindedly consumed with me. Obsessed, even. Just as I have been with him.

He needs me. Those are words he's given me freely, passionately. Leaving no room for doubt.

But love? That's the one threshold he hasn't crossed.

There's a part of me that's not even certain he can.

Every time I see the torment in his gaze, I wonder if it's going to take him away from me one day. Every time I see the hauntedness—the scars that don't ride his skin, but lurk inside of him—I worry that I will never be enough to heal him.

That he won't ever let me get that close.

But that doesn't mean I'm not going to try. After all that we've been through these past few months, the one thing I'm sure of is that I want Nick in my life. I need him in my life, just as he needs me.

I have to trust in him.

I have to keep proving that he can trust me.

That's a task I intend to devote myself to completely now that I have the chance.

My phone rings on the table next to me. It's Nick, which doesn't surprise me, even though we've already spoken a couple of times since he left for the office this morning.

Since the confrontation with Rodney, Nick's been even more protective than usual. As much as I would have chafed against that kind of dominance and control at one time in my life, now, with him, it comforts me.

Tasha starts to get up. "Go ahead and take it. I have to get back to work, anyway. Tell the bossman he's my new hero. Just don't let Tony know I said that."

I'm laughing as I grab my purse and slide out of the booth to answer the call. "Hi, baby."

"I sure like the sound of your smile," he says. "What's got you so happy?"

"You." I glance over my shoulder and wave goodbye to Tasha. "I miss you."

"What a coincidence. I'm missing you too, Ms. Ross." He pauses for a moment, no doubt hearing the clamor of the bustling restaurant in the background. "You're still at Vendange?"

"Just leaving. I'm sure Patrick must be bored out of his mind waiting for me the past twenty minutes. You really don't have to make him cart me around on every little excursion or errand I run."

"I'll be the judge of that," he replies, his tone stern. "We've already covered this, haven't we? You're mine, and I protect what's mine."

I smile, warmed by his possessiveness. "Yes, sir."

He grunts. "That's my girl."

I step outside and nod to Patrick, whose holding the backseat door open for me. "Thanks," I say, slipping inside. "So, Mr. Baine, where are you at the moment?"

"Sitting at my desk with half a dozen proposals to review this afternoon and wondering why I'm not spending the day with you instead. How do you feel about dinner?"

"I'm generally in favor of it. I'm pretty fond of dessert too," I add, smiling at the memory of some of our more creative uses for sweets and toppings.

Nick's low chuckle tells me he's in total agreement. "I'll meet you at the penthouse in an hour to pick you up."

"Isn't that a little early for dinner?"

"By the time we get where we're going, it won't be. I'll see you soon, Ms. Ross."

I can hardly curb my grin. "I'll be ready for you, Mr. Baine."

24

Nick arrives at the penthouse looking freshly showered and mouth-wateringly sexy in a pearl gray shirt with the collar opened and one of the dozen or so bespoke suits he keeps in the private dressing room of his office. The black pants and jacket fit him to perfection, making me yearn to put my hands—and mouth—all over the muscled, male beauty of his body.

His dark gaze seems to approve of my appearance as well. "Maybe dinner plans should wait. You look good enough to eat," he says, catching my hand and rotating me in front of him. "New dress?"

I nod, glancing down at the silky, wine-colored halter dress and sparkly designer sandals I bought on the way home with some of the money from my paintings.

It's a splurge I probably shouldn't have indulged in, but I want to look good for Nick.

"You like it?"

"Oh, yeah. Not as much as I like what's in it, though." He lifts my chin and brushes his lips over mine. "We should go before I change my mind and keep you here."

If he thinks I would have complained about that, he's mistaken. I'll go or stay anywhere so long as it means being close to him. "Where are you taking me?"

His smile is cryptic. "You'll see when we get there."

We step into the private elevator and take the lift down to the lobby. The limousine waits for us outside. With a wink from Manny, I feel like a princess being led to her carriage as Nick strolls with me past the handful of well-dressed people who all pause and look our way.

I'm not sure I'll ever get used to the attention that comes with being on Dominic Baine's arm, but right now I feel miles away from the uncertain, out-of-place imposter who stepped through these doors less than five months ago.

Not because of his money or his recognition as one of the most powerful men in this city, if not the world. I don't feel different because of the luxury and all of the fine things that are becoming my new normal.

I am different because of him.

Better because of him.

Stronger.

And, yes, happier.

So in love with him I'm sure it's written all over my face as he links his fingers through mine and walks me out to the waiting car, pausing to kiss me once more before we both slide into the backseat and leave our gawking audience behind.

I notice Nick doesn't give Patrick directions

anywhere. They've obviously already discussed the plan.

I slant a glance at Nick. "You're really not going to tell me where we're going?"

"Someplace I think you'll enjoy."

The car heads into the evening traffic and I settle against Nick for the ride. It doesn't take long for me to realize that instead of navigating deeper into the city, we're driving out of it. Heading for the airport.

I frown at him. "Nick—"

He silences me with a deep, breath-stealing kiss. "Trust, Ms. Ross."

That phrase and the heated, confident look he gives me transport me in an instant to another moment like this one—to another time when he surprised me with an excursion that brought us to the private charter terminal of this same airport, followed by three weeks of tropical bliss and sheet-scorching, adventurous sex.

I sit back and try to exercise patience I seldom have, watching as Patrick drives us around to where a large jet waits. A jet with the Baine International logo emblazoned on its fuselage.

This is not the aircraft we took before. That chartered plane was a ten-seat miniature compared to this sleek, formidable looking bird.

The limo comes to a halt near the stairs leading up to the aircraft. Patrick comes around to Nick's side of the car and opens the backseat door.

He nods as we climb out and wishes us a safe trip.

Nick guides me ahead of him when we reach the female attendant waiting for us at the bottom of the steps. She wears a midnight blue uniform consisting of a vest and skirt and a crisp white blouse. Her smile is both warm and professional as we approach.

"Good afternoon, Mr. Baine. Good afternoon, Miss Ross."

"Hello, Pamela."

I shouldn't be surprised that she knows my name. After all, Nick thinks of everything. And he's clearly clued in everyone but me as to what this trip is about.

With his palm a warm, reassuring presence at the small of my back, he urges me up the stairs ahead of him.

Trying to mask my awe would be impossible, so I simply stare in astonishment at the elegance of the immense, beautifully appointed cabin and its soothing, neutral palette.

"Wow." I glance back at Nick. "This is incredible. I could live here."

He chuckles. "There have been times when it feels like I do. Since I spend so much time flying back and forth from the States to my other business locations and clients, I prefer to do it in comfort. Would you like to look around before we take off?"

"Sure." I arch a brow at him. "So, are we going to be in the air for long?"

"Nice try." His hand comes down with a firm swat to my backside, his look pure wicked amusement. "Come on, let me show you around."

Before we get started, Pamela returns to offer us cocktails or champagne. I opt for the latter and Nick requests sparkling water. With our cold drinks in hand seconds later, he leads me through the spacious home with wings.

Creamy leather sofas with pale gray accent pillows and cocktail tables in a sleek, glass-topped cube design comprise one section of the main cabin. A large, polished wood conference table surrounded by eight chairs is the focal point of another area. Toward the rear of the jet is a wall-mounted, large-screen television with a matched grouping of leather recliners in front of it.

Behind that is a short hallway that terminates at the open doorway of what appears to be an impressive stateroom.

"Saving the best for last?" I ask him playfully as he takes my hand and we stroll into a bedroom that's got to be twice the size of my entire old apartment in Brooklyn.

As soon as we enter, he wraps his free arm around my back and draws me against him. His lips take mine, possessive and consuming, making my blood quicken and my core clench with heated desire.

Somehow, he manages to remove my champagne glass from my hand and sets it down on a nearby bureau along with his crystal tumbler of water. Then his hands are in my hair, disheveling the loose twist I'd worked on for fifteen minutes to get right, but I don't care.

I don't care that we're far from alone right now, with the flight attendant somewhere in the cabin outside and with probably mere minutes before we'll be directed to take our seats and prepare for departure.

I don't care about any of that.

All that matters is his touch, his kiss . . . us.

I am panting when he pulls away from me, my vision hazing over with desire. So much so, that at first I don't register what I'm seeing on the other side of the stateroom. A single work of art has been granted the entire wall.

It's far from remarkable.

Just a simple self-portrait—amateurish in my opinion—yet it hangs there like a cherished treasure.

"Nick . . . " I swivel my head toward him, stunned.

Confused. "That's my painting."

It's the first one I'd ever done when I came to New York. The first—the only—piece that sold out of all of the work I'd had on display at Nick's gallery. Which means he's had it for more than a year.

Including the nearly five months we've been together.

"You're the one who bought it?"

"Yes."

"Why?" I have to ask. At the time, he hadn't held my art in very high regard. "You said you didn't like my work."

"This piece was different. It wasn't like the others."

I frown, acknowledging the truth in that. I painted the self-portrait just after I arrived in the city. It was meant to be an experiment, a diversion. Just me and a mirror and a pot of black paint.

The brush lines are crude, hasty. The image is more suggestion than accurate reflection, my downcast face and tumble of loose hair the primary focus, as if the rest of me were dissolving into the canvas.

Nick takes me back into his arms. His expression is sober, his voice earnest. "This painting is good, Avery. This was the gift I saw in you. The gift I see in you even more now."

"You never said anything. You never told me you had it."

I'm astonished to think that he's been seeing my painting—this personal expression of myself—each time he's been on this plane . . . in this room.

He holds my shocked gaze as he smooths a loose tendril of hair from my cheek. "You've been mine longer than you know, Avery. I didn't plan on any of this happening between us. Ah, Christ . . . I didn't plan on falling in love with you."

My breath catches at his soft confession, my heart swelling, soaring inside my breast. "Nick . . . I love you too. I love you so much."

I wrap my arms around him as our lips meet, emotion swamping me. I've never known this joy, this hope, this soul-deep love. I'm so swept up in Nick's kiss, his embrace, that I hardly register the quiet sound of approaching feet on the carpeted cabin outside.

Pamela's awkward inhalation breaks through my haze. "Oh, excuse me, Mr. Baine, Miss Ross. I'm so sorry for the interruption."

Nick clears his throat. "It's all right."

We glance at the attendant, who stands sheepishly at the open doorway of the stateroom. "The captain says we're cleared for the runway. We can begin departure as soon as you're ready."

"Thank you, Pamela."

As she leaves us, I look back up at Nick and his cryptic smile. "Are you going to tell me where we're going, or am I going to have to wheedle the information out of the crew?"

He smirks. "I already told you. I'm taking you to dinner. I know this nice little place with a great view and a duck specialty that's out of this world."

I tilt my head, brows raised. "The last time we flew to one of your favorite places we ended up in Miami."

He kisses the tip of my nose, then pulls something out of his back pocket.

My passport.

"Tonight we're going a bit farther than Miami."

25

You certainly do know how to impress a girl."

It's morning in Paris—although, admittedly, at ten minutes before noon, it's barely morning anymore. After arriving from New York after midnight, Nick whisked me off to a dinner at a beautiful historic restaurant that truly did serve a fantastic pressed duck. Although we had arrived long past closing time, Nick had arranged for a private table to be waiting for us with a spectacular nighttime view of Notre-Dame Cathedral and the glistening Seine.

As if my introduction to the City of Light wasn't jaw-dropping enough, Nick then brought me home to his penthouse flat on the other side of the river, where he proceeded to make me come no less than three times before we both finally collapsed into a heavy, sated sleep.

I sigh just thinking of it, my body still thrumming and eager for more.

Nick walks out of the kitchen to join me at the open French doors of the rooftop terrace. He looks decadent and far too sexy wearing just a pair of loose black lounge pants, his dark hair sleek and damp from our recent shower.

He presses a steaming cup of coffee into my hands and kisses my temple. "Learning to love surprises, are you, Ms. Ross?"

"I'm learning to love a lot of things where you're concerned." I sigh and lean against him in a fluffy white spa robe, not yet motivated to think about clothing.

Just beyond the terrace, the postcard landscape of the Paris skyline spreads out in all directions for as far as my eyes can see. From Nick's premium location on a picturesque side street off the famed Avenue des Champs-Élysées, our multimillion-dollar view is flanked by a soaring Gothic church spire to one side, and, to the other, the bronze-colored, delicate wrought iron latticework of the iconic Eiffel Tower. On the avenues below us, countless five-star hotels and world-renowned designer boutiques stretch from one end of the pavement to the other.

"Hungry?" he murmurs, his arm wrapped around me.

"I shouldn't be, but whatever you're making smells delicious." The buttery, vanilla aroma has my mouth watering in spite of how much food and wine we indulged in last night.

I follow him back to the kitchen where he whips up a batch of crêpes with fresh berries and cream, and another with eggs and ham and cheese. With plates full of sweet and savory temptations, we step out to the little table that's been set for brunch on the terrace.

"Best seat in the house," I say, smiling as we get settled.

Nick returns my smile, his gaze holding mine. "Definitely the best view."

I dig in to the most amazing crêpes I've ever tasted, practically embarrassing myself with the orgasmic sounds I can't even begin to contain. Nick grins, making quick work of his meal then excusing himself to fetch a carafe of coffee.

I've just popped the last bite of strawberry and cream goodness into my mouth when he returns. Instead of returning with coffee, he comes up behind me and crouches at my back. I start to turn, but his low command halts me. "Close your eyes, sweetheart. Give me your hands."

His deep voice ignites my senses. I obey him without hesitation, my pulse thrumming, my skin heating from just those wicked, whispered words. I am attuned to him on a primal level now, eager to go wherever he leads me.

He's ruined me for any other man, and right now there is no fear in that realization. Only desire. Only love.

His fingers push up the loose sleeves of my robe, baring my forearms. He strokes me, his mouth pressing a gentle kiss to the side of my neck. Something cold and metallic wraps my left wrist.

"You can open them now."

My eyelids lift and bring my arms back around, realizing with a gasp what he's done.

Around my wrist is a gleaming gold-and-platinum watch, its elegant face encrusted with glittering diamonds. Cartier. It must have cost a fortune.

I pivot to face him as he moves around from behind me. "Nick, my God. It's incredible. It's too much."

LARA ADRIAN

He takes my hand, turning my wrist so the gold and gems catch the warm light. "It's perfect," he says. "Let's reset the clock, Avery. Let's do everything over again. Starting now. On this date."

"Today?" I look up at him, wondering if he knows what it means to me. But I should know better than to doubt him. He remembers. Of course, he does. I've only mentioned it to him once, but he pays attention. He realizes the significance of this date, what it means to me.

More importantly, he understands what I need to put it behind me.

I need him.

All I need is him.

"Nick." My voice catches as I stand up and wrap him in my arms. He kisses me with such tenderness it nearly breaks me.

When our lips finally separate, his eyes burn into mine, scorching yet questioning.

"I want to do it right with you," he murmurs. "I've never wanted anything more."

I smile up at him, troubled by the bleakness that's crept back into his eyes. "Well, this is a hell of a way to start. Last night and this morning wasn't bad either."

A grin tugs the corner of his mouth. "Shall we pick up where we left off? Paris is for lovers, so they say."

I laugh and smack my palm against the firm slabs of muscle on his chest. "It's also for tourists, and it's my first time here. So I hope you plan on showing me all of the sights."

"I'll show you anything you want."

I tip my head back for his kiss. "I wish you had clued me in yesterday so I could've packed some extra clothes and shoes."

"You'll find a selection of things in your sizes already waiting for you in the dressing room closet. I've had it stocked for weeks."

"Seriously?" My mouth drops open. "You think of everything, don't you?"

"I prefer not to leave anything to chance."

Shaking my head, I smile up at him in wonder. "How did we get so lucky?" He doesn't answer, but his eyes smolder as I reach up and bury my fingers in his silky hair. "This is a fairytale, Nick. You've slain all my monsters. You've picked me up and carried me off to your castle. You've saved me."

He curses, low under his breath. Something dark flickers across his expression as he caresses my face in his strong hands. "I'm not a prince. God, never hold me in that light. You'll only be disappointed." His touch gentles, even as his gaze goes hard with intensity. "I'm not a good man, Avery. But I am the one who loves you."

They are words I'll never tire of hearing from him. Words I'm still afraid to believe, for fear that I'm going to wake up one day and find this was all a dream.

"I love you too," I whisper, dragging him to me and taking his mouth in a possessive kiss that would banish both of our doubts.

I groan when I hear the muffled ring of his phone inside the flat.

He doesn't seem happy with the interruption either. The ringtone is one I recognize as belonging to his assistant.

"I told Lily I would be out of touch for a few days," he mutters without releasing me.

"If she's calling anyway, it must be important. Why

don't you find out what she wants?" I extricate myself from his arms and gesture for him to go. "I'll clean up."

He heads inside and answers the call. Some of the impatience with the intrusion leaves his voice when I hear him mention the recreation center and problems with one of the construction contracts.

"That son of a bitch. He agreed to those terms months ago, so unless he wants to take me on personally about this—" He rakes a hand through his hair and grinds out a curse. "No. On second thought, forget it. I'd rather cut the bastard loose and go somewhere else. The center is the most important thing. Can you forward me the file with the other bids, Lily? Thanks."

He meets my gaze as I carry the last of the dishes in from the terrace and start filling the dishwasher.

"I'm sorry," he tells me, muting the call. "I need to take care of this right now. I could be a while."

"It's okay. Do whatever you have to. I'll finish cleaning up the kitchen, and then I think I'll take a little walk outside." His brow rankles, but before he can voice an objection I walk up to him and silence him with a brief kiss. "I'll be fine. You took care of all my monsters, remember? Besides, what kind of trouble do you think I can run into on a street full of haute couture and luxury hotels?"

He doesn't look enthused with the idea, but he doesn't argue. With a tight nod, he steps into the other room, resuming his conversation with Lily.

26

I head out a few minutes later, wearing cropped black pants, ballet flats, and a cap-sleeved striped shirt that makes me feel a bit like Audrey Hepburn. The tree-lined Avenue George V outside Nick's building is bustling with pedestrians and street traffic. Shoppers and tourists and residents of all types stroll past me as I meander on the sidewalk, admiring the city's historic architecture, from the residential buildings and famed designer boutiques to the charming bistros and cafes.

Paris is a feast for the senses and I soak it all in, feeling transported and alive, and so very in love.

My stroll has taken me to the end of the long boulevard before I realize how far I've wandered. I turn back, eager to explore the city with Nick once he's finished with his business. I'm nearly to his building when I spot a flash of strawberry-blonde hair and a familiar face up ahead of me on the shady sidewalk.

Claire Prentice.

She's stepping out of a Rolls Royce limousine with an older gentleman just outside the entrance of the Four Seasons hotel. She's dressed expensively, draped in an elegant champagne-colored dress that accentuates every curve with understated, but unquestionably sexy, style. She's much taller than her obviously moneyed companion, whom I guess to be at least twice her age with his thinning dark hair and rounded midsection.

She glances my way but doesn't seem to notice my wave.

"Claire!" I try again, hurrying toward her to say hello.

My shout halts her. She turns her head in my direction and I see the surprise register on her beautiful face. Her expression freezes, her smile held in place as I approach.

"Avery, hello. How lovely to see you." Despite the warmth of her voice, I feel a prickle of awkwardness as I near her and the gentleman accompanying her. She air-kisses my cheek, still beaming at me in greeting. "What a surprise to see you here. What brings you to Paris?"

"I'm here with Nick. His apartment is just up the street from here."

"Oh. I didn't realize he kept a place in Paris."

As she speaks, I glance at her companion, whom I notice seems more businesslike than intimate with her. "What about you? Are you here on an acting job?"

The man smirks, then murmurs something to her in French before stepping away from us, toward the doorman standing at the entrance of the pricey hotel.

"Uh," Claire stammers. "I'm here with my friend."

And then I realize I must be an idiot. The fancy hotel. The older, wealthy man. The sense that he and

Claire have possibly only just met each other. It all adds up and now I feel worse than awkward. I wish the pavement would open up and swallow me.

"I'm so sorry. I had no idea—"

"Of course, you didn't," she whispers. Then leans in close, adding wryly, "In a way, what I do *is* acting, right?"

I blink at the odd statement. The inadvertent admission that has just told me something even more unexpected.

"This is what you do for a living?" It makes so much more sense now. The multimillion-dollar apartment in the Park Place building. The closet filled with designer clothes and shoes—a wardrobe I marveled at during my stay as her house sitter while she was in Japan those several months.

But if she isn't an actress—

"What about the game show pilot?"

Now her smile falters. She swallows, glancing away from me. "I really shouldn't keep my friend waiting. It was so nice to see you, Avery."

"Claire. There never was a job waiting for you in Japan, was there?" My face feels numb. My heart is thudding heavily in my chest, a sick awareness washing over me. "Why did you lie about that? Why not just say you were going on a trip or vacation? Why the need for the elaborate story when you hired me to housesit your place?"

She takes a step away from me, her lips pressed flat. Refusing to answer any more of my questions.

"Claire, please. I need to know." The doorman and her companion are staring at me now, everyone looking uncomfortable with my suddenly rising voice. They can't possibly feel as disturbed as I do. "Claire, tell me. Why did you lie to me?"

Finally, she pauses. Pivoting to face me, her expression is wooden, resigned.

Apologetic.

Even pitying.

"Maybe you'd better ask Nick."

27

I hear Nick's voice in another room of the flat when I enter. It takes me a moment to realize he's talking to me. My mind is numb. My body is moving as though in a trance.

No, not a trance.

A terrible dream, where I am engulfed in a fog so thick I can barely force my lungs to breathe. Each heartbeat feels as though it is cracking my chest open, exposing me to a chill I feel all the way into my bones. Down to my soul.

"Baby? Hey, there you are. Why didn't you answer just now?" Nick is smiling as he comes to the living area to greet me. His handsome face and tender gaze only breaks my heart open even wider. "Sorry to abandon you like that. I hope you enjoyed your walk."

He draws me into his arms. I'm too shell-shocked to fight the contact, but he notices my wooden stance as soon as he touches me.

He pulls back, frowning. "What is it? Are you okay? Is something wrong?"

"I ran into someone we know." At the sound of my toneless voice, a flicker of unease enters his normally unflappable gaze. I don't wait for him to ask the question. "Claire Prentice."

"Here in Paris?" He grunts, clearly taken by surprise. "That's interesting."

"Yes," I agree. "It was interesting. She was just arriving at the hotel next door with a . . . client, I suppose you'd call him."

"Client?"

I scoff. "Are you going to tell me you have no idea what she does for a living?"

"What are you saying? That Claire's a call girl?"

"She's definitely not an actress. She just admitted that to me on the street a minute ago."

I hold his gaze, feeling some of my shock dissipate, morph into something sharper when I see how deftly Nick can craft a dodge. Doesn't he realize? I am the master of lies and obfuscation.

At least, I was before I met him. He tore down all of my old defenses. He left me bare.

Dear God, I can't believe I'm only seeing it now. He's played me like no one ever has before.

"Why, Nick?"

He stares at me in a lengthening silence. "Tell me what's going on, sweetheart."

"That's what I want to know. What the *fuck* is going on?"

His brow furrows deeper as he reaches for me. This time I jerk away, well out of his reach.

"There was no acting job in Japan," I tell him, searching his eyes for confirmation of the truth. "There was no friend who stood her up that night she came into Vendange and told me she needed someone to watch her apartment for four months. Her apartment, which is in your building, Nick."

He says nothing, but I see a tendon jump in his jaw. His lack of denial is all the evidence I need. Maybe I should feel some satisfaction that he's not going to lie to me some more. But I don't feel anything except pain.

And confusion . . . .

I think back to my painting—the self-portrait he bought more than a year ago. The image of me that he's kept with him all this time.

I think back to his words in the stateroom of his private jet—his declaration that I have been his for longer than I know.

"It started with your art," he admits quietly, knowing me so intimately now, not even my thoughts can elude him. "I saw your gift, Avery. It spoke to me. I've never known that kind of pull before. I saw your face in that painting and it touched something deep inside me— something that had been dead for a long time. I felt a connection that I wasn't ready for. Christ, I wasn't equipped to feel that kind of pull to another person. I've never had that before. I've never wanted another woman the way I've wanted you."

"No."

I shake my head, pushing his explanation away. I don't want it. Not when I'm feeling so foolish. So naive that I had convinced myself this was all some kind of fairytale.

That fate had put us together because we were both

broken and alone.

A choked laugh tears out of my throat. "God, what an idiot I am. You actually had me believing that all of this was real. That we were real."

"We *are* real." His voice is a lash, crisp and sharp. "What we have together, Avery . . . it's real."

"You set everything up!" My chest is heaving with my gasping breath. My heart is banging, fury and anguish throbbing in my temples. "How did you know I would take Claire's offer? How could you be so sure that I—"

The words dry up in my throat. Because I know. The answer hits me with the impact of a physical strike.

"The condo development company. The one that bought my apartment building in Greenpoint. It's one of yours, isn't it."

He takes a step toward me, his face slack with regret. "I never said I was a good man, Avery. I'm controlling and arrogant. I'm used to getting what I want. I'm possessive as hell, but never more than when it comes to you."

"You used me! You took my life apart piece by piece until you had me in your hands. In your bed. You manipulated me like a fucking pawn on your chessboard!" A sob rakes me. "Damn you, Nick, I trusted you. You let me fall in love with you!"

"That was never my intent," he replies solemnly. "When this all began, I only knew that I wanted you. I wanted to see your art blossom. And, yes, I wanted you in my bed. Love was never part of the equation."

"Finally, honesty." I swipe angrily at the tears that are coursing down my cheeks. "I've heard enough, Nick. I can't do this anymore."

I step past him, walking swiftly into the bedroom. I

grab my purse, my passport—the only things that truly belong to me. Nick is blocking the doorway when I turn around.

"I never intended for things to end up like this, Avery. When I said I wanted to start the clock over again, I meant it. I planned to tell you everything while we were here in Paris."

"And then what, Nick? Pick up again as if none of this has happened?"

"Yes." His tone is firmer now. The look in his eyes is dark with demand, even as it implores me to listen. "That's exactly what I hoped we could do. Neither one of us came into this without secrets, without lies. Neither one of us expected this to last, but it has. I need you, Avery. I love you."

"No!" My reply explodes out of me. Hearing those words from him now, when I'm standing in the rubble of his deception—his betrayal—is too much for me to bear. "Don't say that to me, Nick. I don't want to hear it. Not ever again."

I push past him, desperate to get away before he is able to make me into an even bigger fool.

He grabs my arm, halting me.

"Avery, goddamn it. Don't do this!"

I bark out a broken laugh. "I'm not the one who did this, Nick. You did."

He curses when I pull out of his grasp. He says my name one more time, imploring and raw, but I keep running.

As I slam the door of his flat behind me, I hear his bellowed roar.

But he doesn't come after me.

Thank God, he doesn't stop me this time.

I hail a taxi on the street below and climb inside.

Then, with Nick and the beauty of Paris falling away behind me, I put my face in my hands and I weep.

~ * ~

Nick and Avery's story continues in the
suspenseful, scorchingly sensual third novel!

For 100 Reasons

Available Now

"Lara Adrian not only dips her toe into this genre
with flare, she will take it over... **I have found
my new addiction, this series**."

--The Sub Club

Watch for an exciting new novel in Nick &
Avery's steamy, suspenseful saga!

For 100 Forevers

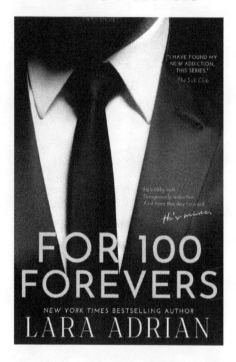

Coming Soon

**"For those of you looking for your next Fifty
fix, look no further.** I know - you have heard
the phrase before - except this time it's the truth
and **I will bet the penthouse on it."**

--Mile High Book Club

You met Baine International security chief and combat veteran Gabriel Noble in the 100 Series. Discover his hidden scars and forbidden cravings in this all-new novel!

Run to You

Available Now

Look for this 100 Series standalone novel in ebook, trade paperback and unabridged audiobook

You met brilliant artist Jared Rush in the 100 Series. Unravel his darkest secrets and desires in this all-new novel!

Play My Game

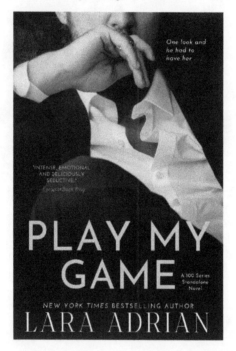

Available Now

Look for this 100 Series standalone novel in ebook, trade paperback and unabridged audiobook

Never miss a new book from Lara Adrian!

Sign up for Lara's VIP Reader List at
www.LaraAdrian.com

Be the first to get notified of Lara's new releases, plus be eligible for special subscribers-only exclusive content and giveaways that you won't find anywhere else.

Sign up today!

ABOUT THE AUTHOR

LARA ADRIAN is a *New York Times* and #1 international best-selling author, with nearly 4 million books in print and digital worldwide and translations licensed to more than 20 countries. Her books regularly appear in the top spots of all the major bestseller lists including the *New York Times*, USA Today, Publishers Weekly, The Wall Street Journal, Amazon.com, Barnes & Noble, etc. Reviewers have called Lara's books "addictively readable" (Chicago Tribune), "extraordinary" (Fresh Fiction), and "one of the consistently best" (Romance Novel News).

With an ancestry stretching back to the Mayflower and the court of King Henry VIII, the author lives with her husband in New England.

Visit the author's website and sign up for new release announcements at **www.LaraAdrian.com**.

Find Lara on Facebook at
www.facebook.com/LaraAdrianBooks

Love paranormal romance?

Read Lara's bestselling Midnight Breed vampire romance series

Discover the Midnight Breed
with a FREE eBook

Get the series prequel novella
A Touch of Midnight
for FREE at LaraAdrian.com!

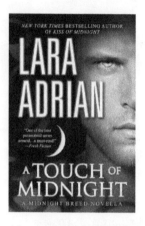

After you enjoy your free read, look for Book 1

Connect with Lara online at:

www.LaraAdrian.com

www.facebook.com/LaraAdrianBooks

https://www.bookbub.com/authors/lara-adrian

www.goodreads.com/lara_adrian

www.instagram.com/laraadrianbooks

www.pinterest.com/LaraAdrian